Let It Go

Also by Yvonne Rodney:

Getting Through

To order, call 1-800-765-6955.

Visit us at **www.AutumnHousePublishing.com**
for information on other Autumn House® products.

Let It Go

a Story of Forgiveness

Look at my hands and my feet.
It is I myself! Touch me and see.
Luke 24:39

yvonne rodney

Autumn House® Publishing
www.autumnhousepublishing.com
A Division of **REVIEW AND HERALD®** PUBLISHING
Since 1861

Published by Autumn House® Publishing, a division of Review and Herald® Publishing, Hagerstown, MD 21741-1119

Autumn House® titles may be purchased in bulk for educational, business, fund-raising, or sales promotional use. For information, please e-mail SpecialMarkets@reviewandherald.com.

Autumn House® Publishing publishes biblically based materials for spiritual, physical, and mental growth and Christian discipleship.

The author assumes full responsibility for the accuracy of all facts and quotations as cited in this book.

Unless otherwise noted, all texts are from the *Holy Bible, New International Version.* Copyright © 1973, 1978, 1984, International Bible Society. Used by permission of Zondervan Bible Publishers.

Bible texts credited to KJV are from the King James Version of the Bible.

This book was
Edited by Penny Estes Wheeler
Cover art by © istockphoto.com/exxorian
Cover designed by Trent Truman
Interior designed by Johanna Macomber
Typeset: Bembo 11/13

PRINTED IN U.S.A.
13 12 11 10 09   5 4 3 2 1

Library of Congress Cataloging-in-Publication Data

Rodney, Yvonne, 1959-
  Let it go : a story of forgiveness / Yvonne Rodney.
      p. cm.
1. Women--Fiction. I. Title.
  PS3618.O3574L48 2009
  813'.6--dc22
                                        2009023006

ISBN 978-0-8127-0494-5

This book is dedicated to women everywhere
who, because of a moment of weakness
or because of a series of choices,
live with guilt that refuses to go away.

It is also dedicated to men
who, under the banner of God, stand strong
in appropriately supporting and
loving the daughters, wives, and sisters in their lives
to be all God designed them to be.

To both groups I say: "God loves you."

Acknowledgements

My T-West (Toronto West) church family: Every week God sends another one of you to give me a card, send me an email, or stop me in the parking lot or hallway to let me know that I must keep writing. Your encouragement means so very much and I thank you.

My immediate family and friends: I do not take you for granted. Thanks for reading my stuff, providing feedback, challenging me, and most of all, keeping me grounded.

The Review and Herald team: Working with you is such a pleasure. Thanks for taking the time to answer my many questions and for preserving the integrity of the "keeping it real" writing that I try to do.

Thanks to God for His daily reminders of His love, and that His grace is sufficient for me.

Introduction

Dear Reader:

Several years ago at my church we staged a play titled *That Thang We Do* in which we introduced Lisa and Luke's story. By the end of the play, 18-year-old Lisa was pregnant and the two teens were facing a life changing moment. Hoping to provoke audience discussion, we stopped right there—a conscious decision not to portray how things turned out. And what a discussion we had! Would Lisa and Luke get married? Should they? Should she have the child and give it up for adoption? How would their lives be affected by this pregnancy? *Let it Go* is the follow up—21 years in the future. But this story is less about Lisa's decision than the effect it had on her life. This is a story about guilt, forgiveness, and how little we know about the damaging baggage the woman or man sitting right beside us lives with every day.

Just recently over dinner with friends we had a discussion about things in life we'd find difficult to forgive ourselves for doing. For example: living with the realization that due to neglect or forgetfulness on our part, inadvertent though it might have been, death or serious permanent injury of someone resulted. What if that someone was our child? How does one live with guilt like that?

Let's face it. We all make mistakes. Sometimes our mistakes are accidental and sometimes they are willful. For the decisions we make against our conscience, we are so focused on the immediate "solution" that we cannot foresee the consequences. And when the consequences unfold, how we flail ourselves. Then to compound our problem, we feel we can't possibly come to God about it because this thing we did was premeditated, willful, and self-serving. No way can we ask God to forgive us, because truth be told, we'd probably do it again given the same circumstances. Furthermore, sometimes the thing we did and for which we suffer was very private. If people knew it, we believe, they'd condemn us too.

But the remorse is eating us up inside. We can't talk about it. We can't get over it. This self-condemnation makes us believe we are undeserving of God's immeasurable grace so we cannot even enjoy a relationship with Him. This self-condemnation also affects our ability to form healthy relationships with others. Thus, when we hear the statement, "God loves you," we cannot believe it. We are not worthy!

I hope that within the pages of this book you might finally believe that God does really and truly love you. Despite what you have done, despite the guilt you carry around with you, despite your sense of unworthiness, God loves you. If you were the only person left on earth, God would still have emptied heaven to come and rescue you. It boggles the mind but it is true. God really does love you. Despite everything. You cannot explain it or fathom it or think yourself deserving. It just is.

Lately, I've decided to give God my drive to work as *our* time. I speak with Him and listen for Him to talk to me. Everyday when I ask Him what He wants to say to me, two messages are repeated over and over again. "I love you, Yvonne." and "Trust Me."

Last week I got really tired of the same old refrain and yelled at Him. (Yes, I yelled at God. I was ticked!) You see, I wanted Him to give me practical directives—do this today or stay away from that situation.

But all I kept being told was, "I love you."

So I lost it and yelled, "Why do You keep telling me that You love me? Everyday the same old thing?"

His answer came: "Because you do not really believe it."

I argued that I did.

He was equally insistent that I didn't.

And He's right. For if I believed it, really and truly believed it, I would walk prouder, worry less, have greater peace, act more purposeful. When you know you're loved for who you are, it gives you confidence. And lately I've been dragging my feet and feeling inadequate. Underneath all my bravado lurks a little girl who feels not beautiful enough, not strong enough, not bright enough, not capable enough, not lovable enough. But God, the King of the universe loves me. Whenever I allow myself to believe it, I feel my face smiling with the joy of it. God tells me He's going to keep reminding me of it until I believe it all the time. Every day. Once I fully believe it, then the trust part will be a piece of cake.

I see the connection now.

Will you join me in this discovery of love? No matter what you've done. No matter what has been done to you? God really and truly loves you. Give yourself permission to try it on for size. Just allow your mind for even a minute to believe. See! Your face is smiling too.

Now just imagine the wattage of our smiles if we believed that for even half of each day! Folks would be blinded by the light of His love shining through us and they'd probably want some for themselves.

The guilt, the remorse, the self-condemnation, and feelings of inadequacy. Let it go. Let God love you, and bask in it. You are precious in His eyes.

Cheers!
Yvonne

Prologue

Journal

They made me come in for the pre-counselling—counselling that I did not want. I knew what I had to do. So much depended on me making the right decision, and this was right for us.

The place where I had the appointment had such a normal look to it. It might have been a comfortable old house for a good family—not a place where secrets were kept and shame lived. The person with sympathetic eyes who met with me explained the procedure. It shouldn't hurt too much. She said that afterwards I'd get something like a period and maybe some cramps, but if I took it easy I'd be back to normal in a day or two. She looked like she knew what she was talking about.

I paid the money and signed the papers (why shouldn't I sign my own papers? I was of age), indicating that I was of sound mind and intellect. I question the latter for getting me in this mess in the first place. We had no right to do this thing. No, I'll take the blame. I had no right to acquiesce. I should have known better, being a good girl and all. Everyone said I was mature for my age.

But what I am is foolish. And weak. And pregnant.

So I signed the papers to preserve our reputation and our future. Not too bad a trade-off, given the alternative. If only I hadn't . . .

Water under the bridge.

I woke up the morning of the day of on the same side of the single bed that I usually wake on. It was May 5, two days before Daddy's birthday. I lay on my bed, flat on my back, listening to but not hearing the same old morning sounds. With a seeming will of its own my hand moved from its cramped position behind my head and meandered slowly down to my belly. Fingers splayed, it tentatively started to feel . . . for what? Five weeks! Could there be movement this early?

I jumped out of bed and gathered my resolve tightly around me. Hurry me up, I begged the morning. "God, make Your face shine upon me and be gracious unto me. Please forgive me for I have sinned and will sin again today, but please understand, I have to do this for us." I headed for the shower before another part of me could ask questions I did not wish to answer.

I fluffed my hair, got dressed, and prepared for my day as usual. Nothing (well, almost nothing) about this day would be different from my regular routine.

I prepared some oatmeal for the family, poured cups of tea, and called everyone to breakfast. *That was my job on Fridays—I made breakfast for the family. I then fetched the paper from the front porch, took the lifestyle section, leaving the hard news for my folks, and sat down to read and eat.*

I was deep in the middle of reading an article when a drop of fluid fell from my face on to the paper, blotting out a word. No one noticed. We were not an alert family first thing in the morning. I blinked to help me focus on the rest of the article but the missing word started to speak to me.

'The.'

Such a tiny word! Not a noun, not a verb, not any part of speech but an article. Yet, while I still could understand the meaning of the sentence without that little article, the sentence had lost something. I became aware of a burning sensation at the back of my throat and tension in my jaw, but I kept it inside and finished my meal. Then I got up from the table, kissed my folks goodbye, and got on with my day as planned. The procedure would be done at 3:00. My plan was to be there at 2:45.

I really had no choice.

Chapter 1

What goes on in the mind of a man as he watches his bride walk down the aisle toward him? Does he feel a momentary flutter of panic— a sudden urge to bolt? Does his heart fill up with tenderness and love?

Derek Clarke was feeling all of the above. Panic because he wondered if he was equal to the task of being a good husband and because so many before him were providing daily statistics that 'till death do us part' was the impossible dream. And tenderness mingled with love because walking toward him was the woman without whom he could not imagine life.

He couldn't stop staring at her. *Dear God*, he prayed as he waited, *make me capable. Show me how to keep that shine in her eyes. Enable me to build her up, support her, be tender with her, and not crush the spirit of the person You created her to be. Keep my eyes from straying and my mind from unfaithfulness. Dear God, please enable me.*

His prayer felt like a plea, but it gave him peace. He remembered his dad's favorite text: "Remain in me and I will remain in you. No branch can bear fruit by itself; it must remain in the vine. Neither can you bear fruit unless you remain in me" (John 15:4). He knew what that meant. In order to be the husband he prayed to become and the one God expected, he would need to abide in God. Constantly. Through thick and thin.

As Derek watched the woman who affected the beat of his heart walking toward him, he experienced a profound feeling of happiness. Yes, this joining of his life to Marissa's was good. It was very good. And the look on his face was such that if the Holy Spirit needed a photograph depicting human joy in all its purity to post in the heavenly album, Derek's provided the perfect Kodak moment.

Marissa, on her slow walk down the aisle toward her soon-to-be husband captured that look. It moved her more than she could say. And she tucked it away in the special place she reserved for beautiful things and would view it again and again in the days and weeks and months and years to come—love's promise.

An older couple, Thomas and Catherine Charles, sitting in pew seven with shoulders touching, had their eyes fixed forward on the radiant young couple repeating their vows.

"I promise you, Derek, that I will love you all the days of my life. I will look after you, sleep with you, hold your hand, encourage and support you during good times and bad. I will keep you always at the center of my heart like you are right now—"

The bride's voice broke. The groom wiped the tears from her cheeks with his thumb. He then kissed the fingers still wet with her tears as she, eyes riveted on him as if he was the anchor to which she was tethered, valiantly eked out the rest of her pledge.

Thomas reached for the hand of his beloved Catherine and clasped it. They looked at each other and that look communicated a lifetime of shared experiences. She stroked his hand. It was dry. But the sound was as soft and comforting as a whisper.

The groom then spoke. "I, Derek Clarke, take you, Marissa Hamilton, to be my wife. I will be your protector, your champion . . ."

Catherine liked that. It was good to hear a young man these days promising to be protector and champion to his wife. She believed that women wanted their men to be strong, despite the fact that they themselves could be tough when needed. But yes, a champion in a man is a good thing. Men need something to fight for. Why not have it be for their women?

Help them God, Catherine prayed. *Help them to stay true to the promises made today. Amen.*

· · · · ·

Lisa loved weddings, and this one was no exception. But she was the first to confess that they always made her cry. Even though she knew that the promises made were easily broken the next day or next year, she loved the hopefulness of it all. Maybe this time . . .

There was Derek all grown and taking himself a wife. So handsome and solemn he looked, as if every word was a pledge. Lisa looked in the direction of her friend Yolanda, the mother of the groom.

She felt her eyes filling up. Any minute now her husband Donald, helpless around her tears, would take her hand and squeeze it. From the corner of her right eye, she saw the hand coming just as predicted, and she remembered her promise given many years ago to have and to hold, come what may. The tears overflowed and raced down her cheeks.

In the process of squeezing his wife's hand, Donald remembered with a start that he'd forgotten to bag the yard waste and put it by the curb in preparation for Monday's pickup. Taking his trusty notepad from his breast pocket he wrote himself a reminder. Then he reclaimed his wife's hand

and squeezed it again. He wished she did not cry so much at weddings. He also wished he knew what was making her cry. And how to make it stop.

. . . . .

Yolanda Clarke absorbed it all. Her only son Derek caressing the cheek of his soon to be wife, wiping the tears and kissing them better. Her heart ached with loneliness. It was at moments like these when she railed at God for taking, far too early, her sweet husband Jackson. And there was Derek, looking so much like him, getting ready to leave her too.

She felt the tears threatening and willed them back. Sitting up even straighter in her seat, she focused on the beautiful flowers she'd volunteered to provide. One of her many gifts to help make her son's wedding day as perfect as possible. An abundance of color making the church a garden.

Yolanda glanced at the faces of her two daughters who Marissa had given the honor of standing by the altar with her. Her three beautiful children. All three married now, and come Monday morning each would be off to their own homes leaving her alone in an empty house.

God, help me!

The vows ended. Promises and pledges meant to last a lifetime or until "death do us part." The pastor pronounced the blessing and the kiss that was shared by the newlyweds was tender and sweet. The peal of the organ signalled the end of the ceremony.

They were now husband and wife, two joyful faces making their slow procession down the aisle, stopping to greet the many well wishers. Yolanda smiled till her face hurt and accepted all the congratulations that also came her way.

God, help me, she prayed again.

Chapter 2

Lisa hummed her way through the door and up the stairs into their private living room. A front facing second-floor living room tastefully decorated with a couple easy chairs, a handful of plump, pliable cushions and carelessly tossed afghans that invited a snuggle. This was her favorite room in the house to do just that, but tonight she felt like dancing. Seeing Donald coming up the stairs, she danced over to him and encircled his waist in preparation for her version of a waltz.

"Wasn't that a beautiful wedding?"

Donald, still thinking about the garbage that had to be put out, looked at her with tenderness but resisted the lure of her dance. "You say that about every wedding you go to, Lisa."

"But this one, oh, you can just feel it. It was so tender, so passionate, and so absolutely romantic!" Lisa breathed a sigh of deep contentment. "Oh, Donald, don't you just feel like breaking out into song? Come on, put something nice on the stereo and dance with me."

"You know I don't dance, Lisa."

"But why not? I've never understood what you have against dancing, honey. It's so liberating! You feel like you could just float off."

"Well, I prefer to have my feet firmly planted on the ground. Floating off is not my style."

"Come on, honey, just one dance with me." Lisa snuggled her face close to his cheek and whispered in his ear. "Dance with me, my love. There is no sin in dancing with your wife. Please dance with me tonight."

Donald, getting more anxious by the minute about the neglected garbage, gave her a quick peck on the cheek. "OK, give me five minutes to change and to put out the garbage and then I'll be right back."

"Forget the garbage, Donald. Leave it for once till morning."

"Five minutes. I promise." And he dashed down the hallway to their bedroom.

Lisa could hear him frantically tossing off his clothes. But of course, he couldn't just leave them on the bed. He would take time to reform the creases in his pants, toss the shirt in the laundry hamper, and hang up the suit.

In three minutes he was headed at a fast clip down the stairs toward the back door. Lisa knew also that he would not be back for a while. Her husband did not do anything in life fast or haphazardly. Sighing again, she flopped onto the couch, but her feet still felt like waltzing and so she got up again, sashayed over to the stereo, and selected the soulful voice of Luther.

Grabbing a cushion for a partner, she did a slow waltz around the room, letting the music, the words and the beautiful voice fill up the empty places in her. She danced to the song about the little things that mean the most in life. At the end of the song she placed a tender kiss on top of her pillow, tossed it back on the sofa, and headed for the shower, there mingling fresh tears with unsalted water.

She was lying in bed, propped up against three pillows by the time Donald returned. He had the grace to look sheepish.

"I guess I took a bit longer than I said, didn't I. Sorry about that, but I knew they wouldn't pick up the stuff if it wasn't packed just right so—" He stumbled to a halt. "The dancing moment is gone too, I guess?"

Lisa nodded.

"Would you like me to make you a cup of tea?"

Lisa moved her head from side to side.

"You need your back rubbed?"

Lisa shook her head again.

"I should just let you be then."

Lisa opened her mouth, thought better of it, and closed it again. She nodded.

"I'll go grab a shower. If you need anything, let me know. OK?"

Lisa nodded once more and Donald retrieved his pajamas from where they were neatly folded under his pillow, took fresh underwear from the third drawer of the armoire, and headed for the shower.

Lisa knew he would make sure the shower was spic and span by the time he was done, the bathroom floor and counter free from all traces of disorder. She reached for the novel she'd been reading the day before. As she reached across, her hand paused for a moment over her Bible, the same one she'd promised herself at the start of the year that she would begin to read more frequently, but she picked up the novel instead and was soon lost in the continuing story.

• • • • •

After cleaning up the bathroom and discarding the used towels, Donald padded over to the bed where his wife slept. Again she'd fallen asleep with a book lying facedown on her chest. Before turning off her bedside lamp he placed a gentle kiss on her forehead. But he did not immediately walk away.

He stood there and stared at her face in the soft shadow of the bedside lamp. He loved her so much. But it frightened him that no matter what he did, it seemed as if he was failing her in some way. After 14 years of marriage, she remained a mystery.

He'd met her, no he corrected his thoughts, he'd been observing her for a while as she, new to the area, had started coming to the church he attended. She always came in at 10:30 or so. Always with head held in a way that invited a greeting, she sat in approximately the same seat week after week. There was something light and free about her, like a butterfly trying hard not to flutter. He'd been drawn to her from the beginning.

She'd joined heartily in the singing and discussions of the medium-sized congregation. He would listen specially for her voice and even when he could not see her, could identify its timbre from a babble of many. So after thinking and praying on the matter, and unbeknownst to her, he made the decision to woo her.

He still remembered the moment she'd agreed to marry him. Up to that point he'd been thinking that he'd not made much progress in his quest. But on that wonderful day in September, September 25 to be specific, he'd taken her for a ride in the country.

The trees were just on the cusp of welcoming the paintbrush of fall and they'd gotten out of the car to stroll along a path that beckoned. Right there and then, he'd asked her. He had surprised himself. He'd not planned on doing it at all this soon. But something he'd said to her had caused her to throw her head back and laugh with full-bellied glee, and out had popped the plea.

"Marry me, Lisa. Tell me you will marry me."

He still remembered the look she'd given him. Half-pleasure and something else. Something that looked like a surrendering or a yielding. Exactly four months later they'd been married at a small ceremony with a few friends, church family, and both their parents.

She was a fairly new lawyer back then, and he'd encouraged her to take time to build up her practice. By then he'd been in the dental business for a few years and was ready, but not to the point of anxiousness, to start a family. But he'd wanted her to have time to give her career a solid foundation first.

Their lives were scheduled and full. They traveled as often as their respective careers allowed and maintained a peripheral involvement in church activities. Lisa, of course, whenever she got the time, welcomed friends and lost souls to their home for one of her catered culinary extravaganzas.

The longed-for children had not materialized. There were two seasons of hope and two passages of grief, and without saying a word to each other, they'd stopped trying. She went back on the pill and he—well, he continued to put out the garbage, order their lives, and concentrated on making her if not happy, at least content.

Donald thought about all these things as he looked at his wife and re-membered again to thank God for his blessings. He tucked the comforter under her chin and was turning to leave her side when she murmured some-thing.

"What's that, honey?" he asked.

"Dance with me." Her request though mumbled was decipherable.

But before he could respond, he saw her smile, as if whoever she was talking to in her dreams had gladly taken her up on the invitation. On her face he could see that she was floating, floating, happy and free in the arms of her partner. Donald hoped the partner was he, blessed at least in her dreams with Fred Astaire grace.

Chapter 3

Derek eased a sleeping Marissa off his shoulders and whispered softly in her ear. "Hey honey, we're almost home."

Marissa's eyes snapped open. "Oh no, I fell asleep?" She blinked her eyes into alertness as the airport limousine pulled into the driveway of the duplex that was to be their first home together.

Derek hated the fact that they had to rent. He'd even suggested that they live with his mother for a little while so that they could save faster toward buying a house. That however was the last thing Marissa wanted. She liked her mother-in-law but at times had gotten the distinct impression that Yolanda resented her for taking her last child and only son away. This duplex apartment, while a bit on the small side, was not too expensive and afforded them the luxury of being on their own to make their own growing mistakes as a couple away from the watchful eyes of others.

Derek paid the driver and hefted the two large suitcases that Marissa had packed full of treasures she'd found in Costa Rica. It had been an idyllic honeymoon, the kind you read about but never dream of having. Her husband could not have been more attentive, more loving, more romantic, more made to order. Their hotel room had overlooked the ocean and each morning they dined on fresh pineapple, papayas, mangoes, and all the fruit this tropical paradise produced. There on their private balcony her husband had loved her with words that affirmed, supported, and titillated her mind. Then in the intimacy of their room, he demonstrated the physical side of his love for her. It was far greater than she'd ever dreamed or imagined, with no previous bad or good memories to mar what she came to see as absolute perfection. This was heaven!

As she trudged up the long flight of stairs (the other down side to the duplex) behind her husband, her honeymoon memories floated her up the remaining steps and to their front door—apartment 205, right at the end of the hallway.

Depositing the suitcases on the floor, Derek retrieved the keys and opened the door. Marissa made to go through but he stopped her. "Stay," he said.

"Stay?" parroted Marissa. "Why?"

Derek looked around as if searching for an intruder. "Let me take the bags in and make sure everything is OK. Wouldn't want any surprises lurking in there to threaten the safety of my best girl now, would I?"

His lean brown cheeks, the ones she felt the need to caress again, were set in lines of playful seriousness. Hoisting the two suitcases again, he backed into the apartment and when Marissa made to follow he stopped her with a look. Deciding to indulge his machismo, she stepped away from the entry and the door swung shut in her face.

In less than a minute her husband was back. "May I have your bags please?"

She handed them over. The door closed again and this time he was gone for a lot longer. Marissa really needed to use the bathroom. Just as she put out her hand to knock on the door, it was thrown open. Her husband emerged and after bowing deeply from the waist, he swept her up in his arms. Much taller than her five-foot six-inch frame, he was strong as an ox. A sports fanatic, Derek took pride in his trim, muscled physique. Marissa did too.

Looking into her eyes, he murmured in his sexiest bass, "Welcome home, my love."

Something about the rumble of his voice had the effect of melting Marissa's bones. When he used it to turn on the charm, she was a goner. He lowered his head to give her a "cross the threshold" kind of kiss when Marissa kicked out her leg and snagged the door that was about to click shut.

"What are—?"

"I'm sorry to do this to you, honey, but please tell me you have the keys."

"Of course! They're right there on the table . . ." His voice trailed off as his brain kicked in, widening the brown pupils of his eyes.

Not taking her eyes from the door, Marissa said. "Don't worry. I got this one," Extending the toes in her shoe until they hurt, she was able to keep the door open, barely. "All I need you to do is to back up two steps and we'll be saved."

Derek complied speedily and soon had her over the threshold, into their home and still in his arms. "Thanks for saving the day, Mrs. Clarke."

Marissa inclined her head and bestowed on him a sweet smile, the kind that always had the effect of lifting his spirit.

This time when he leaned in to kiss her, she was glad there was no door to distract. This kiss required a response in kind, but that too had to be cut short when Marissa's bladder reminded her that some things in nature can only wait so long.

Later after she had unpacked their bags and refreshed the room she'd left in good shape in anticipation of their homecoming, Marissa went in search of her husband. There he was sprawled on the living room couch totally immersed in the hockey game. The Buffalo Sabres were playing the Ottawa Senators. Derek was a Sabres fan.

She snuggled beside him, kissing his cheek. He pulled her close mumbling "Hi, honey," while his eyes stayed glued to the fast moving game on the screen. The score: 2 to 1—Senators.

With only three minutes of regulation time left to play, a sloppy Senator line change put the Sabres in a two-on-one situation. In less time than it took to blink, the two Buffalo players had crossed center ice and were headed for Senator territory. For a moment it looked like the play was going to get an off-side call at the blue line but the anticipated whistle did not blow.

Quick as lightening the player who had control of the puck passed it to his partner across the ice. Without missing a stride the partner took a one time shot a split second before the lone defenseman hit the ice in a vain attempt to block the shot. Derek rose from the chair, body taut with tension, willing the puck toward the tight angle of the net. Quick as a snake's tongue, the goalie's glove flashed out. But the speeding puck bounced off and dropped on the ice right in front of the net. The waiting Sabres player tucked it in the corner of the net to tie the score.

The Sabres bench, along with Derek, erupted in cheer. Only 90 seconds of regulation play remaining.

Derek eventually sat back down but the tension of the game kept him perched tightly on the edge of the couch. "C'mon Buffalo. You can do this. Go for it! Go for it!"

They must have heard him. With momentum working in their favor, Buffalo won the face-off at center ice. Not a team to allow much sloppiness, the Senators regained control of the puck keeping the play within Buffalo territory. A pass, however, to a fellow Senator missed its target. The Buffalo player got a piece of it and headed down the ice for a breakaway. The Senator goalie poised for the assault. The skater faked left. The Senator goalie dived in that direction. As if turning on a dime however, the Buffalo skater manoeuvred the puck to his other side and slapped it hard—straight for the unprotected side of the net. The puck was well on its way when a Senator defenseman came out of nowhere and body checked the Buffalo player hard. He went down, eyes still fixed on the net where the puck had made contact, shining the red light for all to see. Then he lay still.

This time the shrill of the referee's whistle could be heard. Penalty against the Senators! Two minutes for interference.

Derek whooped and hollered, and hauling Marissa up from the couch, danced her around the living room as Buffalo with the man advantage went on to score again, winning the game four to two.

"Man! What a game! Wasn't that great, hon?" Derek asked. He whooped and hollered some more.

"How come the game is on so early?" asked Marissa

"This was last night's game. I programmed the VCR to tape it while we were away."

"All the hockey games?"

"No silly. Just this one. The Senators are a great team. I wanted to see how the Sabres would do against them. If they keep playing like this, they might just make it to the playoffs this year. Anyway, I'm hungry. Do we happen to have any food? Better yet, since it's still early, how about I take you out to dinner? We could be back home by 8:00."

Marissa thought about it. "What we need to do is some grocery shopping. How about we grab something quick to eat and then go get the shopping done? That way, I'll have all my ingredients on hand to serve you breakfast in bed in the morning."

"Now that's a tempting offer—not the shopping part but the breakfast in bed."

"Well in order to get that one, you have to do the other."

"At your service, madam," said Derek as he kissed her on the lips. Then slapping her lightly on her bum, he commanded, "Don't just stand there, woman! Let's get going."

Marissa ran back to bedroom to fetch her handbag and a light sweater to guard against the slight chill of the September evening. She then made a quick inventory of the fridge and cupboards to see what was needed. Thanks to her preplanning in equipping the kitchen, it was mostly fruit, veggies, and dairy that she needed to shop for. She looked longingly at the bread machine resting in the corner of the counter and promised herself she would put it in service as soon as they got back.

The ring of the telephone interrupted her musings. "Could you get that, honey?" Derek called.

"Hello."

"Oh, great! You're back. I missed you guys. So how was everything? Did you have a good time? Is Derek OK? Not full of mosquito bites? I made dinner if you want to come over. Tell Derek I made his favorite lasagne and there's a loaf of garlic bread warming in the oven."

Marissa, after trying several times to interject a response, gave up. The sudden pause in Yolanda's monologue caught her off guard.

"Are you there, Marissa?"

"Yes I'm here. I was just waiting to talk."

"So will you and Derek come for dinner?"

"Well we were just . . ."

"Never mind! Put Derek on. Maybe he wants me to sauté some mushrooms as well. I know he loves those too."

Derek walked in the room and Marissa handed him the phone, making negative motions with her head. She wanted this evening home with her husband.

But you've had his undivided attention for the last 10 days, Marissa. Are you going to begrudge him a meal with his mother?

While Marissa's conscience warred with her want, her husband made the decision. They were going to his mom's for dinner. Surrendering, Marissa insisted however that they still needed to get the groceries and therefore couldn't stay too long to linger after the meal. She hoped that this jockeying for Derek's attention against his mother would not be a long term situation.

Chapter 4

Yolanda well knew that she'd manoeuvred the situation to get Derek to come over for dinner. She'd heard the hesitation in her daughter-in-law's voice, but too bad. The girl had had her son's undivided attention for the past two weeks and it was only fair that Mom have some time too. She'd missed him so much. Plus what was wrong with wanting to have your son over for dinner. Yolanda felt justified in her self-talk.

The little voice in her head told her she was treading down a slippery slope but she quashed it. Did anyone understand how hard it was to be living alone? How the house squeaked in unusual places at the weirdest times of the night? Her greatest loss however was that of being needed. What pleasure was there in cooking for yourself or in sitting down at a table set for one?

Her Jackson used to compliment her on the meals she prepared. He enjoyed his food and she'd taken pleasure in preparing delectable dishes to please his palate. And just like that, he was gone. How could she have known that a stroke was waiting for him? And then, when it looked like he was going to pull through that, he was hit by another, leaving her a widow in shock. But she'd gotten through the days.

Her daughters had come home and Derek had taken time off from his articling job and they'd gotten through. When Derek passed his bar exams, he'd come home to stay with her and she'd been able to keep cooking and having her efforts appreciated. But these past two weeks with Derek gone had been the loneliest of her life. It was as if Jackson had passed away all over again.

Last night she was sure she'd heard his voice speaking to her as clearly as anything. He was calling for her to bring him the nail clipper. One of his few bad habits was clipping his toenails at the couch as he watched TV. He'd put his foot on a paper towel or Kleenex and clip away. Yolanda had hated the habit. And last night she'd heard him call for her to bring him the clipper. She'd been so glad to hear his voice again that she'd eagerly run to retrieve it from the bathroom drawer only to dash into the room to find it empty and the bed sheets tangled against her feet, trapping her need to run.

Yolanda slapped the skillet on to the stove top and turned on the gas, another one of Jackson's ideas. Why use electricity when you could use gas? If the power went out you could still prepare a meal, plus gas was cheaper.

She washed the mushrooms and crushed the garlic, then opened the oven to check that the lasagne was not drying out. After adjusting the oven temperature lower, she decided to turn off the burner under the skillet. She'd do the mushrooms while Derek was washing up for dinner. Then she corrected herself—Derek and Marissa.

Father God, let me love her and not resent her, she prayed as the doorbell rang.

Grabbing a dish towel off the oven door, Yolanda dried her hands. With spry movements she descended the three steps leading from the kitchen through the family room and opened the front door. She was immediately engulfed in a tight hug from her son.

"Derek, let me go you bear! Are you trying to squeeze the life out of your mother?" She slapped playfully at his arms until he did. "Plus what are you doing ringing the doorbell to your own home?"

Raising his brows rakishly Derek teased, "Who knows, you might have had a gentleman caller over to visit and I wouldn't want to catch him in the act of stealing a kiss now, would I?"

Joy took over Yolanda's heart. Her son was home. "Gentleman caller my foot! Pshaw! Where's your wife?"

"You mean Marissa?"

"Did you happen to marry another wife that I don't know of? Of course I'm talking about your Marissa."

"In the car. She's giving us some alone time to say our hellos."

"Oh that's nice and thoughtful of her," replied Yolanda.

"I'll go get her," said Derek.

Yolanda watched her boy jog with the ease of youth round the corner of the house toward the side entry driveway. She heard the slam of a car door and prepared a widened smile of greeting for her daughter-in-law. And there they were coming toward her—hand in hand, Marissa and Derek looking radiant, sun-kissed and loved. Yolanda closed her eyes against the vision even as she opened her arms to greet her unasked-for gift of a daughter.

"Hello, Mrs. Clarke," greeted Marissa as she released her husband's hand and moved in to receive the hug her mother-in-law offered.

"What's with the 'Mrs. Clarke'? Call me Mom. All my kids do and you're now one of the family. Now come in and help me eat this feast I prepared for your homecoming. You can stay for a while, can't you?" Yolanda asked the question of Derek even as she ushered Marissa into the house.

Marissa rushed to answer. "We can stay for about an hour and a bit but then we need to get some groceries before the store closes. Milk, juices, fruits and veggies, stuff like that."

"An hour?" wailed Yolanda. "But that's not enough time to digest a meal and to catch me up on your holiday news!"

"Sorry, Mom, but we didn't know you were planning to have us over tonight," Derek said. "We'll come for a longer visit soon—spend a whole afternoon. Plus I want to have my wife all to myself for a while on our first night home." The look Derek directed at his wife softened his eyes to the point of intimacy and Yolanda felt like an intruder in her own home.

"Well then, let me get the rest of the meal ready. Just go wash up and dinner will be ready in five minutes flat." She bolted to the kitchen and tossed a frantic prayer somewhere in the direction of heaven. *God, help me let him go. And help me love her.*

She was still tossing solicitations heavenward when a soft voice asked, "Would you like some help, Mrs. Clarke, I mean Mom?"

Did I tell her to call me Mom? It feels so wrong!

"Actually, you could take the lasagne out of the oven for me and set it on the dining table. Oven mitts are hanging over —"

"I see them." Marissa interrupted as she retrieved the mittens. Turning around she saw Yolanda's lips moving. Hesitantly she asked, "Are you OK?"

Yolanda focused. "Just talking to God. I do that sometimes when I'm by myself. Bad habit to be doing that with people around. They might think I've gone off the deep end."

"What do you talk to God about? Oops, personal question! Sorry. You don't have to answer that," Marissa back-pedaled.

"It's OK," replied Yolanda. "I talk to Him about whatever is on my mind. Mostly about stuff that's bugging me."

"Something is bugging you now?" asked Marissa quietly.

Yolanda added an unhealthy amount of butter to the hot skillet and watched it sizzle. She then tossed in the crushed garlic along with a bit of vegetable seasoning and then added the mushrooms.

The sizzle was fierce and fragrant. Marissa's tummy rumbled in anticipation. She wondered if Yolanda had heard her question and was ignoring her or did not hear it at all.

"I hate living alone." *Now why did I go and say that?* Yolanda asked herself.

27

"And here I come taking away your only son." Marissa's tone held no rancour or accusation, just a matter-of-fact statement.

Yolanda's conscience brought heat to her cheeks. "Yes you did. But that's the way it's supposed to be. A man should leave his father and his mother and cleave to his wife. The Bible states that quite clearly and I am in complete agreement. However I expected to have Jackson here with me to grow old with and enjoy this time of our lives. Oh the plans we had!" Yolanda felt the burning in the back of her throat giving notice to her tear ducts. "This is ridiculous! What am I doing? I brought you here for a meal, not for a therapy session. Now come along, get that lasagne out of the oven and let's go and have ourselves a feast."

Acting more briskly than she felt, Yolanda turned off the stove and dumped the still sizzling mushrooms into a shallow serving dish. She was just about to turn around when she felt herself being embraced from behind. Her body froze even as her heart broke. This gentle giving of comfort without words.

Then she was released.

She kept her back turned as Marissa opened the oven door, removed the lasagne and garlic bread, and took it out to the dining room. She unfroze her body, patted her short curly grey hair, tossed another prayer heavenward and followed.

Half an hour later most of the lasagne was gone. Two wrinkled mushrooms remained, looking like rejects in a pool of congealed cholesterol death. The salad bowl was empty. Derek pushed back from the table and exhaled his gratification. "That was good, Mom. I don't know what you put in your food but it's always excellent."

"Thanks, son. I love cooking. Better yet, I love to watch people enjoy what I cook."

"You're going to have to give me lessons, Mrs. . . . Mom," remarked Marissa. "I hope that someday I'll be able to prepare meals at our house half as well as this."

"Get Derek to make some of those meals. Doesn't mean that because you're the woman you should be doing all the cooking. I taught him how to cook and take care of his wife, so don't let him try to pretend otherwise."

Marissa threw her napkin at Derek. "You little miscreant. You told me that you couldn't cook!"

"I did no such thing," Derek retorted, a smile hovering around his lips.

Marissa stood up, her arms akimbo. "You did too."

"Children!" said Yolanda.

"Well, he did say he couldn't cook," quipped Marissa, having the last word before she sat back down.

"Derek Clarke! How could you tell such a flat out lie?"

Holding up his hands to ward off the female assault, Derek confessed. "I did not lie but I did lead Marissa to believe that I couldn't."

"But why?" questioned Marissa.

"Because I love when you cook for me. I love how you set the table just so and the love you put into every meal. I love how you pamper me at mealtimes. I feel like a king of the castle. Now tell me, why would any man with an ounce of sense want to tamper with that?" He walked over to Marissa, pulled her to her feet and looked deep into her eyes. "Will you forgive me if I promise to make you dinner at least twice per month and breakfast every Sunday?"

Yolanda watched as Marissa melted against that deep voice-rumbling charm. Before she got more information than she cared to know, she took that opportunity to quietly exit with dishes for the sink.

That night as she prepared for bed, Yolanda reviewed the evening in her mind. There was no doubt her son loved Marissa. It was sweet and painful to watch. She was now truly usurped in her son's affection and she had no place to express the aching in her lonely heart. She picked up her toothbrush and applied the gel containing breath freshening strips to the brush. Methodically she brushed six times in all directions and spat.

After rinsing her mouth she dried the water droplets from the counter and made her way to her bed. Sometime last year she'd begun to center her pillow in the middle of the bed to convince herself she was coming to terms with Jackson being gone. But she still fell asleep on her side of the bed and many cold nights caught herself searching for a snuggle against his warmth. But he was gone and never coming back. Three years next Friday. Tonight, however, she wanted no painful memories haunting her.

She reached for a book of poems lying beside her bed. Maya Angelou would certainly have something bracing to say that would put her feelings into perspective. And as her eyes fell on "A Brave and Startling Truth" the phone rang. Yolanda glanced at the clock. It was 10:15.

"Hello."

"I know you're still probably sitting up in bed trying to figure which of the books piled on the bedside table you're going to read tonight. So what is it?"

Yolanda chuckled. "Are you sure you're not psychic? There's money to be made in that business, you know."

Lisa's grin could be felt through the line. "It only works on you, my friend. You lead a structured life so I can make educated guesses with you and be right a good percentage of the time."

"In other words I'm boring and predictable. Is that what you're saying?"

"I called to say hello and to check in on you. How are you doing? Is Derek back as yet?"

"Derek is back. They got back this afternoon. They were here earlier for dinner."

"And he showed up on his first night home to have dinner with his mom? What a thoughtful boy. I thought he'd want to spend his first night home with his new bride."

"Well, they came and had dinner. So there! It didn't take long and then they went to do some shopping before going back to their place."

"Somebody is sounding a bit defensive. What did you do, Yolanda? Did you make them come over? Guilt them into it? You're such a sneak."

"What's wrong with wanting to see your son? And anyway, I was just about to read one of Maya's poems."

"Red herring in my path! Help me, somebody! So how are they?"

"Very much in love."

"That's so sweet. I still think about that wedding—so intense, so romantic. Ah! To feel like that again. The passion of youth!"

"Oh shut up, Lisa. You have a wonderful husband who loves you to death. I, on the other hand, have only Maya's poems lying on my pillow."

"Well, if Maya doesn't satisfy, you can always turn to the Good Book," replied Lisa.

Yolanda sighed. "I should and I could, but to tell the truth, the Bible sometimes baffles me. I find more things in there to annoy than to comfort. I suppose I should try harder but I much prefer to read inspired writings of regular people. Most of them I can at least understand."

"You know, I was thinking the very same thing the other day. Lately my life has been feeling kind of hum-drum. So a couple of nights ago I couldn't sleep and instead of picking up a novel, I decided to try the Bible. I flipped through Psalms and got to reading chapter 22. There was David telling God how he felt about being forsaken and ignored by Him. Am I supposed to talk to God like that? It seems sacrilegious somehow."

"What's that saying, Lisa? We're long-standing women in the church and we don't know how to relate the Bible to our life needs! What does that say about our faith?"

"Faith has nothing to do with it," Lisa said, her voice rising. "I believe in God. I practice good values and return a faithful tithe. The Bible is just too cumbersome."

Yolanda sighed. "I think we need to do something about this. The Bible is supposed to be one of the ways for people to know who God is. If we don't know Him, how can we have a relationship with Him?"

"Well you're the older and wiser one with time on your hands. So you figure it out and let me know. I need to get home before my hubby sends the search and rescue out to find me."

"What! You're still at work! Are you crazy?"

"Don't you start yelling at me! I'm going. I'm going. Bye."

Yolanda looked at the dead connection in her hand and hung up. "Yeah. Bye, Lisa." She scooped Maya off her pillow and replaced her on the bedside table. After casting a glance in the direction of her Bible, she opted instead to talk to the ceiling again about all the things that were bugging her.

Interlude

Journal

I guess I should write about the day itself. I need to get it off my chest but this is not easy. That Friday afternoon, still resolute, I arrived at the clinic with 15 minutes to spare. I was immediately shown to a room with instructions from a kind woman with a gentle voice to change into a surgical tunic and relax.

Relax!

I sat stiffly on the side of the bed and waited.

While I waited, 100 butterflies took up residence in my stomach and began to flutter, tickling my resolve. I couldn't breathe. The walls of the room seemed to be closing in on me. I heard a whimper escape with one of my ragged breaths. That got my attention. I was having a panic attack! But remembering my commitment to stay the course, I talked the panic down.

"Be strong. Remember that you do not need the complication of a child in your life right now. Think about both of your reputations. Think about your life! In less than an hour it will all be over."

But my heart refused to listen and I think my body went into auto destruct. My breathing difficulties intensified. The room began to close in on me. That sterile, beige room with the florescent lights and a single white-sheeted hospital bed with a too-flat pillow. How many heads had rested there?

I can still see the potted cactus on the windowsill, designed to survive in desert conditions, mocking me with its thorns. I can still see the ruffled half-curtains, undisturbed by my hyperventilating, and the closed, locked, and fully-blinded window.

"Open the window, please! I can't breathe," I choked.

The nice woman with a gentle voice was suddenly at my side. "It's OK, dear. You're going to be OK. Just breathe deeply. I'll help you. Watch me. Now inhale, exhale. Inhale, exhale . . .

I locked eyes with her and sucked in air through tightly clenched teeth but my lungs panicked, increasing the wild fluttering of my heart.

"Open the window," I wheezed.

The voice, no longer gentle, shot me an intentional slap of restoration. "Snap out of this!"

"I'm sor-ry, I rea-lly can-not, breathe. I think I'm going to faint . . ."

From seemingly way up in the ceiling, I watched my body respond to the gen-

tle beckoning of that cold, beige floor.

It was 3:50 when I opened my eyes. I still remember the clock on the wall to the left side of the bed with the white face, black minute hand, and a red second hand ticking with quiet insistence.

I felt my tummy. No pain. That's good, *I thought.* No pain is good. I don't like pain. They must have given me some great meds. Thank God! It's over, *I thought.* The deed is done.

The nice woman who must have been watching and waiting, smiled at me. Her canine teeth were a bit shorter than the rest of her other teeth.

"I see you're awake, dear. How are you feeling?"

"OK, I guess. I thought I would have a bit more discomfort. I hardly feel any pain at all. Can I go home now?"

"We didn't do the procedure because you fainted, dear. Unfortunately the doctor had to go, plus she wasn't sure you would be up to doing this today. We have scheduled you to come back tomorrow morning at 9:00. We don't want to wait too much longer you know. It's always best to get these things attended to sooner rather than later. Less risky you see. So if—"

I can't recall the rest of what she said because my mind was screaming. It started to yell again. I fainted? I fainted? The thing is still in me? O dear God! Well, I'm not going to faint now. What's she saying? Something about tomorrow morning at 9:00? So be it then!

". . . feeling well enough, we can call you a cab and make sure you get home all right. Should I do that, dear?"

What's with the "dear" business? It's not like I'm the first person ever to faint. So I panicked a bit. But I'm OK now. No need to "dear" me to death.

I don't remember saying thanks or goodbye. That's not good. She seemed a nice lady. Somebody's mother—her with the short canines. I recall getting off the bed, getting my clothes on, finding my shoes and jacket and walking out of the room, the dear nurse speaking gently to me while I dressed—as if I was a fragile cookie still too hot from the oven to be picked up. She mentioned something about taking the night to think some more about my decision. Make sure I wanted to do the procedure.

I rode the subway home and joined the family for worship. I didn't pray for God to make His face to shine upon me.

Chapter 5

In the garage of her home, Lisa turned off the engine but made no attempt to get out of the car. It was almost half past 11:00, and though she was bone weary she felt a reluctance to enter her house and the patient understanding of her husband. More than 14 years ago, she'd asked God to send her a good, kind and loving man, and for once God had answered her prayers. But they should have had children. Children would have provided a buffer or another outlet for their love. And she did love him, but . . .

Blame it on pre-menopausal symptoms. Blame it on her demanding job. *While we're at it*, she thought, *blame it on the moon!*

But it was not the moon or menopause. It was her. There in her garage and in the privacy of her sensible Volvo, she could not be anything but honest. She was bored with her marriage and her life. Where was the passion, the connectedness, or the fire in the belly? What was the point of it all anyway? She could certainly relate to King Solomon: "Utterly meaningless! Everything is meaningless!" (Ecc. 1:2).

Lisa rested her head on the steering wheel and made a valiant attempt to take stock of her blessings. She had a loving husband. She had a beautiful home. She had a great job and she had friends. And even though their relationship at this point was mostly one-sided, she knew that she had God. So why this yearning after what could not be? Why this feeling of heaviness?

Guilt.

Lisa sat up. Guilt? She'd dealt with that a long time ago. Yes she had. So what if she hadn't told Donald? Not everything from one's past needed to be discussed with one's spouse. It happened long before them and she'd made peace with it.

Did you? Have you really?

Lisa's mind dodged the questions. She had gotten good at dodging. But this time she was tired and on this September night, the security detail she'd judiciously selected to guard the entrance and man the ramparts of her defenses, yielded ground against the probing pressure. Rusty hinges of memory creaked open a door locked from the inside by a girl who was and is no more.

Lisa felt her head turning first left, then right, left, then right.

No! her mind screamed. *No memories. No! Oh God, it was just the one time!*

She was surprised by the wail. It was the same lament she'd cried out to her parents when she could no longer hide the . . . one time that changed her life.

But you chose the change, Lisa. You chose the life you have.

No, no! I mean yes I did. I did and I made the right decision. I had to do it. I did the right thing!

Lisa is a liar, Lisa is a liar.

The sing-song refrain of the children's taunt chanted in her head. Relentless and mean.

Lisa is a liar, Lisa is a liar.

"Dear God and Father of all, help me. Help me."

Lisa felt her head pounding, dull thudding hammers rapping insistently against her compromised defenses.

"Honey, are you OK?" Lisa looked out her window. She was hearing voices. Dear God!

"Honey!"

She focused.

It was Donald, knocking against the window on the passenger side of the car, his face a predictable photograph of concern—a face that could bring her out of this round of haunting. Clapping her mental hands, she directed her sentries back on duty. She posted extra guards at every doorway, window crease, and crevasse to the past, and opened the other door to the here and now.

"Hey," she said to Donald as she turned the key to lower the passenger side window. Her voice sounded false to her ears.

"Rough day?" he asked, his eyes searching her face with their typical look of love mingled with concern.

"You could say that."

An imp in her head with a sleepy voice sang itself to sleep.

Lisa is a liar, Lisa is a liar!

"What you need is a relaxing bath to get rid of all that stress. It's hot and waiting for you, scented the way you like it." He walked over to the driver's side of the car, opened the door, and guided her into his embrace.

"Oh, Donald. You're so good to me. I don't deserve you."

"You deserve all that and more. You're the woman I love. Who else would I squander my affections on but you?" Then as if assisting a delicate patient back into her hospital bed, he walked Lisa slowly up the four steps from the garage into the house.

"We should have had children."

Lisa felt Donald stiffen. Now why did she say that?

She heard a soft swoosh of breath detach itself from her husband's nostrils as he gently closed the door and locked it. Heading up the stairs he said, "Come on up. I'll help you to the bath."

"Don't ignore me, Donald. I hate when you ignore things that are important to me. You always sigh and act as if I'm some kind of fragile china. I said that we should have had children and you just stiffen and sigh. Don't you have any thoughts on the matter?"

Donald stopped his progress up the stairs. He did not turn to look at her. "Lisa, you've had a long day and you're tired. I'm tired too. Let's just go upstairs and relax. We can talk about what's bothering you another time." He resumed his climb.

"What's bothering me? Who said something was bothering me!"

Dear God, Lisa's mind cried. *Why am I trying to start a fight? Why am I persisting in this tirade?*

"Donald, don't walk away from me when I'm talking to you!"

Lisa watched her patient, kind, loving husband continue his climb up the stairs and away from her. She ran after him. At the door to their bedroom she caught up to him and ran around to look him in the eye. Clutching at his arm she entreated, "Donald, please don't be mad. I'm sorry. I'm so sorry."

She saw no yielding in his eyes. Felt no softening in his muscled arm, but he did not pull away. "Sweetheart," she begged, "I don't know why I said that. I wasn't thinking."

Lisa felt a shudder run through her husband's body as if he was setting loose a great weight. He sagged into a sitting position on the nearby chair, looking suddenly old.

The pinch of Lisa's conscience was sharp. She had done that. By her unthinking words she had hurt the man she'd promised God to love for all times. Kneeling at his feet, she lowered her face on to his knee. "You married a basket case. Did you know that? Certifiable, that's what I am."

The tears came then, unexpected and sudden. "I'm really sorry, honey. I don't mean to hurt you. It's just . . ." Her throat clogged up with shame and her head fell again on his knee.

And then his hand was under her chin, raising her face to look at him. He searched her tear-filled eyes as if trying to discern the soul of her. What he saw or did not see seemed to leave him baffled and unsatisfied. "I love you, Lisa Jones Westwood. I don't claim to understand you, but I love you."

"And I love you too, Donald. So very much."

Donald pulled her up onto his lap and kissed her lips. It was a passionless kiss—the kind meant to bring comfort. "And yes, I would have loved to have children with you, but it's not in the plans. I try not to blame myself for not being able to give you children."

"But this is not your fault, Donald. I got pregnant two times."

"And nothing came of it, Lisa. I know I didn't tell you this before, but after our second miscarriage I went to see the doctor. He told me my sperm count is low. Maybe that's the contributing factor." Donald rubbed his hands across his face, wiping away his discomfort.

"That's so like you. There you are hurting about something, yet you hide it away. How long have you been blaming yourself? You could have shared that with me."

"I talk to God about it. Most days, He gives me a measure of peace. But you, Lisa, you would have made a wonderful mother."

"Oh, Donald!"

"Enough 'Oh, Donald.' Go freshen that neglected bath. No more looking inward tonight. I'm too tired and you're too spent." So saying, he hoisted both himself and her up from the chair and deposited her in the bathroom. Then he kissed her lightly on the nose, exited, and closed the door.

The eyes that regarded Lisa from the bathroom mirror seemed almost accusing, as if her image doubted her sanity. Lisa looked away. Donald was right. Enough looking inward.

She peeled off her clothes and lowered herself into the tub. The water, still warm under the cloud of bubbles, cradled and comforted. Her flexing foot encountered a few beads of mineral salts and as she closed her eyes and sighed, she blessed her husband and felt her body also giving thanks.

Chapter 6

Lisa's office phone was ringing as she let herself in the next morning, minutes after 9:00 o'clock. Today, September 25, was her unofficial wedding anniversary. Even though she and Donald had actually gotten married on January 25, he'd always made a big deal of September 25 because that was the date she'd agreed to marry him.

Despite the night of angst, Donald had gotten up early and brought her breakfast in bed. Her guilt level had climbed into the red zone. He'd also given her a lovely card that said all the things he couldn't or wouldn't say out loud. It reeked of love. But when he walked to his closet to take out the blue suit she knew he was going to wear today, she had felt harsh words, dangerous words, hurting words fighting to erupt from her mouth. She'd chewed the toast almost to the point of liquid to prevent letting the venom fly. Dear God in heaven, her husband's predictability was driving her insane.

She'd managed to finish the rest of the breakfast after getting herself under control and lucky for her, Donald who was running behind his normal departure time, kissed her goodbye and headed off to his first appointment. And how his clients loved him! He was the most gentle of men.

The phone's incessant ring stopped, jarring Lisa back to the present. Good. The phone had gone to voice mail. Stashing her purse in one of the drawers of her walnut credenza, she turned on her computer and quickly scanned her schedule. There were no booked appointments this morning. She picked up the phone and confirmed with the jeweller that the gold watch she'd purchased for Donald was ready for pickup. It was. She'd do that at lunch.

Walking out of her office, Lisa saw that Janine had arrived at her desk and Russell, her partner, was not yet in.

"Morning, Janine."

"Hi Lisa, how are things?"

"Happy anniversary to me," replied Lisa. "Today is our unofficial fifteenth."

Janine's look was one of resigned scepticism. "You and your fictitious dates. Fifteen years! I don't know how you guys do it. How can you stay married to one man for so long? Don't you get bored? Don't even answer that. It might incriminate you. But then again, I suppose if I was married to a sweet man like your Donald, I might be tempted to hang around and watch the grass grow with him. My two exes were not worth the investment."

Lisa chuckled. "Maybe you pick the ones who aren't keepers."

Janine looked as if she'd never considered that possibility. "What does a keeper look like?"

"Sweet and reliable," replied Lisa.

"In other words, boring! I need a bit more excitement than that. I want the guy I'm with to cause my heart to race and my nerve ends to sizzle. I want romance, passion, adventure—"

"So go rent a video. It's cheaper and you don't have to divorce it," quipped Lisa. "Anyway, enough about marriage. When's Russell getting in?"

"He's going to see old man McIver. He wants to change his will again."

"That means we won't be seeing Russell till noon. Can you pull me the file on that settlement case I did last week for the Larkin estate? I need to add some closing notes. And while you're at it, let me . . ."

"Excuse me."

Lisa and Janine looked up to find a young woman in the doorway. She looked to be no older than 16, dressed in too-tight faded blue jeans, a size zero sequined black tee, and high top Jordans. Her curly brown hair matched equally brown sober eyes.

Janine answered first. "Hi, how can we help you?" They didn't often get drop-ins or at least not this kind.

"I need to talk to a lawyer today. A woman lawyer." The girl's words were clipped and defensive.

"We don't take drop-ins," replied Janine.

"Well I need som'body to take me." Her eyes flashed to Lisa. "You a lawyer?"

"Yes," replied Lisa, "but as my assistant was telling you—"

"Good. I need to talk to you before 10:00. That's when I have to meet him."

"Meet who?" asked Lisa, and then could have bitten off her tongue.

Looking warily at Janine who'd now stood up, the girl answered Lisa. "The stinkin' lawyer who they hired to pressure me. I can change my mind, can't I? So what if I was kinda freaked when I left the baby at the shelter?" Her voice had risen to a screech. "My crazy mother had kicked me out. I had no where to go, but now I want my kid back. I got a job at Quick Stop Coffee. I can take care of my kid. You gotta tell him that."

"I'm sorry," replied Lisa. "I really am, but that is not my area of specialty. We do wills and estates here, not family law. Let me give you the name of someone I know who can help you."

The girl was suddenly in Lisa's face. Janine moved to intervene but the girl stopped short of grabbing her lapels. "You hafta help me. I don't have no time to go get me no other lawyer. I need somebody today and I want a woman. You can fake it. Please lady. I need my kid." And as she said the words Lisa noticed a wet spot spreading and darkening the black of the girl's top. The girl noticed it at the same time and uttered an expletive even as tears sprang to her eyes.

"How long have you been without your baby?" Lisa asked, understanding softening her tone.

"Two weeks and five days. I keep expressing the milk at her feeding times so that I can keep myself ready for when she comes back. Listen lady, have you never had a baby?"

Lisa shook her head no.

"Then can you think about what it might feel like to want your own baby and can't have it?"

Dear God in heaven.

Lisa closed her eyes against the naked plea as her mouth invited the young girl into her office.

She heard Janine's "This is a big mistake," as she closed the door.

"Thank you, lawyer lady. I'm kinda desperate. So how we gonna fight them? Him especially!"

"Him who?" asked Lisa, inadvertently adopting the girl's spotty grammar.

"The hired gun. That lawyer guy. He's been pesterin' me since the day I went back to find out what happened to my kid."

"Why don't you sit down and tell me everything from the beginning, starting with your name. And whatever you do, do not lie to me. Tell me everything. I can't promise you anything because as I said before, family law is not my area of expertise. However, based on what you tell me, I will see if I can at least go with you to meet this 'hired gun.' Deal?"

Lisa saw the girl's shoulders lower several fractions as tears appeared in her voice. "Deal."

Half an hour later she had a name. Sophie Sahara. She had an age. Eighteen. She also had a working picture that was tragic in its ordinariness. Teen girl gets pregnant. Teen father freaked and fled. Girl looking for love decides to have baby anyway. Brings baby home to a poor single mother who is also looking for love. Not a recipe for happily ever after.

When Sophie Sahara finished her tale, she raised expectant eyes to Lisa's. "I know this is not like lookin' after some dead guy's will or nothin', but can you at least come with me to meet this guy?"

And in that question, Lisa heard hope, terror, and fight. Professionally, she also felt defeat—defeat in knowing that the odds were against this young woman. That a stand-on-your-feet-all-day job at Quick Stop Coffee would provide neither enough money nor energy to raise a child. And defeat from believing in her heart of hearts that the baby would probably be better off being adopted into a family that had the means, the love, and the time to break the cycle of poverty.

But it was the expanding wet stain on the too tight black top and the milk being expressed in anticipation of an uncertain homecoming that decided Lisa, against all reason, to accompany Sophie to see the "hired gun." She would do this and no more.

Chapter 7

"D erek, wake up!" cried Marissa, jumping out of bed. They had slept way past the time to rise.

In five seconds flat Derek went from total unconsciousness to full alert. He threw off the sheets, bounded out of bed, and was in the shower. Knowing him, he'd be out again in less than five minutes. Marissa having witnessed this kind of fast dressing once during their honeymoon when they had almost missed a booked tour, knew she had no time to waste. She dashed out to the kitchen to try to prepare some breakfast but one glance at the clock told her that there wasn't enough time. So much for the sit down meal with freshly squeezed orange juice, scrambled eggs, warm bread, and preserves.

She settled for the boxed orange juice and poured herself and her husband a glass. They'd stayed up late into the night talking with and loving each other, reluctant to put an end to the last day of their vacation and the too short visit to paradise.

And here he came. From his crisp white shirt and dark suit accented with a subdued paisley tie that screamed establishment, he looked every inch the handsome, force-to-be-reckoned-with lawyer that he would one day become. Of this Marissa had no doubt. Derek loved the law. It was a career choice that fit him to a tee. As he walked toward her, white teeth gleaming and face freshly cleansed and shaven, Marissa felt her heart skip a beat. This honey of a man was all hers—till death.

"My, for someone who woke up less than 10 minutes ago, you're looking especially handsome," she remarked.

"Some woman is to be blamed. She did it, not me."

"Anybody I know?" Marissa teased, sidling up beside him.

He reached for her and kissed her lips. "H'mmm, you taste like orange juice."

"I'm afraid that's all you have time for this morning. Sorry about not having the breakfast I promised you."

Derek glanced at the clock and kissed her again. "I already miss you, you know that. These past two weeks have been the best weeks of my life. Thanks to you. Now it's all over."

Marissa briefly rested her head on his chest. She wished she was taller. "I'll miss you too. Here comes real life 101."

"So what are you going to do with your day today, Mrs. Clarke?"

"I guess I should start on my job search."

"Take your time. I love having you within easy reach." He kissed the top of her head. "Sorry, honey, I have to run. And please don't look at me like that. It makes it so much harder to leave."

"Looking at you like what?" asked a puzzled Marissa.

"I'm going. After I'm gone, go look at your face in the mirror. You'll see what I mean."

Marissa watched him dash off across the hallway and down the stairs. When she could no longer hear the noise of his footsteps, she closed the door and leaned against it. She missed him already too. Curious about his earlier statement, she locked the door and went to the bathroom to examine her face in the mirror. Warm brown eyes stared back at her. Full lips that looked to be the recipients of many kisses and hair tousled from sleep gave her the look of a well loved woman—and one wanting more of the same. She sighed with contentment and bent to wash her face. After drying it, she began to contemplate her new life and the things she needed to get done today.

First priority, she needed to find a full-time job. The one-year research position she'd had with the government had provided enough funds to help her and Derek pay for their dream wedding. Her parents did not have much to contribute and she and Derek had wanted to fund their wedding themselves, even though Yolanda had insisted on helping. Marissa did not plan on living off her husband's income, however. She wanted her own career. Her degree in epidemiology would not go to waste.

After cutting herself a slice of the freshly baked whole wheat bread and smearing on a thick layer of apricot jam, she sat at the table with a notebook and the rest of her juice. Forty minutes later she had produced a list of things to do and leads to follow up on to find a job. Not one to let time go by unoccupied, she picked up the telephone and started to make calls. The first one would be to her most recent employer. Who knows? There might be another project in the works. A job within the Ministry of Health would be right up her alley.

Halfway through dialling the number, Marissa disconnected. She hung her head. "Sorry about that. Here I go again, jumping into things without talking them over with You first."

She and Derek had promised each other they'd incorporate God in everything they did. And that had been so easy to do while they were on their honeymoon and had time on their hands and no busy schedules to interrupt.

But here it was their first morning back to real life and Derek had gone without them taking time to thank God for the morning and put their plans for the day in His hands. So now she prayed.

"Father in heaven, please forgive my neglect of You this morning. Help me to remember to put You first in everything I do. Thank You for Your patience and understanding as I try to grow my relationship with You. Guide me and direct me this day so that the decisions I make and the words I speak will be pleasing to Your eyes and ears. I don't have to tell You that I need a job. I want to be a true helpmeet to Derek and well, I want the independence and security too. I like the challenge of work and want to do activities that will help others. So now God, You see this list that I've made of places to call and people to see. You also know where You can use me best. So as I call, first help me to represent You in my conversations, then open the doors You want me to walk through so that Your perfect will can be done in my life, not just today but always. And now I will listen, so that Your Holy Spirit can speak to my heart."

With her head bowed and mind turned to the place where inner voices can be discerned, Marissa heard a faint chuckle. Her eyes flew open but she kept the inner connection.

A soundless voice with a bit of laughter left in it, replied, *"Good morning to you too, Marissa."*

"What's so amusing, God?"

"You." said the kind voice. *"I love our conversations. You get straight to the point. You say what you want and then ask for My blessing."*

"Is that a bad thing?" Not quite used to this kind of conversational prayer, she found it equally challenging and invigorating.

"It's what makes you, you. Even though I created you and know you inside out, I am still pleasantly amazed to see how each of My children is different. I like that."

"Oh."

"That's an enigmatic word. You give Your maker joy, Marissa. Today You made Me smile. Rest assured that today and always, when you ask and even when you forget to ask, I will be with you and lead you to become all that you were created to be."

"Wow! Thank you. So I take it you don't have any advice for my job search—like who to call and where You want me to be?"

The smile was in the voice again. How could a soundless voice contain the remnants of a smile?

"Make your phone calls and trust Me. I am always here and you can tune in anytime you want."

Marissa slowly closed the conversational door and heard a faint squeak in the hinges. She needed to use that door more.

Taking a few minutes to process her conversation with God, she decided to exercise the trust that on most days was so hard for her. She made the first call. Thirty minutes later, she had one interview lined up with her previous employer for a two-year contract doing the kind of research she was trained to do. She also had an informational meeting with one of the principal researchers at Sunny Glen, a teaching hospital affiliated with her alma mater. She made no attempt to contain her excitement.

"Thank You, God," she exulted. "Thank You! I don't have a job yet, but I have something to look forward to. Thank You."

"So what about those other items on your list?" It was the voice again.

"I'll call Derek later and yes I will get started on the thank you notes this afternoon. Oh. You might have been referring to the Bible study plan? Well . . . to be really honest, I'm not exactly looking forward to that part."

"You've had it on a lot of your lists."

"I know, God. And it's there and keeps appearing because it's something I know I should do. But as You know, I start and then get bogged down. The Bible is not the easiest book to understand."

"But it's an important tool for getting to know Me. Isn't that important to you?" The Questioner was gentle.

"You know it is, God, but if You'll forgive my boldness, couldn't You have inspired the writers to make the Bible a bit more straightforward? In one book, You instruct the Israelites to go kill off a whole bunch of people and then in Your commandments You tell us not to kill and to love our enemies. That's contradictory, so how do I know which part of the Bible is You talking and which part is just some ancient Jewish documentation? And another thing. In the New Testament, when the apostle Paul—in one of his letters—told the people to search the scriptures, which scriptures was he referring to?"

The totality of the silence stopped Marissa's venting. She could have cut off her tongue. Who was she to be running her mouth off to God like that?

"Forgive me, Father. I don't mean to hurt Your feelings."

The silence continued. This time it felt absolute. Marissa persevered however.

"God, are You still there? Please don't hide from me."

"I'm thinking how to explain the unexplainable to you. Some things are hard for humans to comprehend."

Marissa felt her head nodding. She was willing to concede that point. "Was it Peter who said something about us seeing through a glass darkly but when we are face to face a lot of things will become clear?"

"It was My son, Paul. But that's kinda what it's like. That's why faith is so important. It allows you to persevere even when all the questions cannot be fully explained."

"You speak slang!" Marissa accused.

"What do you mean?"

Now she was sure He was playing with her. "You said 'kinda'. I wouldn't have expected it."

She felt Him chuckle again. *"How is God supposed to sound?"*

"I suppose I expected a lot of 'thee' and 'thou' and stuffy talk like that," she answered truthfully.

"Look around you next time you're outside. Look at the trees, the flowers, the sky, the birds, the oceans, and seas. Look at the people I've made. At our next long chat, tell Me which parts of My creation look either stuffy or boring. And if you're serious about wanting to get to know Me through the Bible, then keep your eyes open."

The ringing of the telephone interrupted Marissa's conversation. Reluctantly she said "so long" to her Voice and picked up the instrument. It was Derek.

"Hello, sweet Marissa." His voice across the line was like a caress. "I miss you so much. Tell me you're sitting at home pining for me."

Marissa laughed. This is love. "I do miss you, but no pining as yet. I've been having the most fascinating conversation."

"Who with?"

"With all due respect, honey, you're nowhere close to the league this Guy plays in. He speaks to my heart, my mind, and my innermost being," Marissa teased.

"My first day away from you and already I have such stiff competition? I thought I was your one and only!"

"You are. But this Guy just has a lot of stuff to teach me, you know. Stuff that you can't help me with."

"Like what?"

"Like how to love you even more than I do now."

"Oh. *That* Guy!"

"Yeah, that Guy!"

"How come you never have these conversations with Him when I'm around? I could get jealous you know."

"Trust me. You wouldn't want to mess with that relationship. Get your own. Plus we talk about private stuff. And you can't fault a system where you come out the beneficiary every time I talk to Him, can you?"

"I'm still jealous and I miss you, Mrs. Clarke."

"I love you too, honey. By the way, I have an interview with the Ministry tomorrow morning at 11:00."

"That was fast! I was looking forward to having you home for at least a few more weeks. Try to negotiate for a late start date."

"Derek, I haven't even been offered the job as yet."

"You'll get it!"

"Honey, is there something we missed talking about in premarital counseling?"

"What do you mean?"

"My working. Is that going to be a problem?"

"Of course not. Well, truthfully, I would prefer if we had some more together time before we get too busy with our various careers. I like having you to come home to."

Marissa smiled at the petulant tone in his voice. He could be such a baby sometimes. "OK, I'll see what I can negotiate if they make me an offer. But don't get too used to the idea. I want to be out working too. So until we have a child, that's what I'm going to do."

"Yes, ma'am. Do you still love me?"

"Who said I ever stopped? I'll see you later, honey. Come home early. I might just have a surprise waiting for you."

Derek's tone was eager. "Does it involve chocolate? You know how I feel about chocolate!"

"Which part of surprise don't you understand?"

"OK. I'll see you later. Gotta get back to my boring briefs."

Marissa had a comeback. "You could always switch to boxers."

"Ha! Ha! I married a comedian."

"'Bye Derek." Marissa hung up the phone and counted her blessings, which were many.

Chapter 8

Yolanda parked her car beside the space reserved for the pastor. Today she'd come early for church because she wanted to join the women in the prayer group. Tossing frantic prayers to the sky had its place but more satisfaction could be found from praying for and with other women. She didn't do this often enough. Today however, she needed it.

She opened the door to the prayer room and found that someone had arrived even earlier than she had. The welcoming smile of Grace Wilson greeted her and warmed her heart the way it always did.

"Yolanda, so good to see you," greeted the reserved middle-aged woman. "I've missed you at our prayer group."

"Well, with the wedding plans and the children and relatives arriving from out of town, it was a bit frantic for the past few weeks. But I've missed it too, so this morning I decided to throw off the covers and come."

"I'm glad you did. And how are you doing, I mean really doing?"

Yolanda frowned. She resented the question even as she welcomed the care behind it. "The bald truth is that I'm lonely, Grace, and I'm having negative feelings toward this wonderful woman my son married." Biting her lip, she continued, "There's a part of me that cannot yet fully embrace her. She's a really nice girl, the kind you'd want your son to marry, but every time I see her I want to scream. You can see why I need prayer."

Grace gave her a look of understanding. "It's hard to lose those we love, isn't it? And then you get these unreasonable bursts of anger, so strong you could set a forest on fire. Anger at them for leaving you, anger at yourself for not being able to handle it, and sometimes anger at God for putting you in this position."

"Why Grace, how could you understand what I'm going through? That's exactly how I feel. And then I feel so crummy after I've behaved badly that I get angry at myself for being such a wimp and such a faithless child of God. I'm afraid I'm a major disappointment to Him, Grace. I should have peace. Doesn't He promise peace that passes all understanding? So how come I'm so not at peace?"

". . . for it is God who works in you to will and to act according to his good purpose" (Phil. 2:13).

Grace and Yolanda turned at the sound of the soft voice. They had thought themselves alone in the room. "I didn't mean to startle you, ladies. But Yolanda, I couldn't help overhearing your conversation."

Yolanda, still in the grip of her emotion made room for Catherine Charles to join them. The older Caucasian woman lowered herself slowly on to the chair. "What are you saying Sister Charles?" asked Yolanda.

"We can't have peace without faith. And by faith I mean trust in God. Can we trust Him to carry us through the difficult situations in our lives? Can we trust Him to give us the power to be Christ-like in our behavior even when we don't feel like doing the right thing? It's all there in the Bible. Hundreds of examples of people just like us who struggled with faith, but 'without faith it is impossible to please God'" (Heb.11:6).

Yolanda could feel a great weight of defeat pressing down on her. She could not do this. Coming here was a mistake. Tears of frustration filled her downcast eyes.

"You make it sound so easy. Just read the Bible, trust in God, and you'll have peace." She blinked rapidly. "It's been three years since Jackson died. Three years that I spent trying to put one foot in front of the other. Do you know how hard it's been?"

"I have some idea," replied Catherine.

"How can you have any clue?" Yolanda said bitterly. "You still have your husband. You don't have to face a lonely bedroom, watch all your children leave, and try to paste a smile on your face each day to signal to the world that you're on top of things?"

Catherine gathered Yolanda close to her and just held on. Grace came to sit on the other side and began to pray.

"Loving and most understanding Friend, Creator of the universe, Redeemer of lost souls and Savior of us all, You who were in all points tempted like us, You who understand our human frailties and have been touched with the feelings of our infirmities, please attend to us here in this room. We come to pray, to seek Your wisdom, Your strength, Your embrace. O mighty God, we ask You to incline Your ear to the pain of Your daughter and our sister Yolanda. As we put our arms around her Lord, we are asking You to use us to stand in the gap so that she will feel embraced as if by You. You see how much she's hurting, You who have experienced the most absolute kind of abandonment at the cross, know exactly the extent of her loneliness, the empty spaces that death has left behind.

"Heal her wounded heart, merciful Father, and we pray that she will, from this day forward, start seeing You in a marked way in every area of her life. That the things she wishes to overcome will be done through the might and power of Your Holy Spirit. Show us how to help her, Lord, how to be the support and friends we need to be so that she can truly experience this peace that the world does not understand. Peace that comes from knowing that You are holding on to her and will hold her up no matter what. We pray for healing for us all, for mercy for us all, and thank You for Your absolute and amazing grace. Amen."

The arms around Yolanda tightened and relaxed but did not let her go. Catherine began to speak and Yolanda could feel a slight tremor in the older woman's arm still draped around her shoulder.

"How are you doing spiritually, dear Yolanda?"

Yolanda had never been asked a question like this before. "I'm not sure I know how to answer your question." She did not appreciate the quaver in her voice.

"How is your relationship with God?"

How was her relationship with God? Good question. What was the answer? Head still bowed Yolanda asked, "Do you want the truth?"

She felt Catherine's smile. "I wouldn't recommend lying in the house of God. I know I'm asking a really personal question, but please humor an old woman. You see, lately I've been talking to God about ministry, what God can still use me to do, and it came to me that we very rarely inquire about each other's spiritual condition. Why is that, when our eternal salvation is at stake? If I knew you were diagnosed with a terminal illness or even if you had a common cold, I would do something to help you bear it. I'd make you chicken soup or visit your hospital bed, or massage your back if it would help to ease your pain." Catherine gave her a last squeeze and let go.

"How right you are, Catherine," Grace said. "We care about each other—we truly do—but we rarely ask about each other's spiritual condition. I guess we're not sure how to broach the subject. It could be perceived as some kind of censorship, invasion of privacy."

"But if we don't ask, we do not know," Catherine stated. "And if we don't know, how can we help? It could be that the spiritual battle someone is facing is something we have fought and gained the victory over through Christ. I think there is too much at stake for us to keep silent on this topic."

Grace nodded. "You're so right, Catherine. So much."

"I don't like reading the Bible."

There, she said it. To no one other than Lisa had Yolanda confessed this. Not even to Jackson. "I've been in the church for most of my life. Read the Bible when I have to, but I find a great reluctance to pick it up voluntarily and read it. Sometimes I make myself do it but it's much easier to read my devotional book, or a book on prayer, or any other inspirational writing. What does that say about my Christianity, ladies?"

"It says that we have been neglectful of you. It says that you're being honest. And I have a confession to make to you as well. I did not always have a love affair with the word of God either." Grace smiled at Yolanda's look of shock.

"You?"

"Me too," echoed Catherine.

"Well how did you get to like it? What did you do? How long ago was this?"

Catherine looked up to heaven and laughed in glee. "OK, so You were right, again. Thank You for Your faithfulness."

Yolanda glanced toward the ceiling and then at Catherine. "What was that about?"

"That was the ministry I was talking about, at least part of it. How would you ladies like to come to my house one or two Sunday mornings each month for a feast?"

"You mean Sunday brunch?" asked Yolanda

"Food both for the body and the soul. We'll have a wonderful breakfast at each meeting and then we will feast on the word of God. Now while I can't guarantee that the physical food will always be spectacular, I can guarantee that the soul food will not be boring. We will explore the word of God together and tackle some of the issues we all have with the Bible. Say you'll come. And . . ." Catherine added with emphasis, "if after four meetings you still think the Bible is boring, you don't have to come back ever."

Grace was the first to say yes. "I enjoy the Bible, but it's much more fun to share it with others. Count me in."

"And you, Yolanda?" Catherine prompted.

"Well, it seems that God has an interesting way of answering prayers. Recently Lisa and I were talking about getting into the Word of God, and she told me that since I was the older one I needed to do something about it. So yes, I'll come. And I think Lisa would be interested as well."

Catherine clapped her hands, eyes shining with excitement. "Excellent. We'll start with a small group of five to six women and then we shall see. We shall see."

Yolanda spoke. "I haven't answered your question about my spiritual condition but I'll think on it. Off the top of my head I'd say that it's in se-rious need of an overhaul."

Grace got up and walked toward the window. Her back suggested a need for privacy and as she gazed out the window, she said, "We all could do with either an overhaul or a tune-up for our spiritual condition, Yolanda. I read somewhere that our faith is only as good as each day's trial. We never know when something is going to test us in a way we've never been tested before. Then there is no borrowing from yesterday's faith in-vestment. It's a whole new exercise in trusting."

Interlude

Journal

I went back the next day and got it done. I skipped church and did what I had to do.

When I told _____ what I had done, he got very upset. How could I have done this thing without even talking to him? I told him I did it for us, for our future. Men don't understand that sometimes women have to make tough decisions for the greater good.

From the first time I saw him I felt as if I'd been reborn. We were both in our late teens when we met and I can't recall ever being so happy in my entire life as when I was with him. Being with him made me more of me. He was so handsome—closely cropped hair, lean, bow-legged, and sexy. The planes of his face were just beautiful . . . and the look in his eyes. He loved the Lord just as much as I did. We were . . .

Once the deed was done, _____ never talked about it much after that. And then, well, he . . . I'll come back to that another time. It's too painful even now to write about.

Chapter 9

Two minutes into the meeting with the so-called hired gun Lisa knew her decision to accompany Sophie was not one of her better ones. She judged the lawyer as too cocky. He talked too much, looked at her too closely, and seemed dismissive. His office did not shout opulence, but from the ordered mahogany desktop to the matching burgundy chairs strategically placed in front of his desk, the space exuded masculinity and authority. The almost coal black eyes from which he regarded her gave little clue to his thoughts.

Knowing that she was somewhat out of her depth on this mission of mercy (or stupidity; after all, what did she know about family law?) Lisa felt her defensive muscles flexing. Bad sign! This almost sent her feet flying in the direction of the exit. Before she could put thought to action however, Sophie took her by the arm and requested a seat. She then calmly outlined her rights as a birth mother and the obligation of the courts to award her custody of her child even in this situation where she had not so much abandoned the child, but had put her in a safe place until she'd gotten herself in a position to adequately care for her—which she had now done.

Lisa hoped the shock she was feeling did not show. Gone was the frantic, almost belligerent young woman who'd stormed her office an hour ago. She opened her mouth to speak and Sophie gave her an almost imperceptible right-eyed wink. Obviously the hired gun was stumped too. Well, almost.

"Your points are well taken Ms. Sahara, but you did abandon your child. You told the people at the shelter that you could not take care of it and for them to find it a good home. I have."

"With all due respect sir, my daughter is not an 'it.' She's Laurel Victoria Sahara. And as I stated earlier, a birth mother has the right to change her mind."

"And with all due respect, Ms. Sahara, you have already demonstrated that you cannot be trusted with the care of your own child." He scanned his notes. "What kind of job did you get by the way?"

"I'm day manager at Quick Stop Coffee over on Simcoe Drive."

The hired gun smiled indulgently. "And how much money will you make as a day manager, Ms. Sahara?"

"Sir, I assume you are concerned about my ability to take care of my kid while holding down a job. Who will look after her when I am at work? What will I do if she gets sick? And given I'm such an irresponsible teenager, will I change my mind again if things get to be more than I can handle?"

"Well said, Sophie," encouraged Lisa. "Please put this gentleman's fears to rest. I'm sure he's anxious to be assured that Laurel will not be harmed in any way should she be returned to her birth mother."

Lisa felt Sophie cast a quick glance in her direction but kept her eyes focused on those of the hired gun.

"No problem, ma'am," replied Sophie in her pseudo-professional voice. To the hired gun she then addressed herself. "My supervisor is a woman. When she offered me the job, I told her about Laurel. About what happened and explained to her that I would be working to get my daughter back. She suggested that I could rent the apartment above the coffee shop. I then talked to my mom who agreed to come over and be with Laurel during the day while I worked, and of course, I've purchased a baby monitor so that I can keep tabs on her as well. The money I make will keep a roof over our heads and food on the table. We'll not be rich, but we'll have each other."

"And if she gets sick?" the hired gun asked.

"Babies will get sick, sir. It's part of growing up. When she gets sick I will take her to the doctor. I will do whatever is necessary to keep her well, healthy, and happy."

Lisa thought the hired gun was weakening. At least she hoped he was. His next question, however, dashed her little piece of hope. He switched to the "understanding your point of view soft-tone."

"How old are you, Ms. Sahara? And do not give me that 'with all due respect' insolence."

A flicker of something passed across Sophie's face. It looked like irritation but she mastered it and responded instead, "Eighteen, sir."

The hired gun must have seen it too. A chink in the borrowed persona. He decided to worry it.

"You're a very attractive young woman. I'm sure you must know that." His voice was like the lure of honey to a bear, like sugar on a fly trap.

Lisa jumped in to intervene. "Excuse me. Where is this taking us and how is it relevant to my client's ability to properly parent her child?"

The hired gun did not take his eyes off Sophie as he answered Lisa's question. His tone now was as soft as cashmere and beguiling as a serpent's. "Well Ms.," he glanced quickly at her ring finger which today was naked, "Yes, Ms. Westwood. The point I'm trying to make is that an attractive young woman such as your client here will have some difficulty keeping the men away. Who knows, she may decide in a month or two that the responsibilities of parenting are too much for her. All her friends will be out dating and having fun and there she'll be, stuck at home with a colicky baby. She might just want to have some of that fun, too. I'm sure in no time she'll be dating again. Isn't that right, Ms. Sahara?"

Lisa mentally crossed her eyes, and physically crossed fingers and toes. *Please God, if You want this young woman to raise this baby of hers, give her the right words to say now. I feel that everything will depend on her answer.*

For the first time since they entered the lawyer's office, Sophie had no comeback. Her shoulders drooped and her chin, no longer able to point forward with manufactured confidence, dropped to her chest. She swallowed several times, the pulse in her too pale neck throbbing rapidly. Lisa made another observation. For the first time since the meeting began, Sophie looked far younger than her just-turned-18 years, displaying a vulnerability she'd not allowed to come through before.

Lisa wondered what was going on in the young woman's mind. She could hear her own wristwatch ticking. Donald had many times offered to buy her a digital, aka a more silent one, but she liked the ticking sound. Now it marked off time that with each tick became more and more uncomfortable.

The hired gun did not help matters. He'd stopped egging Sophie on and waited, poker faced, chair tilted back.

Please God, Lisa prayed again. *Please give her the right words.*

Sophie expelled a hard sigh and slowly raised her head. Gone was the borrowed personality. In its place appeared another Sophie, this one more closely resembling at least in spoken voice, the young woman who visited Lisa's office that morning.

"I wish I could tell you that I'll never look at another guy, y'know, or that they won't approach me. I've had guys starin' at me from before I was like 13. Even guys your age. So maybe my face is all right to look at but there's nothin' I can do about that. It's the only face I got and it doesn't change what I wanna do."

This time the teenager searched for the words in her heart, not the researched notes in her head. The rhythmic swinging of the office clock's pendulum joined its beat to the softer tick of Lisa's watch, counting off the passage of time.

"I watch my friends goin' out and think about what my life woulda been like without a kid. But thinkin' how things coulda been different don't change what is. I have a kid. Since the first time I held Laurel and felt her grab onto my finger so tight, somethin' changed, y'know. I feel lost without her. I tried last Saturday night to go out. I mean, I did go out. But I left. I felt that I didn't fit there no more, y'know. All I thought about was my kid and that I'd rather be holdin' on to her than to some drunken guy. I miss her, man. She's prob'bly missin' me too."

Two tears leaked out of each of Sophie's eyes. "Maybe one day I'll meet a decent guy who'll love both me and my kid and maybe we'll get a shot at happy ever after—whatever that is. Then again, maybe it'll be my kid who'll break the three generation cycle of single moms in my family. I don't know what I can tell you to convince you to let me have a chance at lovin' and takin' care of my own personal mistake. And it's my mistake, not Laurel's. I don't want her wonderin' years from now why her mom didn't want her, nor at least try to keep her."

Sophie looked fully at the hired gun, all her bravado gone. In its place stood raw honesty. "Mr. Hendricks, sir, right now all I can tell you is I'll love my kid no matter what. Me and my mom talked 'bout our stuff the other day. She told me she was mad at me because she was disappointed, y'know. That's why she threw us out. She'd wanted me to be the one to break the cycle. But it didn't happen, did it?"

Lisa stole a look at the hired gun but his look remained undecipherable and fixed as Sophie talked on.

"Then she, my mom, told me somethin' I haven't heard her say in years. She told me she loved me. And that together we could help each other. My guess is what she was offerin' to do for me was way more than she got from her mom when she had me! So things can change, y'know. It might take a while, but things don't hafta be like they was before. My kid will not be waitin' years to hear love words from me and . . . well . . . that's all I have to say. Sir." Only then did she break eye contact and looked past the hired gun to someplace where neither he nor Lisa could see.

Lisa felt a crying moment coming on and pulled out a tissue of professionalism to stem the tide. "So Mr. Hendricks—"

"Josh, or as my mom would say, 'Joshua Anthony Hendricks.'" He held out his hand to shake hers, his eyes taking her in as a person as if for the first time. "You did a great prep job with your client here. I'm impressed."

"I think my client did an excellent job making a case for why she should have her child back," replied Lisa.

"I had the perfect set of parents ready and eagerly waiting to adopt that baby."

Lisa picked up on the past tense. "Meaning you don't have them anymore?"

"Meaning that they found another child and have gone in that direction."

"But why did you put Sophie, I mean my client through all this if her baby is available and not yet spoken for?"

"Because Ms. Westwood, that's my job. The family courts employ me to do this, and trust me, I am very good at my job."

"With all due respect to your professional credentials, Mr. Hendricks."

"Hang the 'due respect,' Ms. Westwood! Too many of our children are living in home situations that would make your hair curl even more than it's doing now. Teenagers who are still children and looking for love, the love they should have appropriately gotten from their mothers and fathers, thinking they can find it in a baby. And when the baby's demands are too much for them—the earaches, the teething, the croup, the constant wailing—they burn, shake, slap, smother, or abandon their precious 'love gift.' And yes, I have heard all the plans and all the promises: 'I have a job. I will never look at another guy again, I'll get help,' and I've seen all those promises broken when reality meets hard knocks."

"So you're tellin' me that I can't have my daughter back 'cause I'm like all the rest you just talked about?" Sophie's lips trembled.

"You, Ms. Sahara, I will take a chance on. And do you know why?"

Sophie shook her head.

"Because you have awareness. You at least have thought about the difficulties. You have recognized that your past is a big influence on your future and despite that, you want to do it. No guarantees. You have dreams and hopes. But you're not banking everything on them coming true according to some rose-colored glasses you view your dreams through. Please don't prove me wrong."

Joshua Hendricks started to gather his papers together. Sophie did not move. She sat frozen.

Lisa prodded her. "You got your daughter back, Sophie!"

And then Sophie looked at her. Really looked at her.

"I . . . I . . . I . . . hav'er. Have her back?" she stuttered. "I have my daughter back. Oh, if there's a God in heaven He smiled at Sophie Sahara today!"

Like a confused weather day, Sophie's face broke out with the biggest smile Lisa had ever seen. But it was the sound that gurgled in her throat and emerged in heartbreaking sobs that propelled her out of her chair straight into Lisa, who somehow had anticipated the reaction and was braced with arms outstretched to comfort.

While the young woman sobbed out her relief, Lisa crooned words of comfort, her body swaying to the subconscious rhythm of nurturing. Her professionalism deserted her as she joined tears with those of her client and did not care one whit what the hired gun—God's answer to a young woman's prayer—thought.

O God, let her prove him wrong.

Moments later, Sophie had herself back in control. Joshua Hendricks was busy writing notes on a pad as if scenes like these were commonplace to him.

"Mr. Hendricks?"

His eyes when he looked up at Sophie were softer. "Yes, Ms. Sahara."

"Sorry I lost control like that in your office but I was just so scared, y' know. That I wouldn't get her back. Thank you so much."

"You hide scared pretty well, Ms. Sahara. And you are welcome. But I will be keeping tabs on you, young lady. Mark my words."

"So what do I do now? Can I get her today? Oh, Mr. Hendricks, you're such a nice man. And to think I was callin' you all kinda names in my head."

Joshua's eyebrows rose. The expression was enough to make one quake in her shoes but the twinkle in his eyes disarmed the ammunition. Lisa could see how that look could make a client say words she hadn't planned on. Sophie who was looking at the floor in supplication missed the twinkle.

"You're not the first one, Ms. Sahara. I've been called many names in my life. What was yours?"

Now it was Sophie's turn to squirm. "It's OK. It wasn't anythin' really awful. Some things it's better not to know anyway."

"Do you want your baby back today or next week, Ms. Sahara?"

"Today if it's possible," responded Sophie looking like the floor couldn't open up fast enough to take her in or that she could turn back time and erase that unguarded confession.

"Then tell me."

"Oh, all right. It was 'the hired gun.'"

"The what? Did you say 'hired gun'?"

Sophie nodded sheepishly.

Joshua threw back his head and bellowed with laughter. "That one is a first, Ms. Sahara. And not far from the truth now that I think of it from your perspective. A hired gun. I will add that one to my book of names. I collect them you know. One of my weird habits."

"Oh," said Sophie.

Lisa felt her own face smiling. This Joshua Hendricks was certainly a multifaceted man. The clock in his office started to chime. When it got to 11,

Lisa thought she would have enough time to make her appointment at the jewellers, 20 minutes away. But when it continued to 12:00, she looked up in alarm. "Is that the right time?" she asked.

"Less 10 minutes," said Joshua. "I set all my clocks and watches ahead by 10 minutes. Helps me to get to places on time."

"I need to get back to the office by noon. Sophie, I'm sorry to desert you but I'm sure Mr. Hendricks will see to you from here on. Here's my card, Mr. Hendricks. Please call me if you need anything pertaining to Sophie." She shook his hand, gave Sophie a quick hug and dashed out of the office.

Joshua stared at the door Lisa had just closed. "Nice woman. Have you known her long?" he asked Sophie.

"Long enough to know that she has a kind heart." *And something else*, thought Sophie, but she couldn't put her finger on what the something else was.

Chapter 10

Yolanda deftly removed the spinach quiche from Catherine's oven and placed it on the warmer. It was just starting to turn golden at the edges and looked delicious. That completed the bountiful feast prepared for this first meeting of the women's prayer group.

Catherine had insisted on setting the table in style, white linen and china, real cloth napkins, beautifully fluted long-stemmed goblets standing erect beside sparkling tumblers, dainty teacups, and cutlery shined to perfection. Beside each of the six place settings lay a single perfect thorn-free pink rose. And then the food—freshly squeezed orange juice, real apple cider, choices of herbal teas, fresh fruit, scones and preserves, and of course, Yolanda's quiche.

Both women stood back and surveyed the table. Each gave a nod of approval. All was in readiness for their guests. Catherine excused herself to go freshen up, leaving Yolanda in charge of early arrivals.

Yolanda had volunteered to come early to help. She loved to cook and had suggested the scones and quiche. Catherine did all the rest along with the setting up of the cozy living room to which they would adjourn after breakfast for the supposed feast of the soul. Yolanda felt her body tightening up and made herself relax. "Sufficient to each day," Jackson would say when she fretted things to death.

"Hello there, Mrs. Clarke. Something sure smells good in here."

Yolanda turned.

Thomas Charles. She always liked this tall, grey-haired man. An imposing figure until one looked into his face lined with creases from years of laughter and pain. But it was the laughter lines around his eyes and mouth that were deepest. While the top of his head was completely bald, thick white hair crowned the bottom half, giving him a regal imp look.

"Hello to you too, Mr. Charles," responded Yolanda warmly. She considered giving him a hug but checked herself. Instead, she extended her hand but he pulled her to him and gave her a nice fatherly hug. He smelt of Irish Spring and ointment and Yolanda resisted the urge to snuggle her head against his bony chest.

"Why Thomas Charles, I leave the room for two minutes and there you are consorting with my female guest."

Thomas kept one arm loosely around Yolanda's shoulders and with the other pulled his wife close. He kissed her on the cheek.

"Come here you troublemaker. How is the love of my life doing today?" he asked, stroking her back.

Eyes shining like a girl's, Catherine slapped at her husband playfully. "Go on with you, Mr. Charmer. The love of your life is doing just fine and you need to make yourself scarce before the rest of the ladies get here. Next you'll want to hug them all and then we'll never get properly started. Shoo, dear."

Thomas' countenance fell. "I know when I'm not wanted. But those scones sure look good."

"And I've prepared you a lovely tray which even now is waiting for you in your study."

Thomas smacked his lips and rubbed his hands in glee. "Why didn't you say so before? Now that I have a more appealing incentive, I'm going." He kissed his wife's cheek again and gave a salute to Yolanda.

Catherine and Yolanda watched him go. "See that. Food wins over love every time. And for all he eats, I have no clue where it goes."

Yolanda felt that dull ache coming on, a precursor to what she now referred to as her "spooks." Missing Jackson was there in every man's hug and in every couple's taken for granted intimacies. But before the ache could take full form the doorbell rang and Marissa, the first of the soul food seekers, arrived.

Sixty minutes later, the food had been consumed and the table cleared. Catherine allowed five minutes for bathroom breaks and then shepherded everyone with military efficiency into the living room. Lisa, Marissa, Grace, Yolanda, Catherine, and another young woman named Monica, about Marissa's age, formed the small group.

Lisa curled up in one of the rockers and tucked her purple-socked feet under her. "After that lovely breakfast, must we now use our brains? My brain is still giving thanks to my taste buds and tummy for the feast."

Grace, wiping imaginary crumbs from her lips, agreed. "Mine is too, but I can't wait for this course. I've been looking forward to it all week." She picked up her large black Bible and directed a look of anticipation in Catherine's direction.

"Browner," said Lisa out loud.

When Catherine wasn't looking, Grace made a face at her that had them all howling with laughter. It was so unexpected and she was usually so proper.

"Grace, are you making faces?" Catherine asked turning around.

The shocked look on Grace's face sent them all into another howling fit.

"Guilty as charged, ma'am. But I would have you know that there was also a degree of provocation prior to the face-making."

"Snitch!" stage-whispered Lisa. Marissa giggled and even Monica with the serious face broke a small smile.

Catherine held up her hand, the one with the slight tremor, until the room became quiet. "Isn't it nice when we as Christians can get together like this and eat, laugh, and socialize?"

All the women nodded.

Catherine looked over at Grace who was seated beside her on the beige three-seat sofa. "I'm going to disappoint you a bit today, Grace dear. Today instead of starting out with a formal Bible study, I feel impressed to start our meeting with a story. Some might like to think of it as a testimony."

Catherine saw Yolanda visibly stiffen. Monica looked out the window. Only Lisa, Marissa, and Grace maintained open postures, so she was quick to add, "This is not your testimony but mine. And I think the reason why I've been impressed to share this story is so you can see that some of the things you're going through, some of the mixed feelings or guilt you have about the Bible—those things lived in me at one point. And I'm also hoping that as we grow in the Word and also in our comfort with each other, we can share stories of triumphs and battles—ongoing, new, or ones overcome, so that we can help to boost each other. But before I start, let's ask God to again bless our gathering and work through us today."

The heads bowed, but before Catherine could begin praying Marissa started to address the throne of mercy, inviting the Holy Spirit to do His work—guiding them to truth, teaching them, and bringing things back to remembrance. At the "amen," Catherine looked at the expectant faces of the women, wondering about their lives and what sharing her story might set off. A part of her balked at the telling, but urged by the Spirit she opened her mouth. God would help her find the right words.

When she concluded, unchecked tears streamed down Lisa's face. Marissa and Yolanda's eyes shone with extra moisture, while Grace hummed a hymn about how sweet it is to trust in Jesus. Monica excused herself to go to the powder room. When she returned her face had that just-washed look and in her eyes were remnants of pink pain.

Catherine made no attempt to cover up the moment with activity. Sometimes, she'd found, it was better to let silence do the talking. It was Lisa, still crying, who spoke first.

"I feel so . . . I don't know what I'm feeling. But it's just that you never know what's behind a face you know. Sequestered pain, dashed hopes, but I would have never thought you had gone through all that. And to find your way to God again despite all of it. I don't know how you did it."

"Neither do I," said Catherine. "But God is the great enabler. And it's because of this experience and how God enabled me—because there is no way I could have done it on my own—that I'm so excited to hear of your willingness to discover God through the Bible. But the Bible is just one way of discovering Him. We first start with a need in our heart." She took a deep breath as old memories flashed through her mind. "The need is that empty space that nothing or no one else can fill. It's that sense of 'lostness.' That's what drives our quest. I believe that when God created us in His image, He placed within each one of us a homing device of sorts that triggers a kind of restlessness or a longing and sends us seeking for a way back home."

Yolanda spoke up. "So the Bible is like a road map then."

"That's a perfect analogy," replied Catherine. "Yes, the Bible is like a road map. When one of the disciples asked Jesus to show them the way, what did He say? 'I am the way and the truth and the life. No one comes to the Father except through me' (John 14:6).

Monica asked, "So is the idea that because we learn about Jesus from the Bible, by reading the Bible we can discover how to get back home?"

"Not only that," said Grace, leaning forward in her chair, the balls of her feet helping to support the incline of her body, "the Bible contains not only Jesus' teachings but the stories and the perspectives of believers like us"—she smiled—"from Moses to Paul. People who had encounters with God. Through them we can learn a lot about whom God is and isn't. It helps as well if we read different versions of the Bible. Sometimes what's unclear in one version is better understood in another translation."

"I think prayer is another neat way to get to know God," said Marissa almost shyly. "He says things to you sometimes that are just plain wonky and unexpected. And He doesn't sound like what I thought He'd sound like."

"What do you mean by that?" Lisa demanded. She'd been gently rock-ing herself in the chair, feet tucked under her, but at Marissa's last words the chair stopped cold.

"You're saying you talk to God and *He* talks back to you?" Her look of disbelief was comical, but no one laughed.

Monica spoke again. "Tell us more about this, Marissa. I'm curious to know how it works."

Marissa's honey brown skin took on a hue of embarrassment.

"Go on," Catherine gently urged.

"Well, last year I bought a book about prayer from the Christian bookstore on Pine Street. You know, the one that—"

"Get to your point!" Lisa interrupted.

"Well, OK," Marissa huffed. "The author said that many times our prayers sound either like shopping lists or a things-to-do list. We ask for this and that and throw in a few thanks and blessings and that's it. She said that we don't even stop and listen to hear what God has to say about the stuff we asked about. She even went further, saying that our prayers should be more like conversations. We should say good morning or hello or whatever and just talk to God about what's on our minds."

She paused for a breath, and saw Catherine's thoughtful nod. "It doesn't mean we shouldn't make requests," she continued. "After all, He's our Father and He wants to give us good gifts, but we shouldn't just come to Him because of the gifts. We come to Him and talk to Him because we want to. Actually, we should talk to Him even when we don't want to, because the relationship is that important to us." She shook her head. "I'm not sure I'm explaining it very well, but that's the gist of it."

Lisa's foot continued to hold the rocker motionless. "So let me get this straight. You do your 'Hello, God' or what have you and prattle on about your day and all that, and then you listen and God answers? I don't get it. I ask myself all kinds of questions in my head all the time and my brain spits back out answers. How is this different?"

Marissa, too, sat forward in her chair. "I'm not sure, Lisa. Sometimes I think it's my head spitting things back out at me. And if so, that's still all right since I ask God to guide my thoughts and help me make the right decisions. Sometimes the answer to our situation is already in our heads, in our minds, or hearts, but God enables us to retrieve it as we need it. But sometimes, I swear to you, the things His voice suggests to me are things I would not have come up with on my own. And His voice actually has a texture to it that I would not have attributed to God."

"You're making my head hurt," Lisa moaned.

"But think about it, ladies," Catherine chimed in. "Remember the story of Elijah. First came an earthquake, but God was not in that. Then came a fire and something else that my brain refuses to supply at the moment, but God wasn't in any of those big things. The story says that God spoke in a still small voice. It was that small voice that Elijah needed to hear. There he was feeling so sorry for himself—believing he was the only one in the country still faithful to God. He'd just helped to demonstrate God's power on Mount Carmel, but instead of a reprieve for good behavior he'd had to flee Queen

Jezebel because she wanted him dead. He was in an awful state and then God spoke to him.

"The New Testament also describes the work of the Holy Spirit as 'taking from what is mine and making it known to you' (John 16:14). When we receive the Spirit in our hearts—or our minds—we're actually tuning in to God. But we have to open the conversational door so to speak."

Marissa continued. "Derek and I made a commitment to read through the Bible this year and also to make time to pray together as a couple at the start of each day. But I'll tell you, that's easier said than done. It was easy when we were on our honeymoon, because we weren't on any schedule. But the first morning back to work we overslept and neither one of us remembered."

"Things like that will happen from time to time, but don't let one or two little slip-ups discourage you," Catherine said. "God isn't looking for people to put in time with Him based on some obligation. He wants us to enjoy our times with Him as much as He enjoys being with us."

"I don't have a problem praying and talking to God," Yolanda said, almost to herself. "But when it comes to reading the Bible, I find myself doing everything but. How do I get past this phobia?"

"I don't so much have a phobia about reading the Bible," Lisa told the group. "Mine is more like a kind of avoidance. Maybe I need to approach it the way I do exercise, something I'm not very fond of.

"That's an understatement!" murmured Yolanda.

Lisa ignored her. "I make myself work out faithfully at the gym three times per week and once I'm done, I actually feel quite good. So I suppose if we're reluctant to get started reading the Bible, maybe we should just do it, like on a schedule, until it becomes a good habit."

"We're off to an excellent start, ladies. Excellent!" said Catherine. "But I am going to suggest that instead of just reading the Bible, we study it. One way to do that is to approach it from a topical point of view. What does the chapter or book we're reading have to say, for example, about whom God is? What does the Bible have to say about salvation, marriage, children, sin, forgiveness, Christian development—all the practical stuff for our everyday situations? The topics we select should be relevant to us. That's what will make our study meaningful."

Monica raised a hand. "What do we do about the sceptics?" she asked. "There's a lot of stuff in the news these days that could make you doubt the reliability of the Bible and even the resurrection. Some of it makes you wonder if the Bible is actually true or if it's been manipulated so much through the years that we can't trust it at all."

"This is where I disagree a little bit with some of our church leadership," Catherine jumped in. "We don't often deal with these issues in church. But it should be in Bible study classes where members learn about the assault on the Bible. And I truly believe that's what it is—an assault! We hesitate to vigorously question the Bible, learn about its history, what got changed, what's original and what's not. We treat the Bible with kid gloves.

"Listen, for no other book, for no other historical document has there been such pains taken to preserve the integrity of the original manuscript. In the Bible, we have eye-witness accounts from people who lived with Jesus, people who were willing to give their lives to defend the validity of their testimonies—that Jesus lived and died but He rose again!" Catherine said triumphantly, her eyes flashing fire. "So not only should we study the Bible to see what it has to say to us about our situations, but we also need to read *about* the Bible. We need to consider the questions raised about its reliability, study for ourselves the refutations put forward by apologists, and then make up our own minds."

"Oh, my brain is starting to hurt again," wailed Lisa. "I need a snack. Something sweet."

Yolanda who had been quiet for most of the discussion, stood. "I don't know about you ladies, but there's too much at stake for me to continue to plead that I don't like the Bible. While we might not understand the context of everything in it, I want to at least try to understand it better. So if Catherine will continue to lend us her beautiful home, I will commit to cooking up great breakfasts."

"Count me in," replied Grace.

"Me too," echoed Monica and Marissa.

"Lisa?" prompted Yolanda

"Far be it for me to be the only spoilsport. Who knows, maybe this time there'll be a different outcome than my previous attempts."

The words were said in so off-handed a manner that Yolanda wondered if there was more to this for Lisa. She looked closely at her friend but the rocking motion of the chair had started up again and Lisa's face gave no hint of hidden meaning.

"OK, then," said Catherine. "Four weeks from now will take us to the last Sunday in November. Is that OK with everyone?"

Heads nodded and the meeting adjourned at 2:24 p.m. with Marissa offering Monica, who'd taken the bus, a ride home.

Chapter 11

The meeting over and her house quiet, Catherine, feeling exhausted, retired to her room for a nap. Her brain however refused to relax. Something worried the edges of her mind. Somewhere during the meeting something had changed in the room. She retraced each segment of the day.

After the meal all had been well. So, too, following her storytelling. Had the change taken place during the discussion on prayer? Catherine thought not. Unable to put a name to what was bothering her she turned the problem over to her Father. Then adjusting the pillows on the bed she closed her eyes.

She woke up an hour later, refreshed, and went in search of Thomas. She found him raiding the refrigerator.

"Hungry again?"

"Again? You gave me a meal," he checked his watch, "five and a half hours ago. And I, being an honorable man, did not even peek in once to see how things were going with your meeting. Then I heard the quiet and realized everyone had left only to come upstairs to find you sleeping in the middle of the afternoon."

"Do you want me to make something for you?" Catherine asked

"No, you sit for a change. I'm making supper tonight." Pulling up a high back stool, he assisted her to it. "Now sit there and tell me what's on your mind to send you off to bed in the middle of the day."

Thomas poured himself a glass of vanilla flavored soy milk and downed it in one gulp. Catherine shuddered. White liquids of any kind turned her stomach. He then lifted out the whole vegetable tray from the fridge and began a furious chopping of carrots, celery, potatoes, radishes and onions—the latter making Catherine's eyes water and the chopping making conversation next to impossible.

When there was a pause in the chopping, she said, "I told them. The short version."

"So what's the problem? We talked about it this morning as well as last night. You were at peace with your decision then. How did they take it?"

"I kept it pretty matter-of-fact. Lisa cried, of course. So did a few of the others. And the young woman who recently started worshipping with us, Monica, excused herself to go to the bathroom. When she came out she looked like she'd been crying too."

"If our story will help others draw closer to the Savior Catherine, then the telling is worth it."

"I guess," she absentmindedly replied.

Feeling the need to move, Catherine gingerly alighted from the stool and walked toward the sliding glass door that led to the deck. A thin layer of powdery snow covered everything. At the edge of the deck floor, she could see a smattering of animal prints in the snow ending with a large disturbance which told her that Gecko, their cat, had been scaring off the squirrels again. She closed her eyes.

There. The backyard attached to the house where she'd lived a lifetime of memories. There. Where dreams had been born and too many tears shed, where she could still hear the hearty laughter of the children, and where still remained the trunk of the oak she'd made Thomas chop down.

That's it!

A different house than the one she lived in now. A different backyard. But the same feeling.

Turning away from the window she announced triumphantly. "That's it, Thomas! It wasn't the story or the discussion. It was the pain. In that room today, despite the laughter and the hearty discussion, there was pain and it wasn't mine. I felt so exhausted after the meeting, I thought maybe I'd exerted myself too much, but it was the emotions in the room that did it."

Thomas was not unaccustomed to his wife's conversational leaps. Forty-five years of being married had taught him that a raised eyebrow on his part usually was enough to get her to elaborate. But she was looking past him.

"How about catching me up on where your mind just went and what's really been bothering you?" he prompted.

Catherine focused. "After the meeting I had this out of sorts feeling. More like dissatisfaction. It's like I was supposed to do something or say something important but I'd missed it. Close to the end of the meeting I was having one of my rants about how we should tackle the Bible and not handle it with kid gloves, you know how I get! And then Lisa started to complain that her brain was too full. I chided myself for jumping in too deep with the initiates but it wasn't that at all. I'm positive it wasn't."

Thomas resumed his chopping, glad that his wife had worked through her problem. Now she could concentrate on a solution. When she had things on her mind, conversations were next to impossible. Monosyllabic answers, milk in the cupboard instead of the fridge, and salt in his tea. Even if he had not possessed good listening skills, which he did, it was to his advantage to help in expediting a resolution.

Where he was tall and lanky, she was much shorter. The years had added a pleasing plumpness to her frame which she hated, but Thomas loved. Round cheeks, a wide mouth and lively eyes always promising a smile comprised her face. But it was her heart that Thomas loved most. Her kind heart that first introduced him to God—not through a Bible study or a pamphlet distributed, but by her acts of thoughtfulness.

He'd met her at the pediatric hospital where he was interning at the time. She could comfort the most nervous of children while supporting the shaky hands of nervous interns as well. Before he'd completed his three-month rotation in her department he'd decided she would marry him.

And, oh, how she'd made him wait. She had no desire to marry a doctor! He was too tall for her. She doubted she even wanted to marry—ever! They'd have no life with all the interruptions of a doctor's work. She had plans to work overseas in a mission hospital. And most importantly she was a Christian and he was not. More excuses than his poor heart could handle.

But it was in the Christianity department where he thought he might make some headway. Determined to win her over, he'd asked her to invite him to her church. He still recalled how her jaw had dropped.

For one solid year, as often as his schedule allowed, he had kept going. Somewhere in the visiting, singing, praying, and Bible classes, he started to pay attention to this thing that was so important to her. Somewhere along the way, he discovered that he wanted it for himself too. And so he was baptized.

Still she doubted him, wondering if he had gotten baptized just to remove her objection. But thanks to words of encouragement and intentional prodding from a few of the older women in the church who cleared him as fitting for her, at last she agreed to go out with him.

It was to dinner that he first invited her. Then he waited three more weeks before asking her out again. On their third dinner date he'd slipped a ring under her dessert—a slice of pie, cherry—and she'd somehow forked it up with the pie, bit down on it, and almost broken her tooth. Thomas, already a mass of nerves, remembered the horror he'd felt as he saw the ring dangling from one of the tines of her fork beneath the morsel of pie moving daintily toward her mouth. He was sure his heart stopped beating when she bit down and yelped. With pinky finger pointed outward, she'd removed the offending material from her mouth and had burst into tears when she saw what it was.

Thomas, used as he was to dramatic moments in his line of work, had sat frozen in his chair, sure he'd blown any chance he ever had. Finally, he'd made himself reach for her hand. "I'm so sorry, Catherine. I just . . . I didn't . . . I'll take you home now."

He'd signalled for the waiter only to hear her say, "Am I not even worth a one-knee proposal?"

He'd dropped to both knees right there on the restaurant floor and asked for her hand. And she'd said an unhesitating yes which was greeted with exuberant applause from an audience they'd not been aware of having.

Thomas brought his attention back to the here and now. "Do you know from whom the pain was coming?"

Catherine wrinkled her brow in concentration. "I'm not sure. I know Yolanda is missing her Jackson but I think more than one woman today had buried pain of some kind. I know the texture of pain, Thomas, and some of that same texture was in the room today."

"Maybe God is up to more than just Bible study, dear," said Thomas. "Maybe He wants to use you to help heal some brokenness, too."

"Then I guess I'd better listen as hard as I plan to teach at our next meeting. And wait on God's timing." She walked over to her husband and gave him a kiss on the cheek. "Thank you for letting me think in your presence."

"I aim to please." Smiling cheekily, Thomas added the vegetables to the boiling water and replaced the lid. He reached for a loaf of the bread she'd baked early this morning and cut four thick slices, laying them on a plate. Catherine actually felt a rumble in her tummy as the onion flavor from the soup permeated the kitchen. Today, for a change, she was actually hungry. Another one of God's small miracles.

Chapter 12

"Somebody is loved," sang Janine as Lisa returned from her lunch meeting with Russell and a new client.

"Don't tell me," said Lisa, "you've found a new guy. Again."

"I wish!" replied Janine. "You're the one receiving flowers. I tell you, girl, if you so much as even think you don't want your Donald anymore, put me on notice. I thought you said he was boringly predictable or some such implication!"

Lisa scanned her memory banks. She couldn't recall Donald ever sending her flowers on a day that was not an occasion of sorts. Yikes! Was there something happening today that she'd forgotten about? She hoped not because this new client they'd taken on, a contested estate that had to go to probate and for which she was going to need tons of background information, was going to require long hours at work. Why didn't people take time to make wills, or keep them updated? But then again, if they did, she wouldn't have such a busy practice.

Entering her office, Lisa stashed her bag in the usual place and, before hanging up her coat, removed the card attached to the lovely fall bouquet. It read, "A long overdue note of appreciation. I'm proposing lunch and a client update. Please let me know if this Thursday at noon would be a good time. Reservations tentatively on hold at Vinnie's." Joshua Hendricks' card was enclosed.

Checking her calendar Lisa saw that she was free. She hoped Sophie was all right. She felt badly for not keeping in touch with the young woman. Following their meeting at Hendricks' office, she'd called her once to make sure that the follow through had taken place with the baby and had spoken to a tired sounding but happy Sophie. And now more than a month later, the hired gun was calling to give her an update. What could be the problem? Lisa handed the card to Janine to confirm the lunch meeting and for the rest of the afternoon and far into the evening immersed herself in the new case.

At 6:17, gambling that he might be free, she called Donald at work to see how he was. Tuesdays and Wednesdays were his late nights at the dental office.

The office assistant told her he'd just started with a patient but would try to see if he could come to the phone. She came back to tell Lisa that she had not even bothered to interrupt him as he was in the process of freezing the patient. Lisa left a message to say she'd be home late and was soon buried in work.

"Westwood, please get outta here. It's 10:30!"

It was Russell, her partner.

Lisa stretched to rid her back of the kinks. "OK, OK. I've been going over the same sentence for the past five minutes anyway. However, I did find a 1972 precedent-setting case in Fort Erie that might just work for us."

Knowing if he left her she'd likely continue working, Russell waited while Lisa got her coat and then walked her to her car. Only when she'd fastened her seatbelt and started the engine did he leave. Suddenly he turned back. Lisa lowered the window.

"Tell Donald I got his reminder about the cricket game on Sunday and that I'm bringing Kyle."

"Your son is interested in something besides basketball?" asked Lisa in astonishment.

"Not really, but I told him that while cricket lacked the speed and brawn needed in basketball, it was a gentleman's game of strategy and intrigue, something young pups like him could not begin to comprehend. Man, was he ticked!"

Lisa shook her head. "You men and your sport! This is Canada, you know! Home of hockey and curling and other winter games. Paying all that money to use the Skydome once a month just to play cricket is pure ridiculousness."

Russell chuckled and gave her a sceptic's salute. "Don't knock it till you've tried it. Good night. And tell Donald I had nothing to do with you working this late."

• • • • •

At 11:45 on Thursday morning Janine buzzed Lisa to remind her of her noon appointment with Joshua Hendricks.

At 11:55 Janine stood at the door to her office. "I thought we had a policy about not being late for our appointments."

Lisa looked at her watch and gasped. Grabbing her handbag from the drawer she flew out the door almost colliding with Russell.

Janine removed Lisa's coat from the hook. Counting slowly she walked to the front door, opened it and held the coat out. When she got to 12, hurried footsteps could be heard and the coat was grabbed off her hand with a frantic thank you. Russell, who had seen this happen often enough, shook his head and continued to his office. Janine went back to business as usual.

As the server led her to a small table toward the rear of the restaurant, Lisa calmed her breathing. She'd run the whole way. Seated at the table nursing a drink of some kind was Joshua Hendricks.

"My apologies, Mr. Hendricks. It's been a busy morning," said Lisa unbuttoning her coat.

Before she realized what was happening, Joshua stood up and helped her off with it. She thanked him and reached for her chair.

"Allow me," he offered.

When she was comfortably seated he retuned to his.

"Thank you," said Lisa.

He looked her over in that unhurried manner she remembered and said. "We meet again."

"So we do," replied Lisa. "Is something the matter with Sophie and her baby?"

"They're doing just fine, Ms. Westwood. Better than I expected. But let's order our meal and then I can fill you in."

Lisa, familiar with the East Asian menu this Italian sounding restaurant served, selected the grilled tilapia with a green mango salad and Joshua ordered the Malaysian vermicelli with stir-fried veggies. The typical lunch hour conversational buzz at Vinnie's prevailed but wasn't loud enough for them to have to shout to hear each other.

The flamboyantly Italian owner Vinnie, ensuring all his customers were being looked after, greeted Joshua by name and enquired about their choice for lunch. Satisfied they would be pleased with their choices, he left them.

When he had moved out of earshot, Lisa asked, "Do you come here often?"

"Often enough. Vinnie and his family live on my street. Pretty decent guy. His boy was in a spot of trouble a couple years back and I helped him out."

"I see," replied Lisa.

Joshua took a sip of his drink and relaxed against his chair. "Ms. Westwood, before we proceed any further I must confess up front that I had an ulterior motive for contacting you. Ms. Sahara and her baby were just an excuse."

"Oh?" asked Lisa. "And what was your ulterior motive, Mr. Hendricks? An estate you need to have settled?"

"Now why didn't I think of that?" Joshua's perfect white teeth flashed a disarming smile. He leaned toward her. "No. There's no estate to settle unfortunately. A little matter of desperation precipitated my call."

Lisa's brow creased with puzzlement.

Joshua Hendricks, reading her perplexity continued. "Ms. Westwood, I can't think of a way to ease into what I want to say so I'll just get to the point. You've been haunting my dreams for several weeks. I don't usually have women I barely know creeping into my dreams and interrupting my sleep. You've been doing that, Ms. Westwood. So I thought if I met with you I might be able to understand why."

Lisa's mouth formed the shape of an "O" but no sound came out. The waiter, arriving with their meals provided a temporary reprieve. With painstaking precision under the careful and bemused scrutiny of Joshua Hendricks, Lisa arranged the napkin across her lap, took a sip of water, and picked up her fork, her brain frantically searching for a suitable response.

As the waiter added pepper to Joshua's meal, Lisa stole a quick glance at the man seated across from her. She guessed him to be a bit shy of six feet. Her Donald would be taller, yet this guy gave the illusion of being actually taller than he was. Sporting a polished bald pate and skin the color Janine would describe as Mars Bar brown, frame big boned and toned, he looked a force to be reckoned with. His hands, busy twirling the noodles on to a spoon, were almost as nice as Donald's. Tendrils of alarm prickled her skin.

"So what's the decision?" he interrupted her thoughts.

"Decision?" *What*? her brain frantically asked. *Have I missed something?*

"Now that you've had a chance to study me, what is your decision? Your conclusion? Have I been relegated to the category of the 'totally nuts' or the gentler 'mentally unstable'?"

Opting to match his frankness, Lisa said, "Bamboozled. That's what I'm feeling, Mr. Hendricks."

"Now there's a word with texture. It could mean beguiled, entrapped, hoodwinked. You think I've pulled a fast one on you, despite my decision to come clean?"

"All of the above," replied Lisa.

"Did you like the flowers?"

Have mercy! The mental gymnastics necessary for keeping a conversation going with this man! "They were very nice. I love fall colors. But with all due res—"

Joshua reached across the table and placed a finger against her lips, barely touching but effectively shushing her. "No more due respect, Ms. Westwood. I hear enough of that when you appear in my dreams. So now that we are face to face, please, no more. OK?"

His touch left an imprint on Lisa's mind of a memory . . .

Joshua closed his knife and fork and pushed away his barely touched meal. "I'm mangling this meeting terribly. Permit me to try again."

He gathered his thoughts. "I think I've been attracted to you since the day you walked into my office with young Ms. Sahara. But you see, I have lived long enough to know that attraction comes and attraction goes and with the passage of time and no fertilizer, it tends to die a natural death. After all, previous to that meeting I'd never met you and had no point of reference for the kind of person that you are. When you appeared in my first dream a few days after we'd met, I thought nothing of it since I sometimes dream of transactions that take place during my work. But it happened again a couple nights later. Now it's almost a nightly occurrence. So maybe this meeting can be a form of exorcism, h'mm?"

Lisa still had no words.

Joshua sighed and rested an elbow on the table. "Ms. Westwood, you are a very attractive woman. I like the way your hair curls behind your ear and I like the softness of your eyes. Meeting you again I see there is even more to like. You have a half dimple on your left cheek that appears only when you do that lopsided smile of yours. I like the clothes you wear. The oranges and browns bring out the healthiness of your skin. You give off good vibes, and I would love the opportunity to get to know you better— if not for a relationship then for want of sleep."

Done speaking, Joshua sat back in his chair and regarded Lisa. She looked back at him but his dark eyes provided no additional information.

"Is the tilapia not to your satisfaction, madam?" It was Vinnie himself. Seeing the half finished meal on Joshua's plate as well, he encouraged Italian style, "Manjia. Mangia tutto!"

Without taking his eyes from Lisa, Joshua waved Vinnie away. "Give us a few moments, my friend. Some things in life are more important than food."

My answer matters to him then, thought Lisa. *How can this be?*

"I'm married, Mr. Hendricks," she spoke softly.

Something shifted in his eyes.

"I see," he said.

He kept staring at her, studying her face.

Then, "Are you happy?"

Dear God, did he have to ask that question? Was she happy? Donald's kind face appeared in her mind. Tonight being Thursday, he would start the vacuuming as soon as he got home. Well, maybe if it snowed he'd shovel and salt the driveway first, making sure that she didn't slip. And after he ate, he would select the grey pants and the navy blazer, his concession to dress down Fridays and hang them on the closet door ready for the morning. Then he would take his shower, watch a bit of TV, and if she was not home, lay out the bath salts and oils in preparation for her homecoming. The Christmas tree was already up and soon he'd put up the outside lights. Was she happy?

"My husband loves me very much," Lisa replied.

"'For whom the bell tolls?' It tolls for me," quoted Joshua as he folded his napkin. "Wear your ring always, Mrs. Westwood. It helps to keep fools like me from making even bigger fools of themselves. And don't think I haven't noticed that you avoided answering my question. But I understand. There are complications. Now that we've settled that, have you any alternate recommendations for performing this badly needed exorcism?"

"None that come to mind at the moment, Mr. Hendricks," said Lisa, standing and reaching for her coat.

"Call me Joshua. I've disclosed too much to continue to be Mr. Hendricks."

He took the coat from her hands and held it open for her. As he adjusted it around her shoulders, Lisa could have sworn that he leaned in close and smelled her hair. Then he turned her around. His eyes were wistful. Lisa bowed her head but his finger was under her chin lifting her face to look at him. Just like Donald would.

"Have no fear. I will not become a pest. But if you would please indulge me for one more second. Just tell me this, Mrs. Westwood. Let's suppose there was no husband, would I have stood a chance?"

"A chance for an exorcism or a chance for a relationship?"

"What do you think I mean, Lisa?" Her name, in his voice, sounded like a caress.

"You're a very nice man, Mr. . . . uh, Joshua."

"Damning praise indeed! You make me sound like some guy who likes to wear grey and navy. Nice and dull. Go now, Mrs. Westwood, before I succumb to the strong urge to kiss you. Nice man indeed!"

Lisa felt a tingling in her cheeks. But this man was vexing! She tossed one end of her dangling scarf over her shoulder, almost hitting him. How dare he put her in this position? How dare he condemn her life? But she voiced none of those things. Instead she said, "Good day, Mr. Hendricks," picked up her handbag, and left.

Minutes later Vinnie was back. He pulled out the chair Lisa had vacated and sat. "Joshua, what's the matter? You let a woman put you off your feed?"

Joshua's smile was rueful. "Since Deidre and I divorced, I've had no desire to pursue a woman. Once was enough."

"But you met one who looked a worthy opponent, eh?" asked Vinnie, jerking his chin in the direction Lisa had exited.

Joshua nodded. "She's married and her husband loves her very much."

"The good ones are always taken, Joshua. Too bad you're not a hard liquor guy. Good time to drown your sorrows in booze."

"Or work," Joshua said, standing. He reached for his wallet and pulled out some bills.

Vinnie took the money and the wallet. "A pal should never have to pay for a meal where he's been the hearer of bad news. Vinnie's rule number 18."

He tucked the bills in the wallet, refolded it, and handed it back.

Joshua inclined his head in thanks and left.

Chapter 13

By the time Lisa got home that evening her nerves were on edge. She needed the comfort of her husband. Then she remembered that Donald had enrolled in an Egyptology course, his most recent foray into history, and would be going there directly from work. This meant that she had a whole evening to herself. But tonight she needed distractions.

Opting for a light supper, she popped two slices of dark rye in the toaster and hunted for the teapot. After boiling the kettle, she added two bags of camomile tea to the pot and poured on the hot water to let it steep. In the middle of her preparations Joshua Hendricks' face suddenly appeared—his look of wistfulness and the banked desire she'd tried not to see.

The fact that he found her attractive was nice. After all, her conscience reasoned, it was good for a woman, married or not, to be reminded from time to time that others thought her desirable. She didn't have to do anything about it but yes, it was good. Of course she'd done the right thing in walking away.

Lisa took out a small plate from the cupboard along with her favorite mug, the one that read "You are a miracle." She'd bought the pink mug at a cancer survivor fundraiser a few years back. She filled it up with the hot liquid, added a teaspoon of brown sugar and took a tentative sip. Not sweet enough. However, she resisted the temptation to add more but instead lightly buttered the toast and added some jam. A wedge of Havarti completed her supper.

With Donald-like precision she arranged the meal on a place mat and sat down to eat. As she bowed her head to give thanks for the meal Lisa experienced a feeling that made her open her eyes. It was discomfort. And guilt. Again.

Always the guilt coming at her at unexpected times.

She took a large sip of the tea.

Too hot! It burnt her lips.

Stop hiding, Lisa

That voice again. The one that'd been bugging her recently.

Just come clean.

No! There's nothing to talk about. Nothing to come clean about.

She took a bite of the toast.

How old would s/he be now, Lisa?

Her appetite failed.

How old?

Lisa did not stop to hear any more. With unhurried motions hiding an inner urgency she stood up, discarded the rest of her meal, and fled to the shower. Time to wash up and head to bed.

In the shower the voice was there.

Twenty-one this coming March, eh, Lisa?

Lisa switched mental channels.

Joshua. And his nice eyes.

No! Not that!

She pressed her mental remote again but she must have pressed previous channel because there in the static of her mind, the voice with its annoying reasonableness was still throwing out questions she had no desire to answer. But one unexpected question in particular stopped her.

You like him, don't you?

What!

Lisa started to hum. Louder above the hum the voice pressed.

You like that he likes you, don't you?

Lisa broke into song and soaped herself. She washed thoroughly. She took time with the details of her toilette. Between the toes. Behind the ears. Scrubbing of the heels. Singing hard and loud she contorted her body to reach the hard to reach areas and only when she had exhausted all the places to wash and her skin began to rebel against the cleanliness assault, did she recognize the song she'd been singing—*Memories*.

She turned off the tap, dried herself, slipped into a gown, and went to bed.

· · · · ·

Donald came home promptly at 10:00 to find her propped up in bed, reading. His face communicated his happiness in seeing her. It was not often that she was home ahead of him.

"Hi, sweetheart." He greeted her with a kiss, smelling faintly of Jovan musk and tasting like apples.

Lisa wanted to reach for him and allow the comfort of his love to soothe her. Instead she watched him walk off toward the closet, first removing his socks, (he had nice feet, her Donald), and then his shirt. His abdomen still flat, still resisting the middle-aged propensity to paunchiness.

"What a day! Three major fillings and several children with first-time cavities. Too much sugar in kids' diets, I tell you! And parents aren't taking time to supervise their kids' brushings. My Egyptology class, however, was great. I can't wait for next week!"

Lisa knew he was just venting in her presence so she kept silent.

"So how was your day, love?" Donald tossed the question over his shoulder as he aimed the pair of balled up socks in the direction of the open hamper. An overhand toss with a good arch landed them in the basket. A two pointer.

"I had a baby, you know."

Donald's arm, still orchestrating the direction of the balled socks, remained in the air even as his body turned slowly to face her. His face wore a question.

"What did you say?"

"I was 17. He was 18. One night while my parents had gone to church the doorbell rang. I had just come out of the shower so I grabbed my robe and wrapped my hair in a towel. It was him. And well, one thing led to another and I got pregnant. Anyway, I thought you should know."

From the periphery of her vision Lisa saw her husband's arm, the one that had been shooting sock basketball, fall heavily to his side, palm flat. The slapping sound it made against his thigh was soft and hollow.

"Oh," said Donald, still standing. And then he said it again. "Oh."

"Donald?" Lisa prompted.

"Did you love him?"

"Yes. I loved him then," she said softly.

"What about the baby?"

"I had an abortion."

Donald's eyes opened wide. "Oh," he said again. But this time the sound was like that of a deflating balloon, venting air and whispers.

"It was my decision. He was so upset when I told him about the pregnancy but after a few days he talked with his mom and then he talked with my parents. He had his whole life ahead of him, Donald! Yet, he wanted to do the right thing. But *I* knew better. I *did*. I didn't tell him or even my folks. I made the appointment and went by myself to get it taken care of."

"I see," said Donald even though his eyes were closed.

The ringing of the telephone broke the two-way conversation, creating a third place on which to focus. After the second ring, Lisa closest to it reached for the instrument but pulled back her hand. It rang a third time.

Donald picked it up.

"Hello." He listened. "Oh. Hello, Yolanda. Yes, we're still up. No it's not an inconvenient time to call at all." His voice was dead. "You want to speak with Lisa?"

Lisa made negative motions with her head and hands but Donald handed her the phone. Before she could give a proper response to Yolanda, he'd grabbed a sweater from the drawer, pulled it over his head and exited the bedroom closing the door behind him.

And as she sifted through what to say to her friend, Lisa heard the garage door open and close. Only then did it hit her. Her husband had gone out with no socks on his feet and wearing a sweater that did not match. Never in all the years of knowing him and being married to him had he done that. Lisa made some kind of excuse to Yolanda and hung up.

The vigil she kept lasted until the wee hours of the morning when sleep finally came to claim its debt.

The music from the radio penetrated Lisa's sleep. "Turn that off, Donald."

The music played on.

"Donald?"

But his side of the bed was empty. His pyjamas still lay neatly folded underneath his pillow.

Lisa felt an increase in the rhythm of her heart. Memory flooded her consciousness.

Donald!

She jumped out of bed and hurried next door to the guest room. He was not there. She checked the front living room and then dashed downstairs. Donald was not there either. She checked the garage. His car was gone.

Donald!

A voice in her head cried out his name. Lisa rang his cell phone. Something must have happened to him.

She got the voice message system.

Donald! Oh Donald!

The phone in her hand started to vibrate. Lisa punched the talk button.

"Donald?"

"You had an abortion?" Donald's question demanded a confirmation.

"Donald, please come home so we can talk about this."

"What else don't I know about you, Lisa? What else are you hiding from me?"

"Nothing, honey! Please come home, Donald."

"Did you ever love me?"

"Donald, stop this. Of course I love you. Tell me where you are. I'll come there and we can talk."

Her plea was greeted with silence. "Please, Donald."

"I've called the office to tell them I won't be in today."

"So we can talk. That's good. We need to talk, honey."

"You had an abortion, Lisa. What more is there to say?"

"I'm not sure what you mean, Donald. I want to explain. Want to let you know why I—"

"I have to go, Lisa. I can't think of a single thing to say to you right now. Bye."

"But where are you, Donald. Where are you staying—?"

The hum of the dial tone told Lisa that the connection had been severed.

Great! Just lovely! I finally decide to do the right thing. Come clean with my husband about my past and You let this happen. The truth will set you free? Well, look at me, God! See how free I am!

Lisa made herself drink a cup of tea and swallow half a muffin. And 31 shopping days before Christmas she went to work and got lost in old estates and death settlements.

Chapter 14

"Hey, Marissa, is there anything in particular you'd like for Christmas?" Derek asked his wife as they finished a very late Sunday breakfast. It was nice to finally have some time together after the busyness of the last few weeks. And now Christmas was just weeks away.

"You're supposed to surprise your wife, Derek!"

"That's the problem. I don't trust it when females tell me to surprise them. I lived through two sisters and a mother who always said the exact same thing and when I get them the 'surprise,' they try very hard to say something nice about my gift. I'm not going through that with my wife. I want to make sure what I get you is something you'll enjoy!"

"Well, in that case, I don't need anything for Christmas," replied Marissa.

"Come again?" asked Derek.

"I have you. Something that I enjoy. I don't need anything else for Christmas."

"So I'm a thing to you now, is that it?"

Marissa giggled. "Imagine, honey, our very first Christmas as husband and wife. I can't wait for Christmas morning! By the way, is it OK if Mom and Dad come here for the day? Mom promised to help me roast the turkey."

"You're planning to have dinner here?" asked a surprised Derek. "There's hardly enough room for the two of us, love. I just assumed that we'd go to Mom's."

"Why would you just assume that, Derek?" asked Marissa, equally surprised.

"Because that's what I do at Christmas. Go home to my family." The matter-of-fact tone with which Derek responded immediately put Marissa's back up.

"I thought since you and I were now a family, we'd want to create our own memories together."

"But you want to bring your parents here!"

"And is that going to be a problem?"

"Don't be silly. Why would that be a problem? I just don't see why we can't all go over to my mom's place. She's got tons of room, time on

84

her hands, my sisters are probably coming home for the holidays, too. It'll be fun."

"But I don't want to do that, Derek," Marissa said patiently, seeing all her nicely laid plans on the verge of dismantling.

"Rissa, now you're being stubborn!"

"And you're being insensitive!" She could feel herself getting angrier the more she thought about it. "Is that what we'll be doing for the rest of our lives? Going to your mother's house for Christmas every year? When will we be able to have a Christmas at our house? Oh right, I forgot. We don't have a precious house for you to show off. This tiny apartment is not a home."

Marissa flounced out of the room. The slam of the bathroom door told Derek where she'd gone. He sucked his teeth hard.

Women! He fumed. Why couldn't she see how his idea made the best sense? Christmas was about being with family. He could not even begin to imagine all those people here. Just thinking about it made him claustrophobic. Plus, what right did she have to invite her parents without first consulting him?

But she did ask you, his conscience reminded. The more Derek thought about the situation the angrier he felt himself becoming. Dumping the breakfast dishes into the sink, he gave her time to come back and talk sense. When the two long minutes allotted did not result in her showing up, he grabbed the car keys and opened the front door. Pausing to give her another 30 seconds of grace, he finally headed out the door.

Marissa, sitting on the covered toilet, heard the front door open. She waited for her husband to come to her, to say something, but all she heard was the pause at the entry and then the closing of the door. She couldn't believe it! He'd left without saying a word to her. After all they'd talked about not ever leaving the room angry or going out and leaving each other on bad terms. He'd actually done it! Marissa felt her heart thumping in anger, pain, and disappointment.

Lately, Derek had seemed such a bear. She'd tried everything to humor him, flirt with him, make him the meals she knew he liked, but eventually he'd revert to the quiet bouts that were becoming a pattern.

Marissa suspected some of her husband's behavior was a result of her return to work. She'd landed the job with the government, just as he'd predicted she would, and had been working for three weeks. As a result, evenings at home lacked the lazy leisure of the early days and it seemed that her husband did not appreciate coming home and not having her there to greet him.

She'd never have thought Derek, advocate for gender equality, would be so rigid on this matter. But his mother had always stayed at home and who knows, men probably expected their wives to do the things they liked in their mothers. Too bad! He would have to learn differently.

But her conscience pricked her. She was not behaving like a child of the King.

Working hard to rein in her emotions, Marissa let her mind talk to God about everything she was feeling. She held nothing back and took full responsibility for her role in the earlier conversation. Then she rose, washed the tears of frustration from her eyes, and left the bathroom. She'd fix her husband a nice meal and try to create an atmosphere that would in-duce him to talk about whatever was bothering him, and especially settle this issue of Christmas dinner.

Preparing the meal was fun. A relatively new convert to the joys of cooking, Marissa had begun to pride herself on preparing tasty dishes with few ingredients. She took her time with each dish and even the minute de-tails of the table setting, making sure everything was special for this, her peace offering.

Hurrying to take a shower, she fingered her hair into its pre-cut sassy style, donned a simple but elegantly cut black dress, and waited with music turned low and meal simmering for Derek's return. An hour passed. She adjusted the oven temperature lower. Two hours passed. She lit fresh can-dles and picked up a book to read. Thirty minutes later she closed the book and turned off the oven. She blew out the candles and was in the process of clearing the table when Derek walked through the door. He eyed the set table and still smoking candles.

"You made dinner?"

Marissa resisted the urge to give a sarcastic reply. Didn't she always make dinner? But it took two to make a quarrel and she was not going to allow things to deteriorate again before attempting to clear the air.

"Yes," she replied. "I made dinner." She could think of nothing else to say that would not sound accusatory. "You hungry?"

"No. I ate at Mom's!"

Dear Jesus, give me strength, prayed Marissa, hoping to calm her raging emotions. *He has a right to eat at his mother's house whenever he wants. After all, she gave birth to him! He shouldn't have to battle with his wife or feel guilty for doing what a good son should do—spend time with his own mother. But he could have told me. He could have called. He—*

Talking to herself and to God, Marissa searched frantically for something to say that would move them past this impasse, to find a high road with a yield sign at the end.

"I'm sorry I walked out on you this morning, hiding in the bathroom like I did," she said at last. "I was mad and needed to go cool down but I wouldn't mind making another try at talking about things, if you're up to it. Plus I don't like when there's stuff between us. It makes me feel very lonely."

Derek placed the car keys on the edge of the table and faced his wife. Within the foot that separated them his presence was palpable. "I don't like to have stuff between us either. What did I do that was so wrong? I thought I was making a reasonable suggestion."

"So did I," replied Marissa, still working to keep her voice even.

The muscles in Derek's jaws flexed. Obviously he was trying as hard as she not to start another fight.

"Where does that leave us then?" he asked. "I've gone over in my mind how I might have responded differently but I really don't see what else I could have said."

"It's obvious that we want two different things for Christmas, Derek. All I want is my mom and dad and you. Here. In this space that's our home. And you want to go to your mother's house. I wanted to have our first Christmas here. Together. I assumed that you'd want the same thing."

Derek pulled out one of the chairs and sat. He held out a hand to Marissa, inviting her to sit on his lap. "I want to spend Christmas with you too, Rissa. I love your folks and despite what it seems I said earlier, I don't have a problem with them coming over for the day. But Mom is alone. She misses my dad. Even though he's been gone for a while now, Christmas is still very hard for her. So, if at all possible, I and my sisters always try to be home for the holidays."

It felt so good to be talking and not yelling at each other, Marissa realized. "So this puts you in a bit of a bind, doesn't it? You have to choose between what your wife wants and what your mother needs."

Derek sighed. "Something like that."

"Could we try for a compromise?"

Derek shifted on the chair to pull his wife closer to him. He nibbled at her earlobe. "I missed you. Did I tell you that?"

Marissa gave him a playful elbow. "No, you didn't. And we are trying to have a conversation here!"

"OK, I'll behave. You were saying something about a compromise?"

"How about this? I'll do a Christmas supper here on Christmas Eve.

And then we can go to your mom's on Christmas Day."

"Do we have to have everybody over here for this supper?"

"Derek, what do you have against our home? This is making me nuts. Once and for all, why do you keep resisting every time I mention having people here? Are you ashamed of where we live?"

"No, I'm not."

"Derek!"

"I just like space, Marissa. My sister's kids will be running all over the place and getting into all kinds of mischief. I get tense just thinking about it."

"If it's just me, you, and my parents for supper, will that be a problem?"

"I think I can handle that."

"Good. That's settled then. Christmas Eve supper at our place and Christmas dinner at your mom's. Happy?"

Derek nodded. "Yes ma'am. Now can I tell you how much I missed you?"

"Not yet. I want to ask you one more thing."

"OK. Only one more thing."

"Do you . . . no. That's not exactly what I want to ask. Are you uncomfortable with me being back at work?"

"I don't have a problem with women working outside the home, Rissa, you know that."

"I do. But I'm not talking about women in general. How do *you* feel about *your* wife working? Since I went back to work I get the feeling that you're not OK with it."

"Well, I can't say that I'm over the moon happy about it, but I can live with it. I just wish I could afford for you not to work. That's all."

"But Derek, I want to work. I love my job and want to continue doing it. I don't understand why you're having a problem with this. And how come I didn't know this about you?"

"I didn't exactly know it about myself either. Don't worry. I'll get used to it. Now please, no more questions. Permission to demonstrate how much I missed you?"

Marissa wanted to talk a whole lot more. Wanted to know so much. What other surprises were there in this man waiting to be discovered? Plus, he had eaten. She was hungry! But her voice of reason cautioned her to bide her time and so she conceded. "Permission granted."

Interlude

Journal entry #4

Dear son,

I know you will never read this story but I need to write it. Why do I refer to you as son? Because in my mind you are. I know you might have been a girl but I like to imagine you as a boy. Josiah. Just like that boy king in the Bible.

You will notice that this is not a regular diary with daily entries and dates. Sometimes I can go for long periods without needing to write. It's not that I've forgotten you but the ache is bearable and I know that I can come back and talk to you whenever I want to.

Why is it, if I made such a great choice, the best decision for everyone, why do I dream about you almost every night? It's been years. You would have been an adult in your own right by now but everyday I miss you. Does that make sense? How can you miss someone you never knew? My heart longs for the sound of your voice.

I didn't expect the decision to haunt me for so long but I still cannot reconcile my missing you (the heart part) with the fact that given the same circumstances, and despite what I know to be what God would expect me to do, I'd probably make the same choice again.

What does that say about your mother? Does that suggest an inherent weakness in me? In the Bible it says "anyone, then, who knows the good he ought to do and doesn't do it, sins" (James 4:17). What does God do with people like me who will decide to do the wrong thing again and again?

I'm afraid of people finding out that I have feet of clay. I wonder what they would think if they knew my story.

Today in church there was a pro-life/pro-choice discussion at the youth group meeting. I normally leave such discussions to the people who are adamant they know what the will of God is. They speak strongly about the need for sexual restraint. They would never allow themselves to get into a sexually compromising situation and become pregnant or impregnate a woman.

They make me sick!

Many of them should be glad God is not like man, or lightning would fly out of heaven and strike them dead as they stand there full of their sanctified hypocrisy. If only God would reveal the evil they have lurking in their hearts!

So I had an abortion. Yes I did. God already knows that I did, and He also

*knew that I would have done it long before I did it. But mistakes happen and peo-
ple are not always strong enough to face the consequences of their mistakes. So they
make another bad choice to cover up the first one.*

*So what if the young woman cannot deal with the shame or is not prepared to
saddle her life with a child before she herself has left childhood? What of the young
men who pressure the young women for sex—Christian young men, who make
these young women feel that sex is the only way to prove that they love the guy?
That's what I call pressure!*

*Just the other day I heard a sister whose name I shall not mention, talking very
coarsely about a young girl in our church who was "pregnant out of wedlock." The
poor young woman whom she was debasing is such a sweet girl. She was braver than
me. She still kept coming to church with that big belly dominating her middle. I
think she keeps coming because she needs our love and support. Last time I saw her,
she looked so tired and I felt my heart welling up in sympathy. Do we applaud
these warrior young women who brave saintly condemnation and keep coming for
solace to the assembly of believers?*

*These unwed mothers who decide to go through with their pregnancies, while
they take the brunt of the behind-the-back talking, they, at least by the protruding
belly, give us permission to offer comfort. But what of the ones like me?*

*How do we help those haunted by decisions made a long time ago and to which
they are afraid to confess before the people—lest they be condemned as murderers?
Is there a support group in the church of God for well-meaning "baby killers"?*

*I don't have any answers, my son. I reach again for God's grace to quiet the
voices of my own self-condemnation. Forgiving myself, however, is another matter.*

*I feel like I'm rambling and saying nothing. I started with the discussion at the
youth group meeting that ticked me off. But what is it about this one that has so
gotten under my skin? Like I said, I don't usually sit through them. What made
me do so today?*

*I think I want absolution. I want to empty myself of this trash I've carried for
so long and have a fellow believer say "It's OK." But why do I want this thing
which has become almost a throbbing need? Because all this time I feel I have been
suffering from an impostor syndrome of sorts. I am not who I've pretended to be.
People don't know all there is of me. And if they knew, if they knew I had aborted
a child, would they think less of me? But that's a stupid question to ask. Of course
they would. We, the saints, relish other people's mud.*

*But oh, the thought of coming clean! Yes, I know that God is the only person
I need to come clean with. Yet I feel this need to argue for the side of those like me.
That's what made me so mad today. Again I was being flailed by sanctimonious*

do-gooders. *I wanted to add another perspective to a discussion that was too black and white. I wanted not so much to minimize the church's position on abortion but more to provide another set of lenses through which others could look at those who abort.*

And like I said before, I want to find a way to quiet the voices of my own self-condemnation. God has forgiven me. I know that. What I don't know how to do is forgive myself.

Loving you as always,
Mom

Chapter 15

"Is that baked beans I smell?" asked Thomas, strolling into the kitchen where Yolanda was stirring a pot on the stove.

"Good morning, Thomas," Yolanda said, adjusting the flame. "Yes, you do smell baked beans. I hope the ladies like it, but just in case, there are a few other things to choose from."

"Like what?" asked Thomas, eyes gleaming with anticipation.

"Like scrambled eggs, blueberry muffins, and latkes.

"With real sour cream?"

"How else?" replied Yolanda chuckling. "And don't you dare get me into trouble. Catherine will prepare you a tray as usual so you better scoot before she comes in here."

"He'd better scoot now!" replied Catherine entering the kitchen. "Thomas, are you begging for food already? Shame on you!"

Thomas, not looking one bit ashamed, gave his wife a loud smack on the cheek and left the room with a jaunt and a whistle, heading for his den. The ringing of the doorbell turned his steps and, checking to see if he was allowed to answer the door this time, he got the nod from Catherine.

Marissa was the first to arrive and soon Grace and Monica were ushered in too.

Despite Yolanda's trepidation about the beans, they were a hit. But the empty chair at the table had them wondering what was keeping Lisa. Yolanda excused herself and went to call but when she came back, reported that there was no answer at Lisa's house. Just the voice mail.

After the meal had been cleared away and the kitchen put back to order, the women retired to their "study" room.

"How's everyone doing today?" Catherine asked. Her question was greeted with OKs, fines, and all rights.

"How about your week, Marissa?"

But before she could reply, the doorbell rang. Catherine went to answer it and returned accompanied by Lisa.

"There you are," greeted Yolanda with a slightly scolding tone. "I even made your favorite baked beans, and you come late!"

"Morning everyone," said Lisa. "Sorry I'm late, but better late than never."

"Have a seat. We were just about to get started. Do you need to get something to eat before we continue?" Catherine asked.

"No, no, I'm not that hungry. I can grab a bite later. Please."

"Well, today I thought we could pick from a list of topics I made up. Here are the choices: Forgiveness, pain, relationships, or prayer. We'll go with the majority based on a show of hands. And I am going to vote as well."

There were four hands for forgiveness, three for pain, four for relationships, and two for prayer. Another round of voting between forgiveness and relationships found five to six in favor of relationships.

"OK," said Catherine. "Let's see what the Bible has to say about relationships. But tell me, ladies, what texts come to mind when you think about this topic?"

"Love your enemies as yourself," said Monica (Lev. 19:18).

"Abide in me and I in you,'" said Yolanda (John 15:4, KJV).

"Husbands love your wives," said Lisa (Eph. 5:25).

Monica interrupted. "You know that second part of the text where it says that wives should submit to their husbands, what exactly does that mean? I know I'm not in a relationship with anyone at the moment, but I'm not really the submissive type. Even though I look quiet."

Yolanda spoke up. "I think it means that the man is put as priest over his household. He has the ultimate responsibility for the welfare of his family—spiritual and otherwise. His wife, who is like a vice-priest, will have a say, but when consensus cannot be achieved, she should submit to his decision."

Monica replied with some heat. "I'm not sure I buy that. What if you know your husband is making a wrong decision. Are you supposed to sit there and do nothing?"

Grace intervened. "I am the last person to have an opinion on this subject seeing that I am not married and most likely will never be. But the apostle Paul, who had the most to say on this subject, talks about men loving their wives as Christ loved the church. Christ exhibited the ultimate sacrifice by dying for the church, His bride. That's how men should love their wives."

"No man loves his wife like that!" replied Lisa. "Plus I agree with Monica. What if your husband is not the sharpest tack in the box, so to speak? Are you supposed to submit to him? What if he's got a history of making bad decisions? What do you do then? Personally, I think Paul was a male chauvinist."

"Before we go madly off in all directions, I think we need to decide which aspect of relationships we want to cover in today's discussion," cautioned Marissa. "Marriage relationships, our relationship with God, with our families, the people around us, or what?"

"Will you allow me to make a suggestion, everyone?" Yolanda asked. She was given the go-ahead.

"I suggest that we focus first on our relationship with God. I wager that if we start there, some of the other things will become clearer."

"I can live with that," said Monica.

The other women were on board as well.

"OK, then," said Catherine. "How do we go about establishing a relationship with God?"

Lisa had an answer. "I'd think it's the same way you'd do it with anyone you'd like to have as a friend. You'd talk, spend time together, share information, listen. You know, stuff like that."

"Excellent," said Catherine. "In one of Isaiah's visions God sent a message to Judah and Jerusalem. God invited them to, 'Come now, let us reason together' (Isa. 1:18). Then the Creation story told in Genesis seems to suggest that God's habit was to come in the cool of the evening to walk and talk with Adam and Eve. Another text says that we should 'taste and see that the Lord is good'" (Ps. 34:8).

"I love that one," Marissa put in.

"Me, too," Grace laughed. "Makes me think of my favorite foods."

Catherine laughed. "I'm with you." She picked up her Bible and turned toward the back.

"When we open the New Testament we find that one way we can know God is through Jesus. Jesus Himself said that if we have seen Him, we have seen the Father. And when we get to know who God is through Christ, we'll grow to love Him and not fear Him."

"'Perfect love drives out fear,'" Monica added (John 4:18). "Maybe at some time or another, we've all been a little scared of God. Sometimes He's portrayed as . . ."

"Scary," Lisa said. "Fierce. Especially in the Old Testament."

"That's the subject of a whole other study," Catherine mused. "Back to the one at hand, I think also, as we grow in our love relationship with God, He helps us manage our relationships with those around us."

Monica shook her head. "I once worked with a co-worker who, I was convinced, looked for opportunities to get on my last nerve. The woman was relentless. We shared an office, and even though I repeatedly asked her to turn down the music on her computer because it was so distracting for me, she refused. She'd borrow stuff from my desk and not replace it or return the stuff broken. We shared a phone line, and she'd always be on it making personal calls. I had to leave the office to find another phone to use to get my work done. Love your enemies, yeah right!

"But God worked on me, and every day I made it a point to pray for her. Every time she did something to bug me and I felt I was going to scream, I'd pray for her. Did she become a saint as a result? No. The change was more in me. After awhile, the stuff she did stopped bugging me so much. And on days when she made me the most nuts, I'd go home and bake cookies which I knew she liked, and I'd share them with her. I looked for ways to compliment the few good things I could find in her. After a while, I began to see more good in her than bad. The day I left that job, she left a card on my desk which said something to the effect of, 'I will miss you and your kindness.' There's no way I could have done that without God."

"That's a perfect illustration," Catherine added. "As we get to know more about God through His Word and otherwise, we realize that it has to change the way we behave to the people around us. It will change the way we behave toward each other."

"Grace, honey, what's the matter?" Yolanda suddenly asked. She inserted a bookmark in her Bible and pulled closer to the woman who was making no attempt to check the tears running down her cheeks.

All eyes turned in Grace's direction.

Lisa, so easily moved by someone else's pain, deserted the comfort of her rocker and squatted in front of Grace, holding her hands with one of hers and using the other to wipe the tears from the cheeks of the crying woman. "Tell us what it is, honey. I'm sure we can help. Can you talk about it?"

Grace made a valiant attempt to manage her distress. Her voice when she started to speak was more like a hiccup in sentences. "I'm, *hic*, sorry, *hic*, sorry, Catherine. I didn't, *hic*, mean to disturb *hic*, our Bible study."

"Tell us what's hurting you, honey," encouraged Lisa.

"I thought I could do it, but I can't," whispered Grace. "I need to share this with someone before I go crazy."

"Share what, Grace? What's bothering you?" Yolanda asked.

Grace's lips started to quiver, losing the war to remain in control. A whimper escaped, and she clapped her hands over her mouth to prevent another.

Catherine squeezed in between Yolanda and Grace and placed her arm around the woman, gently stroking her back. "It's OK," she cooed. "Tell us when you're good and ready."

Grace struggled to bring her tears under control so she could talk. Finally she managed to say, "I'm ready. I just never . . . had to say it . . . out loud before. Saying it will m–m–make it real you know. Then, *hic*, it will be true."

Lisa was already wringing her hands. "Please tell us, Grace, because now I'm imagining the worst possible things. Like you're dying or something."

Grace took Lisa's fingers and smoothed them into straightness. "Well it's not the 'or something,' Lisa. I have cancer."

"Dear God!" Lisa jerked her hands free of Grace's and cupped them over her face. "Dear God!"

And then they all were around Grace. Surrounding her. Holding her. Full of questions and shock.

"When did you find this out, Grace?" Marissa asked.

"I've known for a couple of months now."

"Months!" cried Yolanda. "But why didn't you say something. You've been a rock for me when you yourself needed a shoulder to lean on."

Lisa asked the question that everyone was thinking. "Shouldn't you be going for treatment, Grace—chemo or radiation? They can do something about it right?"

Grace's pronouncement shattered them. "The cancer is in my liver. There's not much they can do when it get's there. It's just a matter of time."

"Oh, come on!" yelled Marissa with some heat. "There has to be something they can do. This is the twenty-first century!"

"We'll go with you for treatment, Grace, darling," said Yolanda. "We'll do all we can to get you through this. I hear that diet can be a big factor in the treatment of cancer. I have time on my hands. I can go with you or take you."

"That's it!" cried Marissa. "We can take turns. Oh, Grace, please let us help you."

"But you are helping me just by being here. By being so kind. It's just that—truly—there's nothing that can be done. But being here is such a gift from God. You don't know how much it means to have your company in pouring over the Word of God."

"Oh, Grace," wailed Lisa, big droplets running down her face. "I feel so helpless. You talk as if you're going to die soon."

Grace gripped Lisa's hands and holding back her own grief she said softly, "The doctors say a few months. Three. Maybe four."

"No!" It was Monica this time. "Why is it that every time you try to get focused on God, something bad happens?"

Marissa replied, "Maybe our discussion topic should have been about the problem of pain. Sometimes God makes no sense."

Grace halted their remonstrations. "Everyone, listen to me. When I got the news I experienced something that was a first for me. I got royally mad at God. Why would He do this to me? All my life I've wanted things. Not bad things. Just things other people have that I would expect God to want me to have as well. I wanted a husband. I wanted children. I wanted what all of you have and God said no. No! Why not? Wasn't I good enough? Why would He not give me these things that would make me happy? But I'd submitted my will to His, reconciled my wants to His wisdom, and lived with the hope that even though having my own children was not going to happen, He might still send me someone to love me, to hold me, to share life's journey with."

"Oh Grace! Grace! You're breaking my heart," cried Lisa.

"Let me finish, Lisa. The morning you walked into that prayer room, Yolanda, I had gone there specifically to pray for strength to go on. I felt so lonely. So abandoned. I wanted . . . I don't know what. And there you came with your honesty and with your pain. And I could still give comfort. And then came Catherine with her suggestion for a Bible study group and it was my answer to prayer. God provided me a support group of just the right kind of people who needed something I could give and who could offer something I so very much need—love, support, and friendship. That's what you've become. Friends."

"But you're talking about dying, Grace. You're going to die." Lisa continued to wail.

Catherine rose slowly from her perch beside her friend. "Excuse me. I'll be right back."

In the quiet of her room, Catherine searched for the thing she never thought she'd touch again. Her journey-through-pain journal. She breathed a prayer. "Dear Heavenly Father, show me why you want me to get this book out today. I don't want to go back into that darkness."

Fear nothing, My daughter. I will be with you and give you the words that you must speak.

Catherine felt the shaking increase in her hand even as her heartbeat slowed down for peace. This sharing of pain to help someone else was what she'd prayed for and encouraged them to do. She took the unopened book and headed back down to be an instrument for God.

Not my will, but thine be done.

Chapter 16

One week is a long time to live with silence when all you want is conversation. Especially when just two people live in the same house. Lisa worked longer hours. The current job demanded it but she was glad for the excuse. Overnight her husband had become a stranger.

Donald returned home the day after Lisa's disclosure. He was there when she came home from work. He'd set her bath as usual, but the planned Christmas lights did not get hung on the outside of the house. No annual preparation and discussion about Christmas took place.

On that first of what was to become many evenings of silence, Lisa had taken the setting of the bath as a sure sign that all was not lost. After all, you don't set a bath for someone you can't stand. So after she'd bathed, she'd come to their bedroom hoping to talk things through only to discover that Donald had moved his pillows and reading material to the next room.

Lisa followed him there and having had a whole day to process how she'd mishandled the previous night's confession, was determined to put some context to the story. Donald had appeared to be listening but contributed nothing. The explanation that started out with such hopeful earnestness eventually dried up in her mouth from lack of receptivity. He'd given absolutely no response.

"Don't you have anything to say, Donald?" she'd asked.

"Nope," he'd replied.

He'd withdrawn completely from her. And the guilt that had been loitering around more frequently of late became a constant companion.

Lisa had almost opted out of the last Bible study meeting but after driving around for a while she'd made the decision to go. Anything was better than her own thoughts. Grace and her imminent death had provided a reason to cry for them both. Later that week, Sophie with her laughing baby had dropped by the office for a visit, reminding Lisa of all she'd given away and rubbing salt into her reopened wound.

Luke!

Her first love! His mesmerizing smile. His lean build, his . . . She knew they shouldn't have allowed the relationship to progress to sex, but she didn't think . . . she'd hoped that just the one time . . .

How she'd loved him—a love that couldn't have denied him anything. And afterwards when guilt had paid them its first visit they'd promised each other that it would never happen again. They'd kept their promise, too. But alas, it was a promise made too late. Just the one time had resulted in a consequence that neither of them had bargained for. One single moment of weakness had irrevocably changed their lives.

So while Donald slept in the room next door, Lisa lay alone in her bed and her mind brought back all the memories of those days with Luke leading up to the discovery of her pregnancy. Refusing to believe the clues in the morning sickness or the evidence of the pharmacy-bought pregnancy test, she recalled the sick feeling in the pit of her stomach when the doctor had confirmed that she was indeed pregnant. She could still feel the panic that fluttered her heart when the shocked look on Luke's face told her that her news was not welcome, that somehow she'd been to blame. But it was the feeling that she'd betrayed God and her parents by letting down the standard that still riddled her with guilt.

Dear Luke. After a couple days of holing himself up in his room and finally having to tell his mother, he'd gotten over himself and came to see her parents to face up to his responsibilities, wanting to do the right thing. He'd wanted to be different from the father he never had at home. Despite his plans for school and a promising future, he'd been prepared to be there for her and their child.

But Lisa had wanted other options for herself and for Luke; options that did not involve teenage motherhood and hot-house maturation. Without consulting anyone she'd decided she'd save them both. Luke would have his future. She would have hers. And their love would nurture them until they were ready to fully commit to marriage and children.

But nothing had worked out the way she'd planned. When she'd told Luke about the abortion his face had emptied of all its love. He'd looked at her as if she'd suddenly become someone he'd never known and didn't want to know. Her parents, despite their disappointment about her pregnancy had been prepared to square their shoulders and support her. Their bewildered faces when she told them what she'd done would haunt her for a long time. Too late she realized that though it was an unwanted pregnancy, and would have been an embarrassment to the family, the baby was their grandchild. They'd have an emotional investment in the baby, too. Not that that was any reason to have the child! Around and around her mind had gone. She'd had 21 years to rethink her decision. Twenty-one years.

She'd been such a fool! Thinking her act of bravery and sacrifice could turn back time and make everything the way it was. The relationship she'd hoped to save had died not long after her rationalized sacrifice of her baby. That fall, Luke had left Toronto to go off to college in the States.

By shutting down all feelings, she'd shut off most of the pain. She focused on tasks for which she had control over the outcome. With unwavering zeal and single-minded purpose she had made her way through York University, receiving outstanding grades, and then through law school. She'd grown up finally. And then she'd moved to Windsor to give herself a new start. It was there she'd met Donald and finally put the past behind her. And that was that.

But lying in her bed with her consolation prize husband sleeping next door, Lisa thought she could hear demons laughing.

Condemned!

Hung on her own petard! That's what she was.

She wondered where Luke was now. Wondered if he too had periodic visits from the ghost of life past. Wondered if he occasionally thought about a foolish girl who once loved him.

About a year ago out of pure curiosity she had looked him up on Facebook and even LinkedIn but there was no profile there. She heard he'd married and had children. That was all she knew. Twenty-one years was a long time.

For 21 years she'd carried the secret of her abortion in her belly and had overlaid it with good intentions and penance. She would make it up to God for letting Him down. She had found her way back to the church she never really left. And as the various ministers, laypersons, religious books, and friends over the years had talked, extolled, and expounded on the immeasurable coverage of God's grace she would reach for it and come up short. Again and again. Guilty!

Each miscarriage was another piece of the penance. Her husband's silence was just another payment in the life-long debt. Life for life. Another good man she did not deserve.

Tell me, Mrs. Westwood, if there was no husband, would I have stood a chance?

Joshua Hendricks' question came back to her. If only he knew that his look along with his question had resurrected a need she had thought dead by crucifixion: the longing for Luke and for all that she'd lost in him. And while she was being honest with herself she had to deal with the fact that she had never loved Donald with the fierce passion she'd felt for Luke and with which the intrusion of Joshua in her life had—

No! No! No!

Lisa jumped out of her bed ready to throw herself on the mercy of her husband. But the door was shut. No light peeped from under it. Lisa reached for the doorknob. She needed her husband. Needed to make peace in her home. But her hand fell back against her side and she rested her aching head against the cold wood of the door instead.

Guilty!

Taking a deep breath for sustenance, she willed her body back to her bed. Lying on her right side, she looked at the Bible on her bedside table and reached for that too. Again she drew back. It too would condemn her.

Guilty!

With no friend could she share this pain. How could she say the words? How could she tell anyone what she'd done?

Dear God in heaven. How long must I pay?

But I have forgiven you, Lisa.

Lisa's look around the room was frantic. She was losing her mind. Hearing voices.

No, Lisa. Don't look around. Look within. Listen to your heart. I have forgiven you.

This must be what Marissa was talking about! This voice of God speaking directly to you!

Yes it is, My daughter. I have forgiven you.

Lisa again saw grace dangling in front of her like the proverbial carrot to the horse.

Forgiven.

For the third time that night she reached for this thing that was so good for her. And for the third time she pulled back.

Forgiven? How does one forgive oneself? No. She was guilty. That, at least, was a gospel she knew quite well. And so she pulled her self-condemnation close and embraced this most constant and dependable of all her partners.

That night, it was of Sophie's baby that she dreamed. A baby in diapers with perfect teeth and a young woman's face. And in the background of the picture, she saw Joshua Hendricks looking on, asking her again "Tell me, Mrs. Westwood . . ."

Lisa turned to answer him but he'd disappeared.

Chapter 17

Catherine did not use her journey-through-pain journal at the meeting as she planned. When she'd returned to the women, it seemed that it was Lisa who had needed the comforting. Her tears would not stop. And so they'd spent the time comforting the two women—one who knew she was dying and the other whom they assumed could not bear the thought.

The journal had been returned to her room but not back to its original burial place. It lay in the top drawer of her bedside table. And on the night of Lisa's rejection of grace, Catherine awoke from sleep with the distinct impression that she needed to read it. Right now.

She looked over at Thomas and saw that he was fast asleep so, sliding quietly from under the sheets, her joints moaning with arthritic pain, she removed the journal from the drawer and herky-jerked her way downstairs to a couch. Pulling an afghan across her knees, she opened the book and saw her thoughts through older eyes.

August 27.

Today I will start this documentation. I must not forget. If I forget I will go mad. I shut my eyes and I hear their sun-filled laughter. Why didn't I have a premonition when I looked out the window and saw them playing by the swing— that I would lose them in the next 10 minutes? Why did God not tell me that my babies, my darling girls, would be taken from me? He knows everything, doesn't He? Why did He not stop it?

When the girls turned 5, Thomas had hung the rope swing on the strong horizontal branch of the oak tree. A country home was what we wanted. Our own swing, pond, large backyard with lots of places for our darlings to wander and discover the beauty of nature. For two summers we'd had such fun with that swing. Thomas and I would take turns with one of our girls on our laps and swing with them. Rebecca would fuss if it got too high but Mary always wanted us to take her higher.

I'd just looked out at them and saw that Rebecca was swaying gently on the swing and then twirling herself into a spin. Mary was busy with a bucket and water on the ground nearby. And I remember thinking at the time, I am so blessed. A husband who is my world and twin girls bringing us such joy. *I wanted nothing more but to contain that feeling of absolute well-being, hold it forever.*

It was the scream, the scream that shocked me out of my feeling of well-being. There was my Rebecca, pigtails suspended momentarily in midair, face white with terror as Mary, standing on the swing, feet straddling her sister on either side of the seat, pumping the swing high in the air. Too high! Way too high! And before I could run, before I could whisper a prayer that God might have heard in case He wasn't paying attention, I saw Rebecca start to slide as the swing reached its highest peak, and the rope wobble. I saw her grab for her sister. Saw them falling to the ground in a way that did not look right. It took so long for them to hit. And all the while I am willing my feet to move and willing God to intervene because I couldn't make it to them on time.

Dear God in Heaven, save my children!

It was Rebecca's body that hit the ground first. It bounced once. Mary's body when it hit, arched in a way that spines shouldn't.

Nine and 12 days later my 7-year old babies were dead because I was stupidly wasting time praying for a miracle that wasn't going to do them any good. I should have rushed to them. Stories have been told of other mothers single-handedly lifting cars off their children, tossing them as if they were paper. Yet I froze and prayed. What kind of fool am I? Not deserving of my babies, that's what!

I let them die. This guilt I will take with me to my grave.

Why am I left living? I don't want to be here. In my every dream they are still falling. And in every dream I am going to catch them this time. But my feet are always made of lead. My feet will not let me move.

Catherine closed the book. She could not continue. The guilt she'd fought her way through was there again, beckoning still. Who would have thought that joy could come from such pain? Who would have told her that she'd ever smile again? That she could share her story with women and have it become a ministry? That out of such unfathomable sorrow and abysmal guilt could emerge a measure of peace?

Guilty! The everlasting phase of punishing herself, thinking that Thomas blamed her and that he could never love the woman who'd allowed his daughters to be killed! Repeatedly rejecting God's grace, first because she was too angry with Him and then because she could not forgive herself. Guilty of murder!

Call Lisa.

The impression on Catherine's mind was so strong that she didn't try to rationalize it. She looked at the clock and saw that it was 6:27 a.m. December 19.

OK, Father, I'll call her at 7:00.

Call Lisa now!

Catherine did not hesitate. She got her address book, picked up the phone, and punched in Lisa's number, trusting God to give her the words she needed to speak.

"Hello." Donald's voice sounded tired and sleepy and a mite cross.

"Hi, Donald. It's Catherine Charles. I'm sorry to call so early but I just got such a strong impression to call Lisa. Is she OK? Maybe when she wakes up you can tell her to give me a call."

"Just a minute, Catherine."

Catherine thought she heard a door open. Maybe she'd heard wrong. Then Donald was back.

"I think she's already left for work. She's not in bed."

Catherine felt her alarm mount. "Left for work already? But it's 6:30 in the morning! Are you sure she's gone?"

"I don't know what to expect from Lisa anymore, Mrs. Charles. She's been pulling a lot of long hours at the firm lately. Maybe she had to go in early to get some things done."

"But that's not like Lisa not to tell you, is it? Does she have a cell phone? Please call her and let me know. I'll hang up now. Please let me know as soon as you reach her."

· · · · ·

Donald sat on the side of the bed that had become his lair for the last few weeks and held his head. Call Lisa? What did he have to say to her? He was so angry that he didn't know what to do with it. And since he did not have much experience with anger and especially being angry at Lisa, he didn't know how to manage it. She'd duped him.

All these years of living with her, loving her, looking out for her and she'd played him for a fool. How could she have aborted a child? He thought he knew the woman inside-out and that nothing she did could stop him from keeping his commitment to love, honor, and respect her. But her confession, coming 14 years too late, had done just that.

He picked up the phone and called her cell.

No answer.

Then he called her work.

She picked up on the first ring.

"Hi," he said.

And before she could ask him anything or misinterpret the reason for his call, he gave her Catherine's message, bade her goodbye, and hung up. Next, he called Catherine and gave her his update.

There! He'd done his duty.

105

· · · · ·

Thomas found Catherine ensconced in the couch with telephone in hand, mumbling to herself and tapping her teeth with the rubber end of a pencil.

"Isn't it a bit early for one's brain to be working so hard?" he asked, sitting down beside her.

Catherine turned a puzzled expression in the direction of her husband. "I'm trying to work out my next step. I could phone Lisa at work or I could call Donald at home. But I have the feeling that my telephoning is done for now. I think I'm supposed to do something else."

Thomas sighed and settled himself in a more comfortable position. There'd be no breakfast until she worked this through. "And would you mind filling me in as to what telephone calls to the Westwoods have to do with why you're up this early?"

"Nothing really. I got up to read my journal. Then I telephoned Lisa."

Thomas closed his eyes. He loved this woman but she made his brain throb. "But why would you call the Westwoods this early in the morning. It's not even 7:00 yet!"

"I already phoned her. She's at work. Donald is at home." Catherine tapped the pencil against her teeth. "Something is not right with them. Lisa cried so hard last Sunday, I thought it was because of Grace's news. By the way, today Yolanda is having Grace over to spend the day with her. There's talk of some kind of spa treatment. Did you know that Grace has never had one?"

"Catherine!"

"I know. I'm digressing. OK, then. I'll call Lisa. You will call Donald. Then we can compare notes."

"Catherine! What do you mean call Donald? What am I going to say to him? 'My wife thinks something is not right with you."

"No, no. Nothing like that. Invite him to play golf with you. You two do play together occasionally, don't you?"

"Yes, but Donald's first love is cricket, not golf," Thomas protested.

"Come on, honey. Help me. I just had such a strong impression earlier to call Lisa. I was reading about guilt. But when I called she was not at home. Don't you think that's unusual? And Donald sounded dead and mad at the same time—if such a thing is possible."

"Well God did not give *me* any strong impression to call anyone. He woke me up to come and find my wife and maybe to get some breakfast."

"Then let's ask Him then."

"Ask Him what?"

"Ask God what He wants us to do. About the Westwoods' that is."

"Well, you won't get an argument from me on that suggestion," replied Thomas.

Catherine pulled closer to Thomas and took his hand. "Jehovah God," she prayed, "You who know everything and created us in Your image. We come this morning seeking Your guidance about Donald and Lisa. It feels like there is something wrong there and we don't know how or even if we should try to help. Please clearly direct us in what we need to do and use us as Your instrument wherever You deem best. Please watch over them today as they work, travel, and in all their dealings. Help Thomas, if he should be reaching out to Donald, to find the right approach and to do Your will. Help me to represent You well in all my interactions with Lisa. Continue to uphold us, heavenly Father, as we wait for Your direction and thank You for another day with new opportunities to do Your will. In Jesus' name we pray, amen."

With bowed heads and hearts they waited and listened.

When Catherine felt Thomas squeeze her hand she opened her eyes. He gave her a peck on the cheek and announced, "I've been ignoring those reminder notices to go in for a cleaning. I'll ring up this morning and book an appointment."

"You felt it too then?" asked Catherine.

Thomas nodded.

Laying aside her pencil, address book, and journal, Catherine tugged on her husband's arm. "Come, I'll make you breakfast."

Chapter 18

Lisa, her concentration shattered by Donald's call, pushed back against her chair, giving some distance to the desk. What was she to do? The incoming call light on her phone flicked on. Lisa looked at the time. Still not yet 7:00. Who could be calling her now? She picked up the receiver.

"Hi, honey, how are you?" Mary Jones's voice chirped across the line.

"Mama, how are *you*? What are you doing up so early?"

"When you get to my age you don't ask questions like that. I'm up 'cause my body is done sleeping. What are you doing at work this early? I was just about to leave a prayer on your answering machine. Something to greet you when you got in to work."

Lisa's tear ducts started to smart. "Mom, that is such a beautiful thought."

"How are things, honey? You've been on my mind. How are you really doing?" Lisa could picture her mom, afghan tossed across her knees, sitting on the multicolor sofa in the living room of her tiny retirement home apartment.

Mary Jones had resisted as long as she dared the move from her home. But a heart scare last year had forced her to confront the fact that she needed some degree of supervised assisted living. The Villacrest Retirement Community had provided just that and was still within easy access to church, public transit, and shopping.

Lisa wondered how to answer her mom. Even with three hours' drive separating their respective homes, Mary had a mother's instinct for guessing right about her daughter's state of mind and heart.

"I'm doing reasonably OK, Mama. How about you?"

"Forget about me," Mary responded.

Was that a quaver in her voice, Lisa wondered. She did a quick mental math and drew in a deep breath. Her mom was not a "spring chicken" anymore. This December she would turn 78. The slight quaver in her voice was that of an old woman. Lisa opted for a light tone.

"What do you mean forget about you? You're my favorite mother in the whole world so how can I do that?"

"Lisa, what's going on with you? Something is wrong. I can feel it. How is my son-in-law?"

"Donald is OK, Mama. Well I think he's OK. I don't really know how Donald is doing, Mom, and right now I can't say that I care."

"Lisa! How can you talk like that! Donald loves you and as far as I know you love him too. Not as much as he loves you—I've always known that—but in your own way you love him. So tell me what's making you think you don't care about him?"

"It's not that I don't care, Mom. It's just that he won't talk to me. A few weeks ago I told him something and since then he's refused to talk to me. He's even moved out of our bedroom." Suddenly tears filled her eyes and she felt her throat close as if she might choke. She took a deep breath. "Oh, Mama, my marriage is falling apart and God doesn't love me and there's this man that I'm thinking about that I shouldn't."

"You need to let Luke go, Lisa honey. Luke has moved on with his life. You appear to have moved on too, but I know you. You're still haunted by him. And if you don't mind my asking, what exactly did you tell your husband that caused him to stop speaking to you?"

A pause. "I told him about the abortion."

"Forgive me, honey, but did you say that you told him about the abortion?"

Lisa nodded even though her mom could not see.

"Honey?"

"Yes, Mama. I did."

"Donald didn't know about this before?"

"No."

"Oh, Lisa!"

"I didn't think it had anything to do with us, Mama. It was part of the past that I wanted to remain in the past. I thought I could just leave it there. Everyone has secrets, and not all of them need to be shared."

Mary's voice was gentle. "So what made you decide to tell him now, after all these years, love?"

"Oh, Mama!" Lisa's wail was that of a lost child. "Lately it's like I am haunted by memories of Luke and that abortion. There are voices in my head condemning me. I'm sure it's me doing it to myself, but I feel so angry and guilty and unclean. This is hard for you to understand I know but it's . . . it's like I'm haunted, Mama. And then I met this lawyer who reminded me so much of Luke. I needed to talk or burst so I just told Donald, without even any preparation or warning. There he was taking off his socks and I just blurted it out! Stupid. That was so stupid. And then I couldn't stop talking, and when I finally finished he looked at me like he'd never known me and he left. He left. Mama, he didn't even come home that night. He's back now, but it's been weeks and he won't let me talk to him about it. Every night he still sets my bath and does all that he used to—except share our bed and talk to me."

"That's why you're at work so early." Mary's response was not a question. "Yes."

And in that simple word Mary heard an echo of remembered pain. "Why don't you drive down and visit me this weekend? We can talk through this. I'm sorry, honey. I just assumed that you had discussed this with Donald years ago, but together with God we can find a way to work through it. Now please tell me that you'll come. Will you?"

"Yes, Mama. I'll come. I'm sorry to burden you with my stuff but I could really use your advice and maybe a change of pace would help."

"Call me Friday morning and let me know when to expect you. I'm sorry I have to go now, but the nurse will be here in a minute with my meds. I've enough time for a prayer. Is that OK with you?"

Lisa wiped her eyes. "Of course, Mama. I count on your prayers always."

Mary sat up slowly on her sofa and bowed her head. "Dear Healer of Broken Hearts, touch my child where she hurts. She has voiced her pain of regret for foolish words spoken, self-condemnation for things not done, anger at rejection, ache because of her loneliness, and she is seeking solace and peace. Touch my child, who was first Yours and will always be Yours first. Touch her where it hurts, Mighty Healer. Provide her, please, with even a brief respite from her tortured imaginings. Succour and shelter. Hedge and protect. Guide and lead in this period of her life.

"Be with her as she comes home to visit. Give us words to say that will build each other up. Lead as only You can and give us the strength to follow You no matter what happens. Hold Lisa up today. Bless Donald, too, I pray. And in the end, when this period of their journey is assessed through the lens of hindsight, help them to see Your gentle hand guiding them and carrying them through this difficult period. And when they see, remind them to give You all the glory, honor, and praise that is due to a loving and kind Father who seeks only the good of His children. I commit them into Your care and keeping. In Jesus' name I ask this. Amen."

"Thanks, Mom."

"Take care, love, and I'll see you in a few days."

• • • • •

When Lisa turned into the drive of the retirement complex Friday night, a feeling of unreality assailed her. This was home to Mom but not to her. That part of their shared history was gone. Her dad's death a few years back and her mother's failing health had prompted some tough decisions. One of those was to say goodbye to the place where Lisa grew up.

Lisa slowed the Volvo to take in the beauty of the evergreens lightly covered with snow. Christmas lights in blue and white lined the drive and even though Lisa thought them beautiful, she acknowledged her preference for the traditional greens and reds of Christmas. The scene reminded her that Donald still had not put up their lights, the absence illuminating the state of their widening separateness.

Donald took her announcement that she'd be visiting her mom with his recently acquired nonchalance. He'd asked her to give Mary his love, told her to drive carefully and had withdrawn to his new bedroom. Now Lisa parked her car in the visitor's section, grabbed the parcels she'd brought with her, and walked to the reception area. It was almost 7:30 p.m. and Mama would probably be starving herself waiting to eat with her.

A minute later Mary Jones filled the apartment entry, arms open wide to receive her daughter home, and Lisa barely managed to close the door before dropping her bags and falling upon her mother's frail frame. She held on tight, willing herself not to cry.

"It's OK, love. Let it all out. Mama's here," Mary crooned close to her daughter's ear as she gently rubbed her back.

The pent up pain, guilt, and sorrow of the last few weeks would stay banked no longer. Here was unconditional love. Until this moment Lisa had not realized how much she needed to be hugged, and she sobbed her heart out.

"It's all right, sweetheart." Mary Jones became a mother again. Here was her wounded child, broken of heart, needing comforting that she could give. Mary's body remembered the soothing sway of motherhood and without conscious thought her voice broke into the chant she reserved for this type of trouble as it hummed the childhood favorite "Jesus loves me this I know . . ." Only when she'd hummed through the song the third time, did she begin to feel a lessening of the grip her daughter had on her and a gradual abatement of the tears trickling into sniffs.

Mary pulled back slightly so that she could look into the face of her only child. A face that always mirrored its feelings—at least to the discerning eye. And had not Mary been watching that face from the day her baby was handed to her by the nurse in the hospital room just a few years ago? Now the beloved face of her daughter, wet from its recent torrent, was beginning to register regret.

"I'm sorry, Mama. I didn't mean to barge in here and bawl all over you."

Mary pulled a tissue from the right hand pocket of her robe and gently wiped her daughter's face. "Never apologize for crying on your mother's shoulder. When our children get old, we start to feel useless and moments like this give me a chance to indulge my need to nurture and comfort you. Now that we've gotten round one out of the way, I'm sure you're hungry for some pumpkin soup and toast."

Lisa, touched beyond words, felt another prickle of tears. Pumpkin soup and whole wheat toast was her best comfort food. Whenever she was recovering from a cold, a stressful period, or whatever, she'd get a craving for her mother's pumpkin soup, and here it was again waiting to give her some of the comfort she so desperately needed.

"Oh, Mama! That sounds perfect. Thank you! Let me go wash up."

Several minutes later, mother and daughter were sitting down at the small table for two, Lisa with a steaming bowl of soup garnished with crispy shavings of fried onions, and Mary with a cup of her favorite peppermint tea.

"Aren't you going to have some soup too?" Lisa asked her mom.

"I had a bowl earlier. I'm trying not to eat so late in the day. Not good for my digestion. You go ahead and enjoy it. I made it 'specially for you."

Lisa needed no further prompting. She dug in and only surfaced when the bowl was empty. Nibbling daintily at the last piece of toast bite by slow bite, she focused on her mother.

"So how are you doing, Mama? Any more problems with the heart?"

"A little flutter from time to time that takes my breath away but overall, I'm OK. God is good to me and I can still get out to church."

"I worry about you."

Mary's face was gentle. "When you worry, pray for me and let God do His job. I'm in His care, you know. No weapon formed against me will prosper unless God wills it to come my way. And if He does, He always provides the means to bear it."

"I wish I had your faith," Lisa said, with a shake of her head. "You rely on God for everything. How do you do it?"

"Oh, child, I've had a lot of practice with pride followed by pain. My will continues to be a hard one to break. I've fought with God almost all my life to get my way. Now in the late years of life, I don't fight so much anymore because I've learned that God's ways are always better than the paths I've taken. I've learned that if I'd listened more to Him I would have saved myself a lot of heartache."

"I guess I caused a lot of that pain," Lisa responded.

"It's hard for any mother to watch her child suffer. I had to learn to submit you to God too," said Mary with a yawn.

Lisa shifted in her seat, head down. "I never asked how you felt when I told you about the . . . the abortion. And you never brought it up. Why is that?"

But Mary had nodded off. Noting the time, Lisa could have kicked herself for not recognizing the lateness of the hour. Way past her mother's bedtime. Quietly, she cleared the dishes from the table and washed up. Then she woke her mother and guided her frail frame to her bed.

Mary yawned again and kissed her daughter on the cheek. "It's good to have you home, honey. Sorry I don't have an extra bed for you and you know you're welcome to share mine." Sensing Lisa's imminent protest, she held up her hand. "Then you know where to find the pillows and blankets and the sofa."

"Good night, Mama, and thanks for asking me to come. I needed this."

"Then I'm glad. Tomorrow we can spend the whole day just visiting with each other."

"I'm already looking forward to it. Good night." Lisa kissed her mother who smiled sleepily at her.

Later, refreshed from a shower, Lisa fluffed the pillows on the couch and snuggled down, body tired and mind weary. Fear of rejection wrestled with duty about whether to call Donald. Duty won. With heart armoured against his polite indifference, she hoped for his voice mail.

"Hello."

No such luck.

"Hi, Donald. I'm just calling to let you know I got in safely."

"That's good. How's Mom?"

"She's fine. You know her. In bed by 9:30. OK, I'll see you when I—"

"And how are you?" Donald interrupted.

Nonplused Lisa grasped for words. "Me? Oh, I'm OK. You?"

"I'm good. Good."

"That's good . . . that you're good."

Then there was nothing left to say. Too much left unsaid.

"Good night," said Donald.

"'Night."

Donald hung up first. Lisa, already emotionally spent from her earlier tears felt nothing as she clicked her cell phone shut, fluffed the pillows again, and settled down to sleep.

A full bladder that could not be ignored aroused her sometime later. Somewhat disoriented, it took a minute to get her bearings before padding to the washroom. On her way back, she noted the time. Four-thirty! She poked her head in Mary's room to check on her. She looked so peaceful lying there.

Lisa again wished that she had even half of her mother's faith. Then she could just hand over the cares and worries of life to God and sleep in peace like that. Grace and Catherine had that kind of faith too. Never would she be able to live with a death sentence like Grace's and not lose her faith. God could sometimes be such a hard taskmaster, demanding the next to impossible. To have lived through Catherine's life, to lose your children just like that and still go on? Could she ever be that kind of Christian?

With those thoughts on her mind, Lisa trudged back to her sofa bed. Sleep stayed far away for a time. Then she dozed until the brightness of the day penetrated the lids of her eyes.

Oh, no! Her mom must be patiently waiting for her to wake up.

Lisa swung off the couch. Grabbing a few items of clothes from the weekender bag lying nearby, she popped her head in her mom's room to say good morning. Mary Jones sat on a chair by the window, reading.

"You must have been burning the midnight oil these past few days. I thought you'd never wake up."

"Sorry, Mama. I couldn't get to sleep for a while and I guess once I did the body claimed its due. Give me about 10 minutes and I'll make you breakfast."

"That would be nice. I was thinking that instead of going out today, we could just spend the day together here. There is a lovely park right around the corner. How about we take a walk after breakfast and then come back, sit and catch up. I miss my daughter. Plus, you're going to be heading out early tomorrow and we rarely get time to properly visit, just the two of us. What do you say?"

"Perfect! I think that's just what the doctor ordered," replied Lisa.

Interlude

Journal entry #5

Dear son:

The last time I wrote to you I was very upset. I still am but I have been able once again to talk sense into the part of me that keeps the lid on my guilt. After all these years, I am still haunted by guilt.

One afternoon last week as I was crossing the street at a really busy intersection, I accidentally bumped into a young man. As usual these days, my mind was someplace else and I wasn't paying attention to where I was going. The young man steadied me and made sure I was OK before he walked away. I got safely to the other side of the street but could still see his warm brown eyes and feel the gentle strength of his hands. And just like that, there you were again!

Would you have looked like that young man, Josiah? Would you have been that gentle giant? By aborting you I feel that I've killed a promise. A life not lived. A road not taken. It's also possible that you could have turned into a killer or some kind of child molester and my act might have saved the world from that. So many possibilities to speculate about.

I know I've told you that I had good reasons for doing what I did. What's the point of being a bad teen parent and taking out your frustrations of dreams unrealized on your child? Why saddle two unprepared people with another life to wreck?

But what I haven't told you, my son, is that despite my reasons, I am constantly haunted by that decision. I see you in faces like that young man today. I hear you in the cry of a newborn baby. I watch you walk up to the platform to receive your university degree—except it's not you. It's the potential of you that I see. And I'm riddled with guilt that will not go away. So I need a confessional.

What I want to say to those "black and white" pro-choicers, is that some people, no, let me speak for myself. I, as one of those who exercised my choice, live a haunted life. That is my consequence.

You see, every decision has consequences. By choosing to have the baby, I would have faced another set of consequences. And by choosing like I did to abort you, I, too, deal with consequences that are unpleasant. And I have no one but you and God with whom to share them.

On Thursday evening I stopped by The Bookstore. My eye caught a book about prayer and because it was not a formula book (I made sure), I decided to buy it. I have a problem with books on prayer that tell us that if only we would talk to God in a certain way or follow a particular prayer blueprint, we would be seeing more answers to our prayers. I believe that God cares less about our prayer method. Rather, He cares about the condition of our heart. He listens to our hearts and we need to listen to His voice. Anyway, I should not stray from what I was saying.

The author of the book, a woman, openly wrote that she'd had an abortion. The shock of seeing that admission in print made my hands shake. I had to put the book down. What would possess her to say that in a book? You talk to God in secret about some things and having an abortion is one such thing.

Her reason for admitting to the abortion in the book was to show that we need to come clean with God and own up to our sins. But even as my hands were shaking from the shock of what I'd read, I found myself picking up the book again and re-reading what she had written.

She was writing my story.

But you know what I think? I think she, too, wanted a public confessional to exorcise her guilt. This kind of guilt has a cloying element to it. It stays with you long after you care to be reminded of it. It inhabits my pores and as soon as I sweat or exert myself spiritually, its rank odor permeates my body, crippling my ability to lift my arms to worship and praise with confidence.

I am forever guilty. I wish I could write to her, seeking solidarity with a fellow partner in crime. I want to know how she made peace with her guilt. I want to know if she, too, continues to be as haunted as I am.

Once the deed was done, your dad didn't wish to be reminded of it. I remember him quoting the text "visiting the iniquities of the fathers upon the children" (Ex. 34:7, KJV) when . . . never mind. I won't go into that now.

So who do I talk to about this— if not you, God, or . . . maybe this stranger? Maybe my way of dealing with this is all wrong but I wish God would just touch my memories and make the guilt go away. And if I have to live with the memories, I want release from the guilt. How do I pray for self-forgiveness? God does not seem to answer this prayer of mine.

This woman in the book talks about how sometimes we tenaciously hang on to things that are not good for us because we do not think ourselves deserving of God's grace. Could it be possible that I don't want forgiveness? It's possible. But why would I do that? Could it be that I've come to enjoy being a martyr to my own self-condemnation and by doing so I have limited what God wants to do with and through me?

With your dad gone from my life, my mind willfully goes to this place of questions with no answers. I wish I had more faith. Jesus, after His resurrection, ap-

peared to doubting Thomas and invited him to touch and believe. I am like Thomas. I am ashamed to admit that I find it difficult to believe without my own direct experience with touch. Jesus I think understood that some people, myself included, are like Thomas. I believe that's why He made a special visitation to offer Thomas the evidence that he needed even though He would have preferred to have him believe just based on His word.

Despite Jesus' pronouncement of "Blessed are those who have not seen [or touched?] and yet have believed"(John 20:29) my heart bellows in no uncertain terms that I stand condemned. I need to know for sure that He accepts me with all the wrongs that I've done and that He will continue to accept me even though I want this touch evidence. Maybe then I will be able to end this penance, close this journal for good, and live in peace. That's what I want most of all, son. Peace.

Love,
Your mother

Chapter 19

"How is Grace doing, Rissa? Was she at your last meeting?" Derek asked as he joined Marissa in the kitchen. Today being Sunday, was his day to make dinner and he wanted to get things underway before the football game started.

Marissa looked up from the magazine she'd been reading. "That woman amazes me. She hasn't missed a single meeting. We're having such a good time studying the Bible together but given Grace's condition your mom's totally taken Grace under her wing!"

"In that case, you can expect Grace to join our family circle for the holidays. Mom loves to have a full house this time of year and under the circumstances, I can't see her leaving Grace to spend the holidays on her own. Doesn't sound like she has any family around."

"Sometimes I don't know what to say to hurting people," said Marissa. "I feel so sorry for Grace. She talked about always wanting a family—husband, kids, the whole works, but it just never happened."

"She probably was one of those picky women. No guy could ever come close to her definition of perfection so she kept waiting for Mr. Right only to end up old and lonely," Derek responded.

"Derek! That's the most unfeeling thing to say about anybody! Are you implying that the many unwed women around are single because they've been too picky? And even if some are, don't you think that one should be a little bit selective in the choice of a life partner?"

Derek grinned. "Behold, I have roused the feminist."

Marissa made a face at him but he ignored her. "Come on, Rissa. You have to admit that I have a point. Take Adrienne for example. That woman has dated just about every guy around. When I got back from law school I totally expected to find her married with at least three kids. But no, she's still single and getting desperate. A guy can't even say hello to her without her checking his HPQ."

"His HPQ? What exactly is that?" asked a puzzled Marissa.

"Husband Potential Quotient. And let's say the guy scores well on that particular test, and being a gullible fool, decides to ask her out. God bless him! By the end of date Number 1 he's getting the 'biological clock ticking, don't have time to waste if you're not planning to be serious' diatribe along with having to provide a full accounting of his financial and employment status."

Marissa chuckled. "She does come on strong, I agree, but it's kinda sad too. Whatever the reason, if you'd imagined your life with husband and children and then it looks like it's not going to happen, what would you do? I'd probably get desperate too. Good thing I'm in no rush to start a family." Marissa turned her attention back to her magazine article.

Derek halted in measuring out the lentils for the bean stew he was planning to make. "You don't want kids?"

Marissa looked up. "Huh?"

"I asked if you don't want kids."

"Not right now I don't. Sometime in the future. Plus, I am enjoying it being just the two of us for a while. You're just starting out in your career and I want to get a couple more years of work experience under my belt. I'm thinking that in a few years I'd like to go into health care consulting."

"When will you know you're ready?"

"For children or becoming a consultant?"

"Children."

Marissa's brow furrowed. "I really don't know. Maybe one day I'll wake up with a strong urge to nurture a brood of our own. Brood! What am I saying? I can't see me having more than one kid. What about you?"

"I'd love to have at least four."

She laughed. "Well, that's not going to happen with this wife! Do you know how painful giving birth is? You men always talk about how many kids you'd like to have but I'd wager that if any of you had to push one of those darlings out, there'd be no such talk. Four kids!" exclaimed Marissa in disbelief. "How come I didn't know this? I'm sure we talked about children during our marriage counselling classes."

Derek had his back to her. He washed the beans and transferred them to the crock pot, adding onions and a pinch of salt. After plugging in the slow-cooker he joined her at the table.

"I always wanted a large family. There were five of us in mine, and I assumed I'd have something similar when I got married. Of course, we'll need a much larger home to house them in."

"Oh, here we go again!" Marissa slammed shut the magazine and rolled her eyes.

"Here we go what?" asked Derek, clearly puzzled.

"Another complaint against the apartment."

"Where do you see a complaint in what I just said, Rissa?"

"You hate this place. It's not good enough for Christmas, it's not good enough to raise children in, and everything has to be like what you grew up in. This is getting tiring, Derek."

"Whoa! Wait a minute. What's happening here? It almost sounds as if we're fighting and I don't recall starting it. I thought we worked through the Christmas stuff—what's all this about?"

"Never mind. It's all about me. I always say the wrong thing and everything is my fault." Marissa picked up the magazine and started to walk away. Best to leave now before she said something she'd later regret.

Comprehension dawned in Derek's eyes. "Oh, I get it. Is it that time of the month?"

The magazine flew from Marissa's hand, past Derek's head and hit the wall. His wife flounced out of the kitchen after lancing him with a look of pure disgust.

Derek did a quick mental replay of the conversation. It had started with him asking about Grace and then progressed into a discussion of single women and children. Where had he gone wrong? She became upset soon after he came to sit with her. What had he done? Children. He wanted four and she wanted only one and not anytime soon. But he'd wanted them to talk about it. Not fight. He should go after her. Only God knew what he did wrong this time!

Derek looked at the clock on the microwave. Will and want wrestled. The game was about to begin. If he went to talk with Marissa now, he would miss the game. Conversations with his wife on any issue were never short. Yet, if he didn't go see her now, he'd be in the doghouse for the rest of the week. Granted he could tape the game, but that just wasn't the same as watching the action live. Despite the quandary, Derek recalled his wedding vows and went after his wife.

She lay across the bed, flat on her back, staring up at the ceiling. He sat gingerly beside her.

"Is it safe to be here?"

Still staring at the ceiling, Marissa measured out her words. "Never accuse your wife of having a PMS moment in the middle of a serious discussion. It reduces everything she's saying to hormones and dismisses their importance."

Derek treaded delicately in asking his next question. "Is there ever a time when hormones affect your emotional state—and if yes, how will I know when those times are and how should I behave?"

"Just ask," Marissa responded pithily.

Derek swallowed his frustration. "Help me here, Rissa. I thought just now in the kitchen, that's what I did. I asked but obviously that wasn't the right thing to do?"

"'Got that right!" snapped Marissa.

"But what—"

Marissa's hand motioned him to shush and the question petered out into a long silence. She obviously needed to work through whatever was on her mind. Derek thought of the game and how much more tolerable a 10-man topple would be in comparison to this. He must have made a motion or communicated his growing antsy-ness. Marissa sat up, tucked her legs lotus-style under her and faced him.

"Sometimes us women don't make sense even to ourselves. I got upset for several reasons. I keep discovering things about you that I did not know. How come I didn't know you wanted a large family? In all the nights and days we talked till the wee hours of the morning why didn't that come up? It's like trying to handle shifting sand. Just when I think I know you, I have to keep readjusting my perception of you. How come no one told us that marriage adjustment was so difficult?"

Derek sat on the edge of the bed. "Would we have listened? Look honey, we love each other and as we adjust we'll step on each other's toes. I suspect that even 50 years from now we'll still be discovering things about each other that will cause raised eyebrows. I think we'll continue to grow and change and so the adjustment will continue. Right now everything is new for both you and me. For example, I didn't know you were as sensitive as you are."

Marissa's head snapped back. "I'm sensitive? How am I sensitive?"

Derek shook his head and began to laugh.

Soon Marissa joined him. "I'm sensitive around certain topics, aren't I? OK, point taken. You still love me?"

"I must love you a lot because I'm missing the game to make sure that we're OK."

Marissa leaned in and kissed him. "I really should make it up to you, shouldn't I? May I request a few more minutes of your time, kind sir?"

"Well I suppose if you twist my arm, I could be persuaded," replied Derek in the sexy voice she loved.

Marissa playfully twisted his arm and it was half-time when they returned to the living room.

• • • • •

Having completed her light supper, Yolanda sat at the table and reviewed her day with Grace. Then she gave thanks to God. For the past few weeks she'd been so consumed with helping her friend that she had not noticed that her pain of loneliness was not as acute.

Not convinced that all the medical options for treatment of Grace's cancer had been explored, Yolanda had accompanied her to doctors for second opinions and had fast become Grace's health care advocate. Many nights she'd convinced her friend to stay at her place, to help fill up the remaining three empty bedrooms, and they'd talked into the night about life and dreams and most of all, faith.

So much about this woman she'd known for years she was only recently discovering. Yolanda chastised herself. She'd been too preoccupied with her own grief over Jackson's death. But this Christmas would be different. Enough looking backwards and inwards. She would focus on Grace for as long as . . . well . . . till God . . .

But why, God? Why her? Could you not have granted her one of the things she so desperately wanted—a husband even?

Even as Yolanda completed her question, the words of Scripture came to her. "For my thoughts are not your thoughts, neither are your ways my ways" (Isa. 55:8).

She puffed. This yielding to the wisdom of God was difficult business.

The telephone rang. Yolanda contemplated ignoring it but not wanting to miss the call if it was Grace needing assistance, she rose from the table and picked up the wall extension. She really should get caller ID and a cordless phone for the kitchen.

"Hello."

"Hi, Mom," greeted a perky sounding Marissa.

Yolanda smiled. God is so good. Another blessing of focusing on Grace. She did not spend as much time bemoaning the loss of her son to his wife. The young woman, even though she had an independent streak, loved her son and seemed genuinely interested in cementing her relationship with God. Yolanda had been amazed during their Bible study meetings at the earnestness of her daughter-in-law in this matter.

"Hi, Marissa. You sound chirpy! How is my son? Let me rephrase that: How is your husband?"

"He's doing fine. Watching the football game. I can only take so much and then I need a distraction."

"Is that what I am then? A distraction?" Yolanda teased.

"Well kinda," responded Marissa honestly. "Actually, I called to ask your opinion on something but the question might make you uncomfortable."

"Now I'm intrigued," Yolanda said, propping her shoulder against the wall. "Ask away."

"Maybe this wasn't such a good idea."

Yolanda could feel Marissa retreating. "Just ask the question, child. If I can't answer it then I can't."

The intake of a deep breath could be heard across the line.

"Well it's like this. I had a fight with Derek today. I can't recall exactly what led to it but I reacted to something he said and then he asked me . . . not asked really, said something like 'it's that time of the month, right?'"

"And you threw something at him!"

"Mrs Clarke! I mean Mom—how did you know? I had a magazine in my hand and before I knew it, I had flung it at his head and flounced out of the room. It's good he ducked in time, but I felt so bad afterward. Mad and bad at the same time. What I wanted to ask you was this. Derek followed me a few minutes later and asked what he'd done wrong. I told him that implying a woman's anger was a result of her hormones running amok, or some such thing, was to deny the legitimacy of her emotion.

"Then he asked quite innocently, what he should have done instead. To tell the truth, I wasn't very happy with the answer I gave him. I mean, sometimes my hormones do affect the way I feel and might make me overreact to things but other times, my reactions have nothing to do with hormones. I'm just legitimately mad. Am I making sense?"

Yolanda chuckled. "Welcome to the fascinating world of male/female communication. It sounds however like you two made up. How did that come about?"

"Well, the more we talked, the more I realized that I am a bit sensitive over certain issues. I just don't think I was able to make it clear to him why he shouldn't introduce the hormone issue when we're having a serious discussion. I'm not even clear on it myself."

"And you might not always be clear," replied Yolanda. "But listen to your body. You know when those PMS feelings come and the time of month when they're most likely to occur. You feel cranky and out of sorts for no reason. You don't even want your husband to look at you. And if he ignores you, you start feeling like he doesn't care. Jackson made a sign for me that read 'mentally out of commission' and begged me to prominently display it as needed. It really helped. I would put the sign on the bed or on the bathroom mirror and he'd smile at me and keep out of my way till the sign was taken down. One time I had it up for about two weeks. Then one morning I went into the bathroom and there was a note beside it saying 'missing the love of my life.' I took the sign down that very moment."

"That is so sweet," replied Marissa. "I wish I'd known him. Your Jackson sounds like . . . well, he sounds just like Derek."

"Don't get me wrong. We had our ups and downs. All marriages do. Especially in the first year there is so much about each other that you don't know. And while some of the discoveries are fun, other traits or habits you learn about the person can make you wonder why you married them in the first place. But the thing to keep in mind is that you need to talk. Keep talking things through. If talking is too complicated, write letters. Send an email. And when you fight, sometimes you both need a cooling off period. Then come back together when tempers are calmer and talk through what happened, owning your part of the problem and taking responsibility for saying how the other person's words or behavior affected you. Keep your comments focused on the behavior, not the person. And pick your fights. Some things are just not worth the passion!"

"Thanks, Mom. You've given me a lot to think about. I really appreciate it."

"You're welcome anytime. And keep doing what you do so well dear. Continue to pray together and separately. Many problems can be worked out within the prayer closet."

"I will. Thanks again. Oh, by the way, how is Grace doing? She's going to be joining us at your place for Christmas dinner, right?"

"I invited her to come Christmas Eve and stay for a few days. I know the house will be full and busy with everybody here but I don't want her to be alone. I recently realized how much of what I've been blessed with, I've taken for granted and how little she has and yet manages such a lovely spirit of gratitude."

Marissa sighed. She wondered when she'd get to that place of spiritual maturity. She couldn't imagine being as spiritually mature as Grace. "She's a wonderful inspiration, for sure. I'm glad I accepted Catherine's invitation to the Bible study group. I'm learning so much and well, getting to know everyone and finding such support is special for me. Which reminds me, I promised myself to call Monica today. I'll do that right now before the game is over. How's Lisa?"

"H'mm! Good question," replied Yolanda. "I think she went to Toronto to see her mom. I'll call her. I'm long overdue for a call anyway. Goodnight dear. Say hello to Derek and please make sure he doesn't purchase any personal items for his sisters before he gets their Christmas wish lists. Long story . . . don't ask."

Chapter 20

Lisa turned the envelope over and over, mulling over what to do with it. The Bar Association had outdone itself this year. Gold embossed lettering combined with the black insignia of the Association's logo made for a most attractive invitation.

What a difference a year makes, she thought. Last year this time she already had her dress picked out and her appearance at this grand annual Christmas gala a foregone conclusion. The gala provided a great time to get reacquainted with old friends and meet the newcomers to the profession.

The invitation had been sitting on Lisa's desk for the past two weeks, waiting for the right moment when things were patched up with Donald, to discuss it. But other than the briefest flicker of interest when she'd called him from her mom's house last week, things were back to the new normal of separate beds and "pass the potatoes" platitudes.

Coming to a decision, Lisa picked up her phone to call in her RSVP. She was going with or without Donald. Tonight she'd give him an opportunity to accompany her, another opportunity to chip away some of the ice forming over their relationship. If he refused, well . . . well . . . that's just too bad.

Lisa felt again the threat of tears. No way José! No tears today. Enough was enough!

Last week's visit to her mom had done her a world of good. Following a lazy breakfast, they'd strolled down the lane and across to the park bundled up from head to toe to withstand any kind of cold. The day had been touched with warmth, however, and even the light sprinkling of snow from the previous evening had melted by the time they made their way outside.

Sensitive to the fragile condition of her mother's heart, Lisa slowed her stride but Mary would have none of that. After allowing herself first a slow then a medium paced walk up and down the lanes, she'd stepped up her pace and it was Lisa who was huffing and puffing by the time Mary decided that a perch on a nearby bench was in order. Lisa sank gratefully in the seat and tried to catch her breath.

"Too many hours sitting at a desk will do that to you," Mary commented. "There's nothing like God's creation to put the wind under your sails."

"You're enjoying this, aren't you? Watching me huff and puff to keep up with a 70-something wonder woman!"

Mary grinned. "Why shouldn't I? There was a time there when you were running so fast I had an awful time just keeping you in sight. Good thing I had God doing that for me."

"I guess we're no longer talking about physical running, are we?" concluded Lisa.

Mary placed her gloved hand on her daughter's knee. "Why did you wait till now to tell Donald about the child, Lisa?"

Lisa stared across the field. Some distance away she observed a couple squirrels frolicking up and down the trees, their movements quick and frisky. Why had she chosen that moment to tell Donald? Why had she blurted it out to him like that?

"I'm never going to have a baby, Mama. You will never get to be a grandmother. Somehow I'd counted on that. Planned it even. I even had it worked out how I would manage childcare and work responsibilities. I knew the nanny service I'd use and factored in how many hours I would need to work to keep my skills current while maintaining a not-too-demanding work load. I pictured what Christmases with you and Daddy would be like and how Donald and I would dote on this child. She wouldn't be spoiled. No sir. She'd be loved and protected but not spoiled. I wanted her to have a wonderful home life just like the one I had."

One of the squirrels picked up something from the ground and securing it in its paw proceeded to nibble daintily at it, all the while eyeing its mate to see if the treat was in danger of being stolen.

"Holding secrets take a lot of resources," Lisa continued slowly. "You always have to remember that certain subjects are off limits. You must constantly remind yourself to keep manning the ramparts and shoring up the defenses lest in a moment of weakness everything comes flying out." A long pause. "Then where would you be? Stranded. Beached. Washed up with no place to go."

Mary nodded, giving her daughter the space to vent.

"I'm stranded anyway," Lisa continued. "But, oh, Mama, it was such a relief to let down the guard. It was sweet."

Lisa heard herself sigh deeply then turning to face her mother, she admitted sheepishly, "But as the saying goes, for every action there is an equal and opposite reaction—or something like that. So I got my relief, albeit a temporary one, and now I must deal with the consequences."

"You sound just like your father when you said that. He was one for facing up to stuff. No side-stepping one's lot. Just deal with it and get on with the business of living."

"Now that you mention it, I must say that I'd expected Daddy to go ballistic when I told him . . . about the abortion. But if I could find a word to name the look he'd worn when I told him, it wasn't anger or even disappointment. It was more like a look of defeat. After that, he never broached the subject again. I just wish . . . oh never mind. What's done is done."

"You wished he'd have been more upset? Is that it?"

Taking Lisa's silence for a yes, her mother continued. "You think he wasn't? Honey, your father spent many hours with God agonizing over what to do or say. In the end he decided that what he needed to do most was to love you and model God's grace to you."

Lisa bit her lip, pondering. "He certainly did that. But can I tell you something, Mama? The abortion left me with a feeling . . . it's kinda hard to describe. It's like . . . like I've been permanently soiled. Yes, that's it. Not dirty, but soiled."

Mary's eyes took on a look of secret pleasure. "And that's where God comes in, sweetheart. He covers our soiled state with the clean robe of His righteousness."

· · · · ·

Seated at her office desk, Lisa could still see that look on her mother's face. It seemed to say that she had an exclusive relationship with God. The kind in which she, Lisa, could have no part.

Recalling her decision about the banquet this Saturday night, Lisa picked up the phone and called her husband at work. Forget talking to him at home. Calling his work would be the safest thing. Most likely he'd be in an appointment and she could leave a message with one of the assistants for him to call her back.

"Westwood Dental," a friendly voice answered.

"Hi, Denise. It's Lisa."

"Hello, Mrs. Westwood. I guess you want to speak to the love of your life, eh? Well, your timing is perfect. Dr. Westwood just got a cancellation so he's free to talk to you. Hang on. I'll put you through to his office. Have a good day."

Before Lisa had a chance to say "take a message," Donald's friendly and professional voice boomed across the line.

"Dr. Westwood."

"Hi Donald. It's me, Lisa." Her voice sounded breathless.

"Hi Lisa. Is something the matter?"

Lisa could not believe her nervousness. "No, not really. I was just calling to find out if—"

"Could you hold for a minute? They've put another call through. Let me get it."

Before Lisa could agree, the music of FM 102.7 was playing in her ear. She talked to herself.

Come on. This is your husband. You've been married to him for almost 15 years. What's the big deal in asking him to a silly banquet?

However, the more Lisa heard her self-talk, the angrier she became. Why couldn't he just deal with the fact that she'd had an abortion? Who was he to condemn her for a decision she made such a long time ago?

"Sorry, Lisa. A patient I worked on yesterday just arrived complaining of pain. I have to see her. What did you want to ask me?"

Coming straight to the point she asked, "Are you available to go to the Law Association banquet with me this Saturday night?" Lisa could hear the coolness in her voice and yes, the defensiveness too.

"What kind of question is that, Lisa? Don't I always accompany you?"

"Of course, Donald. I just thought that under the cir—"

"Is there anything else?" His voice was still polite and friendly. Nothing to fault in his tone. But Lisa felt like a patient needing to be soothed prior to a major cavity fix.

"No. Nothing else. Thanks."

"Good. I'll see you later then."

"Yes. Later."

So there, she consoled herself. You now have a date for the banquet. A public appearance as husband and wife where you get to make believe you're happy!

• • • • •

On Saturday night, Lisa donned one dress after another. She couldn't make up her mind. Finally, she settled for a black dress with a fitted bodice and flowing skirt. The dress made her feel desirable and at ease with herself. In the past, round about this moment, Donald already dressed and giving her space to do her frenetic dress changes, would have returned to the room to watch her, smiling at her final decision. Not that it mattered to him. He liked her in whatever she wore.

Tonight however, he had come in earlier, removed his navy blue suit, a subdued paisley tie and a crisp white shirt from the closet and had gone to his room to dress. When she made her appearance on the landing, his eyes had flicked over her with a glimmer of interest but all he said was, "You look nice."

That was it.

Nice, I look nice! Lisa fumed all the way to the downtown hotel.

I am drop dead gorgeous in this dress and all he says is "You look nice."

If Donald had any inkling of Lisa's inner quarrel, he showed no outward sign. Slipping a Christmas CD into the player, he allowed the music to fill up the silent night.

They had no sooner pulled up at the hotel entrance when a valet appeared at the door of the car to escort Lisa out and park their car, free valet parking being a perk at this event. With the car gone, her husband offered Lisa a sad smile and his arm, which Lisa took. The evening charade was about to begin.

On entering the banquet hall proper, Lisa's eyes took in the scene in front of her. Dominating one end of the hall was a humongous Christmas tree lit all the way to the top with the popular tiny blue lights Lisa hated, but she admitted that it fit well with the room's décor. Subdued candle-like light stands tastefully arranged at strategic points, created the feeling of a street in Paris—a particular place she'd once visited. Behind the crowd of some of the most influential legal minds in the city, she could hear the bopping sounds of a jazz band, adding the right kind of ambience to the party. Lisa's foot itched.

As she scanned the room, a server dressed in tails, popped up at her elbow with a tray of wine glasses. "White or red madam?"

"A Perrier, please."

"And you, sir?" he asked Donald.

"Just some orange juice for me. Thanks."

"Lisa! Donald! Good to see you." It was Janine with her date for the evening looking for all the world like she was having the time of her life. "This is Gould. Gould, I'd like you to meet my boss, Lisa Jones Westwood and her husband Donald Westwood. Russell is out on the balcony. Rita couldn't come 'cause the baby is sick so go keep him company."

"We just ordered drinks and . . ."

The server appeared at her side. "Here you go Madam, Monsieur."

"Later!" Janine danced off with her partner leaving Lisa and Donald to make their way, with many interruptions for greetings, to rescue Russell.

Halfway across the room Lisa felt Donald tug at her arm.

"I can't do this," he said, voice sounding tight.

"Do what, Donald?" inquired a perplexed Lisa.

"I can't do this night. I just . . . can't. Here are the extra car keys. The valet has the spare. I'll grab a cab home." He thrust the keys in her hand and bolted from the room leaving Lisa gaping after him.

She blinked her eyes rapidly, trying to recover her bearings. Her brain shut down then restarted itself, and finally suggested a plan of action.

Find Russell!

Lisa was turning in the direction of the balcony where Russell should be, when she was jostled from the side, spilling half the contents of her Perrier down the front of her dress.

Great! What else could go wrong in this crazy evening?

"Ma'am, I'm so very sorry," a voice said.

Lisa froze. She knew that voice.

It was the same voice that kept asking in her dreams, "Tell me, Mrs. Westwood, if . . ."

Lisa looked up into the familiar face. His evident pleasure to see her and the brief flash of that illusive something in his eyes that made her pulse, pulse harder, distracted her from the shock of her husband's abrupt departure.

"Hello, Joshua." Her voice sounded breathless to her own ears.

Joshua Hendricks smiled, his teeth their whitest. *Donald would appreciate the dental perfection,* Lisa thought.

"Mrs. Westwood. You look a marvel as always, despite my causing you to spill your drink. May I get you a refill?"

Quick as a wink, he snagged a passing serving staff. He replaced Lisa's order then checked her dress for damage. Luckily none of the liquid had soaked into the material and could be easily shaken off.

Uncomfortable with his close inspection of her, Lisa declared the dress just fine.

Joshua took a step back, looking around the room. "And where is that lucky husband of yours—the one who loves you very much?"

Lisa looked sharply at him to see if he was mocking her but his eyes held no guile. Why had Donald chosen this particular moment to leave her alone with this man? She searched the room, hoping that somehow her husband had had a change of heart. But Donald was long gone.

Feeling Joshua's eyes on her she answered. "He was not feeling well and had to leave. You just missed him."

"That's too bad. I would have liked to congratulate him on his excellent taste in women and encourage him to treasure you always."

And as always with this man, Lisa felt at a loss for words. He rescued her however.

"How about this, Mrs. Westwood? Since I too am without a partner for the evening, how about we keep each other company, h'mmm?"

Lisa eyed the covered balcony where, within one of the cluster of groups, Russell, her friend and partner was.

"Say yes, Lisa. I promise to be the perfect gentleman." With that pronouncement he smiled at her charmingly and proffered his arm.

Lisa took it.

For the rest of the night, Joshua, true to his word, gave her no cause to doubt his promise. Throughout dinner, he sat with her and regaled her with hilarious anecdotes of the antics of some of his more unusual clients. During the Recognition and Awards Ceremony, he joined heartily in the applause as deserving colleagues received their commendations. He demonstrated an appealing boyish bashfulness when he, too, was called to receive an award of his own. Obviously he did not enjoy being praised. Lisa liked that.

Russell, coming in from the balcony for dinner earlier, had found them together. Lisa had introduced them and invited Russell to join them at their table which he did. However, he was obviously missing his wife and concerned about the baby, and had left as soon as protocol allowed.

Following the awards ceremony, the jazz quartet transformed itself into an oldies band which had Lisa toe-tapping to the music and heartily singing along to all the songs she knew. The floor was filling up with dancers and Lisa itched to join in.

She felt Joshua watching her and kept her eyes on the dance floor.

"Will you dance one dance with me, Mrs. Westwood?"

Yes! Lisa's heart answered.

Temptation! A voice in Lisa's head yelled.

Her heart argued back. *I like to dance. What harm could there be in just one dance?*

Don't go there, girl. Don't do this. Don't put a further wedge between you and your husband.

That was not the right thing for the brain to say.

Donald is not here! Donald left me here. Alone! Joshua is here. He wants to dance and so do I.

Holding out his hand, Joshua waited, beguiling her, daring her with his eyes.

"I'd love to, Joshua . . ."

Please, Lisa! Her reason continued to plead.

". . . but I should be getting home."

Joshua, hand still outstretched, pressed. "In that case, dance with me to the door and I'll walk you to your car. I'm sure you can allow yourself to do that. I can tell those feet of yours are itching for action."

Lisa considered his proposal, mentally measuring the distance from their location to the exit, then stood and took his hand.

Joshua's eyes lit, making Lisa want to take back her hand. But the die was cast. Twice, three, then four times he twirled her around the dance floor. Lisa gave over to the music. She really loved to dance. She loved the freedom of it. She also loved the feeling of being admired. For one long minute, she was beautiful.

The minute ended too soon for Joshua. Lisa could feel his reluctance to let go of her hand. She refused to look him in the eye, lest he see how much she'd enjoyed herself. But as she was discovering, Joshua was a man of his word.

A perfect gentleman.

From helping her on with her coat, even on the escalator ride down to the main floor, Joshua took time to watch out for her, opening the doors, his hand splayed lightly against the small of her back, simply a felt presence. Not once did he behave in a way that she could label inappropriate. That was the problem.

The valet, after informing Lisa that it would take a few minutes to get the car, left them to do so. Lisa shivered in the crisp December air. Christmas and goodwill was everywhere.

"Cold?" Joshua asked.

"Just a bit chilly," replied Lisa, adjusting the collar of her coat. "Thanks for keeping me company. I had a pleasant evening."

"Good. That makes two of us." Joshua tucked his hands in the pockets of his pants, observing the decorated greenery all around the front of the hotel. He looked very handsome in the black evening suit. "You know, of course, that this whole evening is going to set me back some, don't you? I'd just started getting over dreaming of you." He turned to face Lisa. "What is it about you, Mrs. Westwood?"

Lisa attempted to make light of his seriousness. "Have you not heard that my name is legendary for causing young swains to cast themselves off cliffs but for a glimpse of my face?" she joked.

Her comment had the desired effect. Joshua laughed heartily and loudly. Lisa liked his laugh.

"Thanks for the warning and the compliment. I don't think I've ever been referred to as a swain. And a young one to boot!" Joshua took a step toward Lisa, holding her eyes. "Tell your husband, Mrs. Westwood, not to tempt fate by leaving you alone like this, sickness or not." The lightness of laughter had gone from his voice and Lisa felt a shiver starting up on her insides. She, too, was unable to break eye contact.

The sound of the Volvo's engine broke the moment. Rescue!

Joshua opened the car door. Lisa seated herself, closed the door, fastened the seatbelt, lowered the window, and turned to say good night.

Joshua reached inside the car and took her right hand in his. Then he turned her palm upward and placed a light kiss there.

Dear Lord! Lisa's mind screamed a prayer.

Joshua placed the kissed hand on the steering wheel, squeezing it so gently. "Good night, Mrs. Westwood. Sweet dreams." Then he straightened up and walked briskly away, not once looking back.

In something akin to a sleepwalker's trance, Lisa brought her un-kissed palm to join the other on the wheel, put the car into drive, and headed home leaving the window down to cool her fevered imaginings. She parked the car in the garage and quietly let herself into the house.

For the first time in a long time her heart didn't leap at the possibility that maybe tonight her husband would be lying in their joint bed, returning their lives to normal. This night, with too much on her mind, she ignored his closed door and proceeded thoughtfully to her room.

Chapter 21

Thomas Charles had purposefully requested a late appointment on the off-chance that he and Donald would be able to talk privately following his cleaning. He got his chance. After Donald finished checking his teeth and declared them in relatively good shape for an "old man," he'd agreed to Thomas' invitation to join him at the nearby coffee shop for something to drink.

Donald looked tired. And unhappy. He dropped his body heavily in the chair, filled his cheeks with air, and blew out.

"Long day?" asked Thomas.

"Long everything," Donald said with a sigh. "I can't believe that with only four days to go before Christmas, things are so busy. Normally we'd get a rush of activity after Christmas as parents use the break to get caught up on missed appointments. Anyway, how are you? I'm surprised you came in for your cleaning before I had to personally get on the phone to you."

"Don't tell me that *you* enjoy going to the dentist! But I'm fine. You, however, look like death warmed over. How are things?"

"How are things?" Donald pondered the question. "Reasonably OK, I guess."

To move the conversation past surface responses, Thomas called on his many years of experience discussing difficult issues with patients. Even though he didn't have the finesse of Catherine, he figured men in general neither required nor wanted kid-glove handling so he got straight to the point.

"Catherine said . . . well you know how women are with their intuition . . . Catherine felt an urgent need the other day to pray for you and Lisa. Then she asked me to talk to you. I, of course, said no."

"Obviously at some point since then your 'no' changed to a 'yes,'" remarked Donald, picking up a small pitcher of milk.

Thomas grinned. "Happened that very morning. Knowing I wouldn't speak to you based just on her 'feeling,' she asked me to do the one thing I couldn't say no to. She asked me to pray with her about the matter. So we did. And as I waited for God to speak, I, too, got the same sense of urgency to speak with you. What about? I don't know. So here I am."

"And here I am." Donald looked out the window. Nothing about the falling snow and the approaching night registered. He only saw Lisa's face. Her words still ringing in his head: *I had a baby, you know.*

"How are things between you and God, Donald?"

"For better or for worse. That's what I promised her. But what do you do when you no longer have trust?"

"I asked how things were between you and God, Donald. Not between you and Lisa. Not that Lisa isn't important, but now that I'm in my dotage, I've discovered that when things are OK with our relationship with God, the other things in life are manageable."

"God!" Donald shifted in the chair. "We used to talk pretty often. I used to listen like you do for His voice to tell me what to do or how to handle a situation. Lately, I just don't feel like it."

Thomas thought paint could dry with more enthusiasm than Donald spoke.

"I see. And Lisa?"

A hard look came into Donald's eyes. "Lisa." He smiled as he said her name but there was no warmth in the smile. How did he tell this man whom he so respected that his wife had had an abortion. That she'd waited close to 15 years to tell him about it. And that when she did, the telling lacked finesse, tact, and sensitivity? She'd cut him open. Laid his insides bare. Had the Queen mother herself announced to the public that she was a Romulan spy, he couldn't have been more shocked.

His one instinct had been to run. Run hard and far, quickly before the voice of his lover divulged any more unmentionables he could not bear to hear. That was the gist of it.

Since then he had done what made sense for his survival. Lock down. He knew Lisa wanted to explain. To seek absolution. But he wanted no heart-to-heart with her. No further baring of her soul. She would not turn him into a priest-confessor. He'd signed up for the husband thing—not that. Did she think him stupid? And to think, he had so revered her. Loved her like his own heart.

And then last Saturday night at her lawyers' banquet. He'd talked himself into doing the right thing. He'd go with her to the banquet. With so many people there, he could pretend with her that things were OK. But the press of people, the laughter, and gaiety had gotten on his nerves and he couldn't do it.

"What has your wife done that you find it so hard to forgive, Donald?"

Donald's head snapped to attention. He hedged. "Why do you think there's something to forgive?"

Despite his seriousness, Thomas felt his mouth smiling slightly. "Knowing the way you love Lisa, she must have done something that has completely affected your view of her. Something you feel you cannot forgive. I don't need to know what it is. That's between you and your wife. But is it really that bad? Is it so awful that it's worth sacrificing your relationship with God for?"

"What do you mean?" asked Donald. "I'm not sacrificing my relationship with God for Lisa!"

"Aren't you?" Thomas tempered his question with gentleness. "You just told me that since whatever it is has happened, you've not felt much like talking with God. So who are you mad at? Lisa? God? Or both?"

"I'm not mad at God," said Donald adamantly.

"Then if you're not, go home tonight and talk to Him, my friend. Ask Him what He would have you do and listen for His answer."

"He's going to tell me to forgive her." Donald caught himself. Pain closed his eyes. His jaw tightened to contain the emotions.

Sensing his friend needed some privacy, Thomas excused himself for a washroom break. When he returned Donald had himself under control again.

Thomas continued as if he'd never left. "Catherine and I have been married for 43 years. Every day I find more things about her to discover. More aspects I didn't know. Some of her habits, not a lot, drive me to the prayer closet to work things through with God. Marriage relationships can be one of the best ways of perfecting our characters for heaven. And us men, we have a lot to learn about our women—how to love them, how to talk with them, and how to let them be the people God designed them to be."

Sensing he still had Donald's attention, Thomas continued, "Talk to God tonight, Donald. Don't let too much time go by. Tell God everything you're feeling. What's making you angry, sad, hurting. Spill your guts to Him and beg Him for help to get through it."

"That's going to be hard."

"Yes, it is. But you must do it. Then you're going to have to do the next difficult thing. Ask Him to make you an example, a role model of Him to your wife. Be the priest in your home."

"What!" Donald's face wore a stupefied look.

"Don't look at me like that," smiled Thomas. "That's our job as 'man about the house.' To be priest to our families. To take on their burdens and offer them up to God as if they were our own sins."

"Like Aaron in the Bible?"

"Like Aaron in the Bible. Like Jesus Christ Himself in the heavenly sanctuary."

Donald had no response to offer.

"Listen. I want to invite you and a few of our men to join me in meeting together. I think it's time we start talking with each other about the role of men in the home and what that means. We can learn from each other as we do our own growing—not a support group but a discussion and debate group. I have a feeling that fantastic things can happen in our homes, churches, and communities when men get together to seek God's will for their lives."

Seeing Donald's hesitation, Thomas pressed. "You don't have to say yes now. Think about it. Pray about it. But I personally would appreciate your presence and help with this."

"Fair enough," replied Donald. "I'll think on it."

The men talked for a few more minutes about sports events, a much more comfortable topic. Then they parted. Each filled with thoughts of his own.

Interlude

Journal entry #6

Dear Son:

I wrote to that author woman and she called me today. Can you believe it? I don't know what prompted me to include my phone number but for once I decided to come clean with someone other than you and God about my past. I was in the kitchen making myself a sandwich when the phone rang. It was a strange woman asking for me. Thinking it to be a telemarketer I was remotely polite but when she identified herself I felt the shaking starting up again. I felt my throat clogging up with many years of repressed tears and I must confess that I couldn't stop them.

Her name is Laura-Ann and she speaks as plainly in real life as she does in her book. She said she called me because as she read my letter, she had the distinct impression to not write, but call.

Josiah, my boy king, I don't know how to describe the last hour I've spent on the phone with this woman sent by God Himself. I talked about the guilt, the pain, the imposterism that I feel, the lack of forgiveness. And she listened, said "ditto" at many places, and then she did something that caused my weeping to start afresh. She asked me if I believed that God loves me. I told her yes. She then told me to say it out loud. I did. I said: God loves me.

But Laura-Ann did not stop. She made me say that statement over and over and over again.

God loves me. God loves me. God loves me.

She made me insert my name and repeat it over and over again. And every time I repeated those words, it was like a piece of a wall pressing down on my chest being lifted off. I could breathe easier each time. Weeping till I felt completely exposed and raw, I kept repeating the words. God loves me. And after each saying of it she asked me if I believed it.

I didn't.

I couldn't! Why would a perfect God choose to love me?

I'm not deserving.

But Laura-Ann kept at me, making me repeat the words like a mantra. And then I did. I believed. The story of the lost sheep, the lost coin, the prodigal son, were all stories about me. God cares what happens to little old me and loves me in spite of myself.

God loves me!

How amazing, how marvelous is it that the Creator of the universe loves me. How awesome that the God who is Alpha and Omega knows me personally and despite all my sins, He loves me.

Me. Me!

Undeserving me.

Me with my issues and guilt and martyrdom. God loves me.

This Laura-Ann, a special angel emissary sent by God to be His hands and His side, touched me in places that were too dark to look at and made me understand that my pain was also hers. That while the memories continue I must not let them haunt me anymore. And so tonight, my son, I released them in the name of the Lord.

I cannot describe the lightness I feel. The weight of guilt has been lifted. I'm floating on grace.

Forgive the tears on this page. My heart is too full. I've decided to let go of the self-condemnation. Put the past in the past. Like Paul, I say, "Forgetting what is behind and straining toward what is ahead, I press toward the goal to win the prize for which God has called me heavenward in Christ Jesus"(Phil. 3:13, 14). I can do this through the strength and power of the Holy Spirit.

So I'm going to be saying goodbye to you soon. I can feel it. Maybe not today or tomorrow, but I must leave this past behind.

God loves me despite what I've done.

God loves me despite what I might do in the future.

God loves me. Period.

And because God loves me, I am doing Him a disservice by not loving me. If He considers me important enough to love, I need to act like I am loved. Laura-Ann pointed out that I have to let go of the constant self-condemnation and start acting as a loved child of God. That is where my challenge will lie. But God is gracious and I know He will help me.

Laura-Ann also told me that maybe my story could help someone else just as how her's helped me. She told me to ask God to show me who needed to hear it. But before she'd finished her statement, I knew my answer. I have someone to tell my story to. And when the time is right, prompted by the guiding hand of my Creator, I will.

Goodnight, my son.
Your mom.

Chapter 22

Christmas came and went. So did the New Year. Yolanda's house had been filled with good family frenzy. The addition of Marissa, her parents, and Grace had provided ample opportunities to expand the feeling of goodwill to all.

On the second Monday night into the New Year, Yolanda, having returned from visiting with Grace, decided to call her friend Lisa. Except for a brief chat on Christmas morning, when Lisa had called to wish them a Happy Christmas, they'd not had time to really connect. And the last time Yolanda had tried to call, following that conversation with Marissa that still made her smile, she'd gotten the answering machine.

Yolanda completed her night rituals, climbed into bed, propped four pillows against the headboard to support her back and picked up her phone. At 10:07 Lisa should be home. She punched in the numbers.

"Hello/Hello." A male and female voice answered at the same time.

"Two for the price of one," Yolanda greeted them. "Hello, Donald and Lisa. Happy New Year to you both! How are you doing?"

An empty space greeted her question. Then both voices rushed in to fill it. "We're doing fine. Reasonably OK."

"Listen," said Donald, "I know this call is not for me so I'll get off and let you two talk. Nice hearing from you, Yolanda. G'night."

"Good night, Donald." The extension clicked off.

"How did it all go with everyone over for Christmas?" Lisa jumped in. "When I called on Christmas morning, the din was unbelievable."

"I felt as tired as a dog by the time they'd all left but I haven't had so much fun in a long time. Marissa's parents had dinner with us. It was nice to get to really know them. I like them. Then you know how Grace is about everything. My grandson took quite a liking to her and chose her over his own daddy to sort through and get working all the toys he got for Christmas. Grace loved it. She told me afterward that the gift of his company was one of the best parts of her holidays."

"That's sweet. How's she doing, Yolanda? I haven't been in touch as much as I wanted to be?"

"You know what? There are days when I have to forcibly remind myself that she's dying. She looks so good and maintains such an upbeat spirit. I told her that she doesn't have to act happy on my behalf but she's just that kind of person."

"Is she still mad at God for not giving her the things in life she wanted and allowing her to get cancer?" asked Lisa.

"We talked about that too. I confessed to her that I also have been mad at God for taking Jackson before I was ready to let him go. Mad, too, at Marissa for taking my son away. So guess what we did? We decided to search the Bible for instances when folk had difficulties accepting God's will. We found David, Jonah, and others. That was so reassuring! Even though we wish to be like Job and say that God gives and takes away— blessed be His name, it felt good to see that there were 'fighting' journeys to submission in the Bible."

"And now?"

"Interestingly, after laying out our stuff before God and owning them, we don't feel so mad anymore, at least I don't. We're moving toward acceptance. I'm not there yet, but closer."

Lisa expelled a hard sigh that seemed to come all the way up from her toes. "I wish I could do that." She paused for a moment. "Yolanda, there's something I want to ask you. I know that you and Jackson were very close. You loved that man! But . . . was . . . was . . . was there ever a time when you felt like . . . you know . . .?"

"Like what, Lisa?"

"During all your married years, did you ever feel attracted to another man?"

"Like wanting to have an affair," Yolanda said cautiously, "or like admiring a man from the point of view of 'If I wasn't married I'd be interested in someone like that'?"

"Yeah, that! That!"

"What?"

"There's this lawyer I met last year. I ended up working with him for a client of mine who really wasn't supposed to be my client as we don't specialize in family law. But she was in a bad situation and I decided to help out. Anyway, that's how I met this guy—Joshua. Then one day he called the office and asked me to lunch. I assumed it was to talk over the case but it turned out that he's been having dreams about me and wanted to find out if I would be interested in going out with him. I was shocked, obviously. I told him I was married then left the restaurant, meal untouched. But then I met him again at the Christmas banquet, and because Donald had left for some silly reason I ended up spending the rest of the evening with this guy. He kissed my hand, Yolanda. I mean he kissed the inside of my palm."

"And now you can't get him out of your mind, right?"

"I'm so glad you understand. I've been so frightened. Compared to him, Donald is so—"

"Dull."

"Yes! Dull. Plus I don't think Donald loves me anymore. He hardly talks to me these days."

"You said that you're frightened. What frightens you, Lisa?"

Another pause. "Is it possible that after all these years I could be tempted to break my marriage vows . . . my husband is not speaking to me."

"Donald?"

"Who else, Yolanda? He's moved out of our bedroom!"

"He knows about this Joshua?"

"No. At least I don't think so. Joshua and I haven't done anything wrong. He's just in my mind. Donald's absence from our marriage doesn't help."

"OK, Lisa, now I'm thoroughly confused. What does Joshua have to do with Donald not speaking to you?"

"Nothing."

"Lisa!"

"I'm serious. Nothing. Donald hasn't spoken to me since I told him about something that happened in my past a long time ago."

Yolanda took a deep breath and slowly let it out. "What did you do a long time ago, Lisa? Did you have an affair? Is that the connection to this Joshua guy? Wait . . . forgive me. I'm sounding like an interrogator. Tell me only what you're comfortable with."

Yolanda felt more than heard Lisa's tears on the other end of the line, so after a moment she urged. "Lisa, come on. What's upsetting you so much?"

"His name was Luke, Yolanda. He was handsome and tall. A really sweet guy that I met soon after our family moved to Toronto. I fell head over heels in love with him and he with me. What we didn't know was that the powerful feelings we were discovering would, one day, overwhelm us."

Yolanda heard Lisa's strangled cough, then her whisper, "I've gotta get a drink of water." She waited through the sound of water running and through the silence that she presumed was Lisa getting a drink and, perhaps, control of herself. And while she waited, Yolanda prayed.

Now Lisa was back. "No way was I going to be one of those teens who fooled around with sex outside of marriage. Never in a million years. I wouldn't have dreamed it could happen," she said, her voice shrill. "But it did. One day—just one time—we did it. Just one time, Yolanda! We were so shocked at ourselves. I think we were embarrassed too. We promised each other and God that it would never happen again. And it didn't. But you know what? We closed the gate after the horses had escaped. Six weeks later I knew I was pregnant—and I was. I was a mess. When I told Luke, he was a mess. My folks were bowled over but they were all prepared to rally around us and make the best of this bad situation. But I couldn't . . . I just couldn't." Her voice dropped to a whisper. "So I had the baby aborted."

"Oh, Lisa. I see, I see. I think I'm getting the picture. All these years Donald didn't know, did he? What made you decide to tell him?"

"My mom asked me the same question," she sniffed. "I don't know. I'm bored with my marriage, Yolanda. Donald loves me, well, at least he used to. But life with him is so predictable, you know. Name the occasion or the day of the week and I can tell you *exactly* what he'll do, what he'll say, what he'll wear."

"So I guess his reaction to your news was not a surprise. You would have predicted that?"

"Are you playing with me, Yolanda? Because I'm not in the mood."

"We never know everything about people, Lisa. Not even the ones we've been married to for years. They keep growing and changing on us. We do the same too. And just when you think you have them pegged, they go do something totally out of character. But to get back to my question. What made you decide to tell Donald now? How did you tell him by the way? Please tell me you didn't just blurt it out in the middle of a conversation. You tend to do stuff like that, you know. Act, then think later."

Phone static spoke to Yolanda.

"Lisa, talk to me. I'm your friend."

"I just blurted it out. And—and—and—then he took off. He didn't even come home that night. I have no idea where he went. And when he returned the next day, he moved his pillows into the guest room. He won't let me talk to him. Do you know what it's been like at home, Yolanda? He still sets my bath and he still makes dinner for us, but come night time, he disappears to his room. He won't let me talk with him about how I'm feeling. I have stuff I want to share with him."

143

Yolanda prayed for patience. She loved this younger woman like a sister but having a conversation with her made for character development. She asked the question again. "What made you decide to tell Donald, Lisa? Why now?"

"The night of Derek and Marissa's wedding, I came home so joyful. I wanted to dance. I asked my husband to dance with me but putting out the garbage took top priority. I long for romance. I'm dying for someone to touch my mind with passion. That's what I had with Luke. I know that at 40-something one can't expect to recapture the pure headiness of that first love experience, but I want romance, Yolanda. I need it. I want passion. And my husband does not emotionally touch me that way. I don't know if he ever did. But after all these years, I want it."

"Lisa . . ."

"*I don't know why I told him, Yolanda! Then, or at all!*" Lisa shouted. She worked to bring her self under control. "Maybe I wanted to shock him. I suppose there's some of that. But you don't know what it's like, Yolanda. Calling yourself a Christian and living with the fact that you had an abortion. The nightmares that haunt you. The guilt that plagues you. 'Thou shall not kill.' And knowing in your heart that you are not deserving of the love of a good man who bores you to tears. What does that make me?"

"Certifiable for sure. Way beyond the reach of God."

"You think so, Yolanda. You really think I'm beyond the reach of God's grace?"

"Come on, Lisa. Don't be ridiculous. I'm just trying for a bit of levity in this conversation. Nobody is beyond the reach of God's grace, unless of course, they choose to put themselves beyond it. We have the power to do that, you know. Put ourselves in a place that completely shuts God out. And since He refuses to force our love, He has to respect our choice. Do you want forgiveness, Lisa? Have you not asked God to forgive you for aborting the child?"

"Yes. Of course. I did that a long time ago."

"Do you really and truly believe that He did?"

"I'm not sure. I think so. But the problem is me. I have difficulty forgiving myself."

"I'm going to tell you a story, Lisa. Something I've never told to another soul. Not even Jackson. You're probably wondering how come I knew exactly what you were feeling when you told me about this man, Joshua. Well, this might explain it. There's a particular phase in a marriage, especially when you have young children, where all your attention is focused on them. They need to be fed, homework assisted, taken to lessons, and that's all your life is.

"Jackson and I had our three children. And until Derek turned about 8 years old, our lives were on this treadmill we'd chosen. Then one day you look up and there is no child immediately under foot. For the first time in how many years, the children can entertain themselves for hours on end and you have breathing space. You notice your husband as a man for the first time in a long time and he's grown a bit of a tummy. He clips his toenails in the rec room while he watches the game on TV, and the clippings fall on the floor. And you realize that you're living with a stranger. The father of your children, the man resembling the one you married mind you—but a stranger."

Yolanda paused to gather her thoughts. "This stranger's eyes no longer light up when you walk into the room. You're not doing much better yourself because it's much more comfortable to walk about the house in baggy cotton pajamas that not even Atilla the Hun would wear. Your tummy and other body parts are sagging, and this stranger husband of yours only wants to have sex with your body without engaging your heart or mind. Are you still with me, Lisa?"

"Yes. I'm listening."

"Round about that time, I'd begun to get more involved in church activities. There was this man who was part of the crew that went out on the third Saturday of each month to take food to the homeless. He wasn't new to the church but I only got to know him while I worked on that committee. Whenever he saw me, he would always have something nice to say. He'd commend my smile or my nice way of dealing with the homeless people, and of course, my sandwiches always got rave reviews. I started to look forward to hearing the nice things he said. I looked forward to being around him. Then one night, after our group had met to pack the lunch sacks for the next day's food drive, he and I happened to be the last ones to leave the building."

There Yolanda stopped. She did not know how to continue. How do you explain to your tempted friend that adultery begins first in the mind? You're preoccupied with how you'll appear to the other. You think of ways to make him smile. You figure out a way to accidentally meet him. Next to the fantasy man living in your head, the stranger within your gates is achingly dull.

"Go on, Yolanda," prompted Lisa.

"Well, this one day he walked me to my car. It was a cold day in

November. I got in and started the engine which sputtered, then died. I tried again but afraid of flooding it, I sat back wondering what to do. The church was locked. Of course, back then we had no cell phones. And silly of me, I hadn't dressed appropriately for the weather so taking the bus was not an option.

"I tried the engine again but this time it didn't even catch. The next thing I knew there was a knock on my car window. It was this same man. For argument's sake let's call him Bill. He motioned for me to move over and he tried to start the car. Nothing. We tried boosting the battery but it wouldn't hold the charge. So we locked up my car and he drove me home.

"In the half hour it took to reach my house I was aware of this man like never before. Every shift he made of the gears, the way his hands held the steering wheel, the way his mouth smiled with me. I was an agony of need. He talked, I laughed. He shared and I reciprocated. In my eyes, we lived on the same wavelength of mutual understanding. We connected."

"Did he feel the same way?" Lisa asked softly.

"I'm sure of it. That night when he turned into my driveway, he cut the engine and turned to me. This is what he said. 'Your husband is a very lucky man, Yolanda. I envy him his good fortune.'"

"Oh my!" said Lisa.

"When I got into the house I found myself shaking. Why? Because when he said those words to me, I had wanted so very badly to have him kiss me. He must have felt the same way too. I saw him looking at my mouth, but one of us must have slammed shut the door to temptation and I bolted.

"To make matters worse, when I got to bed, there was Jackson waiting up for me with a look that told me he was in the mood for love. Not one word of compliment. No thanks for the lovely dinner. He didn't even ask about my day! I tell you, the last thing in the world I wanted at that moment was to be in bed with my husband. How could I when I was mentally wrapped up with this other man? I glared at the man I married, grabbed my pillow, and went to sleep on the living room sofa."

"Didn't Jackson come after you?"

"No, he didn't. Which was a good thing. That night, Lisa, I faced God in the privacy of my living room and did not like what I saw. I had allowed feelings for another man to come between me and my husband. The man I'd promised God that I would love and cherish till death separated us. It frightened me how easy it would have been to stray. Had I let him kiss me, (and how I wanted him to), I'd be . . . well, I'd be . . . an adulteress! Me!

"Then and there I made a commitment to God to stay emotionally and

146

physically true to my vows. I enrolled Jackson and myself in a marriage en-
richment seminar, and it saved us. I'm convinced of that. For the first time
in years, Jackson and I really talked. On that weekend of the marriage retreat
we began to rediscover each other. We shared our dreams, talked about the
people we'd become, and discussed our fears and hopes for our future and
that of our children. We even wrote love letters to each other—"

"But!" Lisa interrupted. "That sounds so artificial. Writing love letters
that you couldn't have meant. Not at that time."

"But you see," Yolanda countered, "I did have the will to love him
again. I'm being bare naked honest with you. It was by sheer force of will—
plus leaning hard upon God—that I fell in love with Jackson again. And I've
praised God for that a thousand times. No, it didn't happen overnight, but
over time. All our relationship needed was time, communication, commitment, and nurturing of each other."

And that's the whole of it, Yolanda thought as she waited for Lisa's response. *God and I did it together, and no one can ever take away from me the happy
years that followed.*

Lisa's voice overlaid her memories. "And the love affair continued till
Jackson died!" she said, wonder in her voice. "Thanks for telling me about
this. It helps." Another pause. "By the way, what became of the other guy?"

"He met a lovely woman and got married a year or so later. When our
church established a new congregation in the east end of the city, he and
his family joined that company."

· · · · ·

In the room next door, after he'd put away his book and turned out the
lights, Donald lay quietly, hoping for sleep. He could hear Lisa's voice in
conversation with Yolanda. Listening hard, he found he could make out
words. Something about garbage taking priority over her. And then, clearly,
Lisa's shout: "I don't know why I told him, then or at all."

Guilt, longing, and rage wrestled. He missed his wife but maybe what
he actually missed was the woman he thought her to be. Then the words
of Thomas came back to him: *Tell God everything. Be a priest in your home.*

Was it such a hard thing that his wife asked of him? To listen to her
confession and have mercy on her? But how could she have aborted a living human being, and now here they were childless! He shifted position,
eyes open in the darkness, his mind whirling with thoughts. His heart told
him that not only was it hard to forgive Lisa. It was next to impossible.

Chapter 23

The women had just finished another sumptuous breakfast and had gathered in the familiar place, each occupying her preferred seat. Lisa on the rocker, Grace and Yolanda on the sofa, and both Marissa and Monica on straight backed chairs brought in from the dining room. Catherine opted today for a firm upholstered Queen Anne chair. She needed the support, her arthritis broadcasting to her body the dampness of the day.

"Happy New Year everyone! Now tell me, ladies, was it only me or did you find this break way too long? I really missed your company."

A chorus of voices agreed with Catherine.

"Is there anything in particular anyone wants to talk about today? Grace has asked to say a few words. Anyone else?"

Marissa lifted her hand in a shy way that reminded Catherine of a schoolgirl asking for help. "I have a question that I need some advice about."

No one else spoke.

"OK. Grace first, followed by Marissa. Then we shall see what the Bible has to say about the things discussed. Grace, go ahead."

"I just want to let you women know how much you've helped me. The phone calls, the prayers, the support. I really appreciate it. I cannot thank God enough for Yolanda. I never had a sister but if this is what it's like, I am blessed beyond measure to have her walk through this valley with me."

"Please don't make me start crying again, Grace," begged Lisa whose eyes were already filling up.

Grace smiled at her. "Yours is a warm heart, Lisa. I do, however, want to talk about a second thing. When I first told everyone about my illness I was feeling pretty sorry for myself. I'm not going to apologize for anything I said because I was being honest with you and God about my feelings. But now I want to share something Yolanda and I discovered in the Bible.

"Sometimes God asks us to do things that make no sense to us. Jonah received a directive to go to Nineveh—a nasty city—to tell them to repent of their evil ways. Imagine God asking you to go to a den of iniquity where no respect resides for laws of any kind? Jonah balked. But God wanted him and no one else to do this job. Moses was another who received a directive to go back to a place where a warrant was posted for his arrest to ask for deliverance of the Jews. He too balked. But it was a job for Moses, and only Moses, to do.

"Where does my death fit within the plans of God? I have no clue. Am I a small ripple in a small river, but necessary to trouble the water; maybe the catalyst to an outcome I could never imagine? Am I some trophy disciple God is relying on to demonstrate to the universe as in the case of Job, that there are those who will stay faithful though they lose everything? Am I just a mere consequence of life in a sin-filled earth? I don't know." She looked from one woman to another as she spoke. "But since I cannot imagine a life without God, and even though I don't always understand what He's up to, I'm going to trust Him and His wisdom. Even though I will soon walk through the valley of the shadow of death, I am determined to trust Him. But I just wanted you to know that the trust is made so much easier because God provided all of you for me for such a time as this. And so my journey is not a lonely one. I have friends to touch my hand and to hug me. God bless you all. That's all I want to say."

"There you go again, Grace," Lisa wailed as she wiped at the overflowing tears. "God bless you too."

Grace received many other blessings and reassurances of continued support, then Catherine gave Marissa the nod.

"Well, I'm interested in hearing what everyone thinks about this. Should a mother stay home so she will always be there for her kids, assuming she can afford to. And if so, why did God give her skills in other areas that have nothing to do with parenting?" Her voice rose an octave. "I don't even know if I like kids!"

"I guess this isn't a hypothetical question, is it?" Monica asked. "Leave it to you, Marissa, to bring up this contentious issue!"

"Why is it contentious? I mean, you're not that much older than I am. Seriously, what do you think?"

"You're not going to like it."

"Well, I asked your opinion. I don't have to like it but I want to hear what you think."

Monica rested her head against the back of her chair and looked at the ceiling. Her voice roughened. "I'm convinced that my marriage broke up because I put my career above the needs of my family. I thought I could do it all, you know. Bring home the so-called bacon and fry it up and all that. But now . . . somehow I feel that if I'd been home more, my marriage wouldn't have crashed. I could have been more supportive to James—my ex."

"You're taking all the blame for your divorce?" Lisa asked incredulously.

"Of course not. It was both of us, but looking back I see things differ-

ently. And now I'm raising my kid all by myself. Sure, my parents help out—
especially like today when I need some time for me—but life gets too crazy
with two people working. It's a constant run: pick-up, drop off, breathe,
sleep, and get up to do it all over again. Children suffer." She stopped for a
deep breath then added, "And my daughter misses her dad."

"But why should it be the woman who stays at home," questioned
Marissa testily.

"Because she's got the womb and men can't multitask," Monica laughed.
"Plus men are not natural nurturers of other people's dreams. They're good
at getting bolstered and not very good at bolstering their women."

"I don't know that I buy that argument," Lisa protested. "Of the two of
us, Donald is more nurturing than me. If I'm to be honest, I'd say that he
takes way better care of me than I do of him. I'm sure if my job required me
to move to another country or even if I just wanted to, Donald would give
it serious consideration and do whatever was necessary to make it happen for
me."

Grace's eyes twinkled as she waded in. "For what an old spinster's opinion is worth, I think if I had a husband and kids, and could afford to do so,
I'd stay home during the critical years of their lives to be with them.
However"—her tone and raised eyebrows made everyone laugh—"I
wouldn't go as far as saying that a woman should stay at home just to cook
for, clean up after, and nurture a man. Their children, yes. And I personally
think that many of the problems our families face these days are due to
parental selfishness."

"That's kind of a harsh indictment," Marissa charged.

"You think so?" Grace asked. "Maybe. But I think if a couple chooses
to have children, both parents need to invest serious time in the training and
rearing of them. That is an awesome responsibility—to be the trainers and ed-
ucators of the next generation. Somehow I think we women have allowed
ourselves to be misled in believing that if we choose to focus exclusively on
our parenting, we're somehow second class citizens. That's hogwash! And the
men need to spend time with the kids too—not work from dawn to dusk,
leaving them to the mothers to rear alone!"

Lisa laughed. "I don't think our Grace has any opinion on the matter at
all. Wouldn't you agree, ladies?"

Grace's neck shrunk an inch within her collar. "No, no opinion whatsoever!"

Yolanda slapped her playfully with a cushion. "Yeah, right! Marissa's
question is a good one. For someone who's from the old school as a stay-

home wife and mother, I have no regrets about my decision. But now that my children are grown and Jackson is gone, I wish I had a job or something meaningful to occupy my time. I still feel that there's much left for me to do with my life."

Grace turned grateful eyes to Yolanda. "For purely selfish reasons I'm glad you're not in a job right now. If you were you wouldn't be available to be the great support you are to me." Yolanda winked her approval, and Grace went on. "Listening to us talk, I'm wondering why we think our work has to have a salary attached to it for it to be important? I ask that despite the fact that I've been a career woman all my life."

"But I don't want to be just a mother or a wife," cried Marissa. "I have a brain. I have skills that the world needs. I can do research that will make a big difference in the health of people everywhere. There's so much value I can add in the workplace! My whole being screams at the thought of being cooped up at home all day with a squawking kid. Catherine, please say something!"

"Objection!" Monica called, turning mock serious eyes on the other women. "Ladies, have we just been dissed? Is it just me or did Marissa's request imply that our opinions are mere second cousins to the wisdom of Mother Catherine Superior there?" She jerked her thumb in Catherine's direction.

Lisa considered the question. "Permit me to speak as the consul on staff. The prosecution's question requires a judgment call which cannot be factually supported. As far as I know, opinions do not have relatives of the familial kind. Objection overruled."

Yolanda deadpanned. "But then again, except in the case of the Man Christ Jesus, I have never heard of a person acting as counsel and judge on the same case. I move that this lawyer/judge be found in contempt."

Lisa jumped off her chair and advanced on Yolanda. "Contempt! Contempt! Woman, you have never seen contempt. I'll show you . . . you insufferable little dweeb?"

"Catherine, stop them!" Marissa begged. "They're out of control."

Catherine rapped her knuckles against the wall. "Order! Order!"

Lisa jive-walked backwards to her chair, continuing to make threatening signs at Yolanda who responded in kind.

"Well, Marissa, there you have two good reasons for not having children," Catherine remarked.

Yolanda and Lisa both gasped.

"I never!" puffed Yolanda.

Lisa's mouth worked furiously to find an equally fitting reaction. "Ditto to that!" she finally managed.

The hilarity that followed had them all in stitches for a while. Finally, Yolanda spoke up amid lingering fits of giggles. "Ladies, this is supposed to be a Bible study group, not a comedy club. We haven't even looked up one text as yet."

"I have one," Monica piped. "'A merry heart doeth good like a medicine'" (Prov. 17:22, KJV).

"A berry heart—where in the Bible does it say that?" asked Lisa.

"I said a merry heart. Merry. Letter before N. I have a bit of a cold that's all."

"Talk about berries, have you guys seen the prices for blueberries lately? This little sliver of a container with no more than 20 sorry looking fruit in it, was selling for close to $5.00. Imagine that! Five bucks!" Catherine complained.

Marissa held her head in her hand. "And there goes our fearsome leader. OK, ladies. You win. I concede. You've done what few in life have been able to do—shut me up. I back down. I yield. Yes, you are all nuts and I must be close to receiving my own diagnosis, because I enjoyed every moment of this . . . this . . . study of . . . God help us."

Grace helped her out. "To paraphrase, 'How good and pleasant it is when sisters live together in unity'" (Ps. 133:1).

Monica broke into song. "Bless be the tie that binds," she sang, and one by one the other voices joined in. That led to prayers, testimonies of praise and thanks, and promises to continue the discussion at the next meeting.

Chapter 24

Donald still had not followed Thomas's advice to have it out with God. How could he? But how could he not? This impasse with Lisa could not continue. Was it true what Thomas said that he needed to be the priest of his home in the real sense of the word—taking on his family's mistakes and burdens as if they were his very own. Such awesome responsibility boggled the mind. He had enough trouble carrying his own stuff!

That night, however, Donald picked up his Bible. Starting with the twenty-seventh chapter of Exodus he reread the instructions God gave to Moses about the sanctuary and the priests that ministered in it—from how they should be dressed to what kind of material and adornments should comprise their garments. The last section of chapter 28:30 caught his attention: "thus Aaron will always bear the means of making decisions for the Israelites over his heart before the Lord."

As he read on into the book of Leviticus, he saw that the meat from both the sin and guilt offerings were to be eaten only by the priest. Donald was not sure he understood what it all meant. Not sure even if any of it still applied to his twenty-first century life. But he felt convicted that he, despite his unwillingness, would be held accountable for modeling God to his family.

Before Lisa's astounding news Donald considered himself a pretty OK guy. Not perfect, but certainly patient, loving, forgiving, and slow to anger. Now everything had changed. He felt a palpable anger that he wanted to hug close and intolerance for choices—and people—that he didn't approve.

And now?

The prodding of his conscience stopped him cold. Could it be true that he no longer loved Lisa because she was human?

Is that what you're saying, Donald? Your wife must be perfect for you to love her? She must have led a spotless life, as you define it, for you to love her?

Donald was not a shouter, neither was he a violent man, but he suddenly felt like smashing something. How dare she show him up like this? Dear God, he *so* wanted children. And Lisa had a child, and had not kept it, and now they could have no more. Maybe the quack of a doctor messed up her insides suctioning out the evidence! No! He must not think of that. But dear God, that woman took away his dream of a family. All this time he'd blamed himself! His fault, his low sperm count, his bad genes—but it was all her!

"That woman," Donald?

Lisa, then. Lisa. And it was her fault!

And now?

His conscience persisted in annoying him.

Now? Now he wished for rows of glass bottles in a squash court. He could see them laid out neatly within easy reach. He'd fling them hard against the concrete wall and watch them cascade in lethal bits to the floor. Then he'd grind his feet into them and take in the pain. Maybe then, he would have something external to distract him from the torment of his heart.

"God, I can't do this. I can't even talk to You. You seriously cannot expect me to forgive my wife for destroying my dreams."

Yes, I do. I know the plans I have for you. Plans to give you hope and a future . . .

"What future? I'm already getting old. I can't start again with another woman and recreate the family I want. I know You're not suggesting that anyway!"

Is My hand short, Donald?

"Then give me what I want God. Give me—"

Say it, My child. Tell Me what you want Me to give you.

To his surprise, his eyes filled with tears. "Give me, God . . . give me . . . give me peace."

Donald surprised himself. Why had he asked for peace? He wanted, needed, a family! Peace? You can't play with peace, read it a bedtime story, tuck it in bed, or teach it to ride a bike!

"My peace I give you . . . I do not give to you as the world gives. Do not let your hearts be troubled" (John 14:27).

While Donald's heart continued to wish for peace, his mind yelled no. And then Lisa's words of the other night slammed into his consciousness, slightly tipping his resolve. Had he in good conscience been the kind of husband his wife needed? When she wanted things that he didn't like as much as she did, had he tried to accommodate her?

"Husbands, love your wives even as Christ also loved the church and gave himself for it" (Eph. 5:25).

For the first time in weeks, Donald felt a flicker of doubt about the rightness of his behavior. But what to do instead? He a priest? He didn't even know what that meant. He only knew this one thing: he did not have the credentials. God help him! He had no idea what to do. He was 51 years old and he needed to learn about the role of a husband in the home. Not sure how to start or what to say, he stuttered his first—in a long time—petition to the throne of grace. Jesus, High Priest in the heavenly sanctuary, would surely know what he ought to do.

• • • • •

Unaware of the battle raging next door within the mind of her husband, Lisa through fitful sleep, battled her own demons. First Luke and then Joshua—both men vying for play time in her mind. She thought of Yolanda's story. But happy endings only seem to favor a few select people. If only she had her mother's faith.

The next day, Lisa went into work feeling like grains of sand were permanently lodged under her eyelids.

"Morning, Janine," she grumpily greeted her assistant and kept walking.

"Morning, Lisa. And how are you today?" Janine looked up from her computer and noticed the haggard face of her boss. "What's the matter with you? You look like—" Lisa's look of venom made her swallow her comment.

"Hello! You look like you could use a hello." Seeing no responding greeting or break in Lisa's stride, Janine replied to the closing door, "And then a goodbye."

Lisa closed the door and heard it slam harder than intended, rattling the framed picture of a park scene in fall. Donald had bought it for her on their first wedding anniversary. He said it reminded him of how the trees had looked the day she'd agreed to marry him. One part of her mind wished the picture would crash to the floor and break into pieces. The other wanted to steady it.

Her head throbbed. Not content to harass her only in the night, her demons had followed her to work, pestering the edges of her sanity. They spoke as if reciting from a script she did not recall approving or writing, fully filling the stage of her mind.

Demon 1: Come on, sweetheart. Face it. Your husband doesn't love you. How long has it been now? Almost three months since he moved out of your bedroom?

Demon 2 *(to #1)*: Of course he loves her. Just like Luke loved her. And her daddy. But they're all gone. When she loves people, they get going.

Demon 1: I like this Joshua. He's so smooth and so cool. I especially love it when he says in that sexy voice, "Tell me, Mrs. Westwood . . ." I swoon every time he says that. That voice is to die for.

Demon 2: And Lisa likes it too. Did you see how she was shaking that night after the banquet? Man, that guy knows how to turn on the charm and

155

leave a lot to the female imagination."

Demon 1 (*to Lisa*): You like him, don't you, Lisa. You want him, don't you? Compared to dull Donald he's a ray of sunshine on a cloudy day.

Demon 2: Compared to Donald, anything is a ray of sunshine. Tell me, Lisa, did you purposefully marry a dull Don Juan? You wanted no reminders of Luke, did you? Did you really love him? Lisa, I can't hear you! *Did you love him?*

Demon 1: What's with the yelling at her? Didn't they teach you nothing in school? No yelling at the client? Gentle, reasoned persuasion, like this: "Lisa, it is quite obvious that your love for Donald is not as strong as the passion you felt for Luke, and if I might be presumptuous, the excitement that the few brief moments with Joshua has stirred in you . . ."

Demon 2 *(to Demon 1)*: I like this. It's subtle. Go on.

Demon 1: You and I both know that you've tried everything to get your husband to talk to you. I mean, look how he walked out on you at the banquet? I saw the defeated look in your eyes when he just left you standing there, car keys jammed in your palm. You have every reason to be upset. No one would fault you for clearing some space in your mind for another man. After all, thinking about Joshua is not wrong. A woman needs to be thought desirable. And then after you took so much time to find a dress that would spark fire even from an iceberg, all your Donald did was say you looked nice.

Demon 2 (*getting a feel for the art*): But look at the difference when Joshua saw you. He wanted you. And look how nice he was about it all. He respected the fact that you belong to someone else. He treated you with such deference. Such tenderness. Yet you know that beneath all that gentlemanliness, he wanted you. See girlfriend, you still have what it takes to capture the attention of a man among men. You got game!"

Demon 1 *(raising her eyebrows at her partner's last statement)*: It's totally harmless what you're doing. Nothing but a mental holiday from everything that's dull and stressful in your life. Enjoy it. Don't let anyone tell you different. Nothing is wrong with a little mental flirtation. Every woman needs it.

Demon 2: And you are every woman.

A sharp knock on the door jolted Lisa back to reality. Her handbag sat on her desk and the coat was still draped from her arm. How long had she been here in dreamland? Thoughts of "every woman" and of Joshua lingered in her mind as she opened the door to answer to Janine.

Her work day had begun.

Chapter 25

On a Friday evening in February, three days before Saint Valentine's Day, Thomas Charles sat in his study and looked at the men who had responded to his invitation. The study had the look and feel of a library. In addition to the expected medical tomes occupying one wall, religious books, science books, and history books as well as fiction and non-fiction on an array of topics filled a second wall. A large mahogany desk with a comfortable burgundy executive chair took up the third wall and the final was interrupted by a set of double glass doors leading out to the side of the house and the garden.

Derek, husband to Marissa had come. Beside him, on the recliner, was Simon, a tradesman, from their church. Bill MacDonald sat in the next chair. He was a quiet older gentleman, a widower and retired, whose mind Thomas loved and whose grasp of the Scriptures was phenomenal.

Yet someone was missing. Thomas keenly felt the absence of his friend Donald. He dropped his head to his chest and offered a brief plea to God to prompt Donald to come. Then he lifted his head and began the meeting:

"Gentlemen, you have done me a great honor in coming this evening. For some of you it's been a rough work week, but here we are. I asked you to come here because there's a crisis in our community and in our families. The more I read the news the more I hear about young men in the city who are killing each other, for what? Because someone 'disrespected' them? Because someone else wants to remain king of the hill? Thirty-six deaths already in our city this year. Six in this week alone! And the more I see stuff like this, the more I think that somehow we as men have failed our boys."

Bill MacDonald nodded. "We have failed ourselves."

Derek gave an impatient shake of his head. "Come on! We spend enough time as it is bashing men. No offense intended to you, Dr. Charles, but . . . "

"Call me Thomas."

"OK, Thomas. I take exception to that position of us failing our boys. What does the fact that there are idiot young men out there killing each other have to do with what you said we'd be discussing—the role of men in the home? That's what I came to hear about!"

Simon raised his roughened carpenter's hand and waited to be recognized. Thomas gave him the nod.

"I know I'm not a fancy professional like the rest of you, but I don't agree with Mr. Derek here that what's happening with our young men is not somehow connected to what we learned about ourselves at home. I mean, a boy learns how to be a man from his dad, right?"

Derek intercepted the question. "That's exactly my point. Many of these young men came from homes without fathers. The have no concept of what it is to be a man—at least none that was learned from a dad. They were left at home to fend for themselves and when that happens, boys find a way to belong to something. These ones grow wild."

Bill MacDonald cleared his throat in preparation for speech. Thomas smiled. They were about to hear a dissertation. But his assessment was wrong. "I hope, Derek, that you're not implying that the absence of a father in the home automatically results in boys growing up derelict."

"I think I am," said Derek. "Like Simon said, boys learn how to be men from their dads."

"Then," continued Bill, "I should be six foot under the ground, king-pin of a mafia group, or serving several life sentences in some prison."

"I'm not following," said Derek.

"I, Derek, am a product of a fatherless household. No, I misrepresent myself. I am mostly the product of a fatherless household. You see, the man who fathered me hung around for the first seven years of my life. He hated kids, me in particular, repeatedly physically abused me, my mother, and my young sister. Our lives were a living hell. When he finally decided to relieve us of his presence, he took all the money—what little we had, and left my mother without a job, without resources for the next meal we would eat. He just left."

"But you had a good stepfather or someone like that, didn't you?" questioned Derek.

"Shut up and listen young man. Learn something for a change. Law school might have taught you about precedents but I'm talking to you about life! There was no stepfather, but there was my mother. She did not even have a high school diploma, but I can still recall the day my father left. She dropped right there on the bare earth of our yard and thanked God for my father's departure. Then she begged God to open a way for her to get a job, any job to feed her children and raise them up, despite the rough beginning, to be the people He designed us to be.

"That woman washed clothes. She ironed, cleaned homes and offices, anything it took to keep life and limb together. Every night, no matter how late it was or how tired she'd be, she would gather us around her, me and my sister Betty, and that woman would pray on us."

"Pray on you?" asked Derek.

"Pray on us. She'd put her hand on our head, one at a time, and petition the throne of God to rain down blessings on us, for God to protect us, keep us from straying. She showed up for every meeting at school that she could. Every day she asked about our homework. She taught me my first scripture verses. I said my first testimony in the church of Adeline MacDonald. I am a retired university professor. Betty got a Masters degree in social work, ran her own practice for a while and then went overseas to make a difference in saving other lost children. She turned down many offers of marriage, a few from some pretty impressive men. You see, Betty was, still is, a looker. But her brain, therein lies her beauty. Her brain is a beautiful thing to watch working. That and a heart of gold. So there you have it my young friend. Two exceptions to your theory."

Derek had the grace to look sheepish. "Well, my life was different. I've always had a dad around. My old man held our home together. He led out in worship. He drove me to my first school banquet. It was he who explained to me the facts of life and taught me about responsible sex. I guess I took that for granted."

Thomas considered Derek's point. "Maybe it wasn't so much as taking for granted but that you assumed what you had was the norm for everyone. However, before we stray too much to the enticing discussion about nature and nurture and gender socialization, this seems as good a time as any to get back to the reason for our meeting. You see, I have this theory, well maybe it's past theory stage by now."

A soft knock on the door interrupted Thomas. "Come."

Catherine poked her head in the room. "Guess who I found stalking our premises?"

Donald's head could be seen peeking over Catherine's shoulder before he straightened up. "Is the meeting still open for latecomers?"

"Come in!" Thomas called enthusiastically.

Catherine withdrew and Donald greeted the other men. He knew them all from church but with the exception of Thomas, he didn't recall having any extended interactions with any of them. He took a seat next to Bill.

Thomas returned to the topic under discussion. "Just before you came in, Donald, I was saying that I believe some of the problems with our society stem from the decreasing influence of men in the homes. These days, I'm not even sure if men know what being a man is all about. Once we started to belittle the role of men as the one responsible for leadership in the home, we left a gap of need for our young men. And by the way, I'm not advocating for us to return to the dark ages of women being subservient to their men." His eyes unconsciously glanced toward the door where Catherine had stood a moment before. "My wife has enough to say on *that* subject so talk to her if you want to go there. What I'm talking about is the role of men in the home."

Thomas paused. He wanted to get this out just right. His heart told him he had something here but how to say it? He sent a thought-prayer heavenward.

"Here's where I'm taking this, gentlemen. Before Christ came to make atonement for us once and for all, God's chosen people—the Jews—had the symbols of the sanctuary. The priests, starting with Aaron (and yes, I do realize there were priests long before Aaron), got to stand in the gap between God and the people. One of Aaron's responsibilities as priest was interceding with God on behalf of the people. Every time the people sinned, they would bring a sin or guilt offering to the priest who would go through these elaborate rites in burning the fat, sprinkling the blood on the altar, etc. That was the role of the priest and no one else. Are you with me?"

Donald's brow furrowed in concentration. "I tried reading through the book of Leviticus the other night to better understand the role of the priest. It was tough going but God was very specific about a lot of what the priests could or couldn't do."

"That's right," agreed Thomas. "But I want to move us beyond the Old Testament. In the New Testament the apostle Paul talks about Jesus taking on our sins and is now in heaven acting as High Priest on our behalf."

Derek asked, "You mean that He's standing in the gap just like the priest of old, between our sins and guilt and the righteousness of a Holy God?"

Thomas leapt to his feet. "Yes, yes, and yes! But the part that I did not want to see for years and that has floored me since, is the part where Paul compares how a husband should love his wife to that of how Christ loved the church and gave Himself, or atoned for it! Doesn't that just blow you away, gentlemen? If Christ so loved the world that He gave Himself, He who knew no sin so that we can be redeemed, then as a man, I am expected to love my wife with that same kind of 'standing in the gap' kind of love."

"Wait a minute," Bill protested. He'd been listening intently and now turned to look Thomas in the eyes. "Somewhere here your logic is starting to break down. Women do not need a husband to stand in the gap for them. What Jesus did on Calvary by ripping the veil between the Holy and Most Holy was to take out the middleman. We can all come boldly to the throne of grace ourselves. We don't need a priest-confessor."

"Not to confess our sins we don't. I quite agree with you," replied Thomas. "My point is that we, meaning us men, we need to love our wives as much as Christ loved the Church and be prepared to represent Christ to them with the same kind of sacrificial and loving benevolence when they need our support, forgiveness, guidance, and advice."

"That's a pretty tall order," said Derek.

Simon ran his fingers through his hair, his face working to keep up with the pressure on his brain. "If I'm following this argument of yours, Thomas, you're saying that we men, no . . . we Christian men . . . need to recapture this role we've lost. It's not about being catered to by our women. It's about giving our all if it comes to that, to ensure our families are right with God. Man, it means we have to love them even when they're unlovely and pray for them when they drive us crazy. You're saying that we gotta support them to be the best they can be for God. Love them like God loves us all. That's our job."

Frustration burned Donald's throat and eyeballs. He bit down hard to control the yowl of pain crouching behind his front teeth, ready to spring out and consume him. He shook his head. No. No. No. No way. Not him.

Not me, God. No man can do this thing that You're asking. I want what I want. I wanted children. I wanted so many things that I'll no longer have—that I'll never have. And You expect me to love unconditionally? Be Your representative in my home?

He must have made a sound or communicated his agitation.

Derek looked at him. "You said something, Donald?"

Donald looked at the young man. Really looked at him. Then his mind returned to the room. "No man can do this thing that you're saying, Thomas."

Thomas beamed at his friend as if he'd just won the blue ribbon for best articulated statement. "Bingo! No man can do it. But Christian men who have submitted their lives to the Lordship (or headship if you will), of Jesus Christ can. They can do it because whatever Christ asks of us He's already prepared the way to help us. That's the calling I want to bring to our consciousness my friends. There needs to be an army of dedicated Christian men who will not be swayed by the media's portrayal of what men ought to be. An army of men—two, three, 60, or 600, who answer only to the General, Christ Jesus. He is the Man we model ourselves after.

"We will plead for our families, we will love the unlovely, we will wrestle with God just like Jacob did and wear a permanent limp if we must, to demonstrate to the world the tenacious, uncompromising, unselfishness of true love. But for us to do that, we must face ourselves and acknowledge before God that we cannot do it on our own. We need to get right with God for ourselves. Then we ask God to show us what we ought to do to begin to heal ourselves, and our families, and our communities. We can show the world—through the enabling influence of the Holy Spirit—what real manhood means."

"That's heavy stuff there, Thomas," said Derek.

"Very heavy," Simon nodded.

"I guess men like Ghandi and King caught a bit of that vision," commented Bill.

"Maybe they did," replied Thomas. "But this is not about them and what they did. This is about us and what we need to do."

"And what is it that we need to do, Thomas? What exactly are you talking about?" Donald could hear the annoyance in his voice.

Thomas wondered, same as Catherine had, if he'd overwhelmed his friends at this their first meeting. He tipped his head backwards and thought for a minute. Then he made eye contact with each man in the room. His words when he finally spoke were measured and deliberate.

"I want you to go home and think about what we've discussed tonight. Study the Word of God and see if you come to a conclusion different from the one I reached about the role of men. Pray about it. Please. Pray hard on this. Then if you're convicted on the matter, call me and let me know. I would like us to start regular meetings—a brotherhood of sorts. We would commit to support each other, pray for and with each other, hold each other accountable and vow to model God in every aspect of our lives. I am convinced down to the bunions on my big toe that despite our fathered or fatherless role-modeling, God will do wonders with our commitment. Gentlemen, that's the dream I have for our men and that I think we can launch with your assistance."

On this Friday night there was no easy slippage into the comfort of sports radio talk. Simon closed the meeting in a prayer that moved Thomas and sent Donald, Derek, and Bill home to their closets. He prayed for God to use them to be lighthouses at home, work, and in their communities. He prayed for release from the baggage of bad role modeling and asked God to broaden their chests with muscles of patience, kindness, gentleness, goodness, and peace. Finally he prayed for strength to be strong men, real men, who understood their commission and who in their strength could also learn to submit without feeling weak.

It was a prayer from the heart—chock full of paradoxes and possibilities.

Chapter 26

Please God, this can't be true!

Marissa rushed out of the apartment. She had to be sure. Fifteen minutes later she was back.

She closed the bathroom door. That other test had to be wrong. It had to be! Thanking the heavens she'd had a lot of water to drink today, she took time to carefully read the instructions. This Best Response brand claimed to be more than 99 percent accurate. *This* one would be right. With trembling fingers she removed the test from its foil pouch. She then removed the cap. A minimum of 10 seconds under the urine stream and then she'd know for sure. She'd know that the first test was wrong.

Let it be negative, God. Please. Please, I'm begging You.

Marissa replaced the cap on the tip of the device and laid it gently on the countertop. That should meet the requirement in the instructions for a flat surface. "Do not move the test while the results are developing." The instructions had that statement underlined and bolded. Marissa made herself breathe deeply. The package promised results in only one minute but recommended waiting for three. She'd force herself to wait so there'd be no mistake.

Turning away from the pending verdict she sat on the covered toilet and talked to her soul. *Relax yourself, girl. Think peace. Think calm. Light ripples lazily drifting across calm waters. Gentle breezes whispering in the trees that all is well. Breathe. Good. Good. V-e-r-y g-o-o-d. Aaahhh! Just wait for the appropriate time to pass. In three minutes you can open your eyes and look.*

Marissa counted off the seconds. "One Mississippi, two Mississippi, three Mississippi, four Mississippi . . ." When she got to 60 she folded her thumb against her palm to indicate the passage of one minute. Then she began again. "One Mississippi, two Mississippi, three Mississippi . . ." Three rounds of counting the seconds to 60. Then she counted an extra 60 seconds just to be sure.

She talked to her soul again. *No need to panic, girl. No need whatsoever.*

But her soul would not listen! Panic! Panic? *There's every reason to panic. What if it's positive?*

Just look, her logic told her.

Marissa shook her head vigorously.

What do you mean you can't do that? Her logic asked.

Marissa sat frozen until logic spoke again.

OK, just open one eye and look. A pink bar line in the results window for positive, no line for negative. Pink line for positive, no line for negative. Got that?

Marissa opened her left eye but couldn't see anything from her perch. She got up slowly, right eye still locked. She felt her heart hammering in her ears. Her breath whooshing out in rapid pants.

No lines, God. Let there be no lines! No pink, blue, or whatever. No lines please.

Her logic ran out of patience. *Get it over with. Look!*

Marissa opened both eyes and peered at the marker. She rapidly blinked her eyes and peered again. Closely! And saw red.

Two extra bar lines. There was one in the rectangular part of the control window and another in the circular part. A million bees began buzzing in her ears, pins and needles prickling her fingertips.

"Oh, dear God. No. No. No. I cannot be pregnant. I must not be pregnant. How could this be, Lord? I never miss my pills. I—"

And then she remembered. The afternoon she'd twisted Derek's arm she'd just finished her period and had missed taking her pill the night before. But what are the probabilities of that time of the month . . . that one time causing this . . . this . . . catastrophe!

Marissa sank to her knees on the cold tile floor. Hot tears gushed out from a broken cistern behind her eyes.

"Father God, *no!* Not a baby."

She did not want a baby. Not now! Then fury overtook her. Grabbing the two indicators of ill tidings, she flung them against the wall. She pounded the floor with her feet, beat at her chest, and for a fleeting moment, entertained the thought of ripping out her insides where lurked . . . what? What was there now? Nothing! No. No. A beginning. That's what lurked there.

"Please, God. I don't want this. Please don't do this to me!" Marissa's prayer turned to sobs. "No, God. Please, I'm begging. No!"

Just then the apartment door opened and Derek stepped inside. He'd been shoveling the snow from his mother's driveway, so bent to remove his boots. The sound of his wife's sobs and stomping put his feet in motion, hurtling his body straight toward the source.

"Marissa!" He flung himself against the door of the bathroom, turning the handle as he did. The door stood firm.

"Marissa!" He bellowed.

The crying eased. Derek jammed his ear against the door. "Marissa, open the door. What's the matter? Let me in so I can help you. Marissa!"

No answer.

"Marissa. Honey, are you hurt? Tell me what's the matter! Honey!" But there was still no answer except for the whimpering sounds.

"Marissa, if you don't open the door right now I'm going to break it down!"

But Marissa could not speak.

Derek lost his slippery grip on patience and drove his shoulder into the wood. It gave way. Fortunately he'd had the presence of mind to check his momentum because there on the floor, almost immediately behind the door, lay the love of his life in a heap. The eyes she turned to look at him dropped him to his knees to cradle her in his arms. "Marissa, honey, what's wrong? Please tell me what's wrong."

But she was beyond words. The weeping and wailing started up again. She clutched at his shirt and buried her face in his chest, breaking his heart with her grief.

Derek made himself comfortable and pulling her onto his lap, rocked her gently for what seemed like hours, cooing words of comfort. Gradually, the tears tapered into hiccups, then sniffles, and eventually stopped. Still she refused to look at him. Derek tipped his wife's face up to him and softly kissed her lips. The action sent her flying out of his arms and across the room.

"Don't touch me. Don't you dare touch me! You'll never touch me again!" With that pronouncement she bolted from the bathroom as if he'd become the notorious Scarborough rapist!

Derek, slow to recover from the shock of her departure, tiredly pushed himself up from the floor. As he turned toward the door his boot crunched against something. Stooping to pick it up, he examined it. What could this be? It looked like a thermometer or a dip-stick. His eyes caught a second similar device in the bathtub. His legal mind began an analytical sifting through of the evidence. The garbage container held a small package. A similar package lay on the counter beside the sink. Pregnancy test kit. There his mind stopped.

Then it hit him, collapsing his legs. Derek sat heavily on the toilet. Marissa is upset because she's pregnant? He felt a leaping in his midsection. Could it be they were going to have a baby? The leaping took over his heart. A grin began to make its way across his face, starting at the corner of his mouth and picking up momentum after it passed his cheeks.

A baby! Thank You, Jesus!

· · · · ·

Marissa's mind could not get past the fact that she was pregnant. Married just more than six months and she was pregnant. In just 40 weeks she would be someone's mother. All the plans she had, all the hopes for her career—gone.

Why are You doing this to me, God? Marissa's mind prayed. *You know I don't want this and yet You've allowed this thing. Why?*

Are you sure you want My answer, daughter?

Marissa nodded. *Yes. Explain it. You've allowed me to have an education. You've given me skills in areas that can make a difference to the world. You—* Marissa ran out of words.

Did you not commit your life into My hands?

Yes, Father, I did.

Will you trust Me to take care of you even when you cannot understand My leading?

Yes, Lord, I do, but . . .

No buts, Marissa. Just trust Me.

Marissa, curled up in a fetal position in the corner of the couch, pushed a cushion against her middle to stop the fluttering in her belly. Butterflies of all description performed their dance of panic there. While the voice of the Spirit implored her to trust, she dropped her head into her hands and shut off her mind.

Derek, having made his deduction and recalling previous conversations with his wife on the subject of parenthood and related topics, took some time to give himself a shower and order his mind past his own elation. Then remembering Thomas' challenge that men be priests in their households, Derek asked God to guide him as he talked to his wife about her—no, their— pregnancy.

The truth of the matter, now that he had time for second thoughts, was that this was not an ideal time for them to have a baby. Another year or so would be just right. By then he would have paid off his educational debts and have some money put aside for buying a house. But life did not always cooperate with one's plans. But how to broach the subject to his wife who seemed devastated by the news?

Armed with prayers, a clean body, and good intentions, Derek located Marissa on the couch. From the head resting in the palm of her hand to the droop of her shoulders, her whole body communicated defeat and dejection. She rocked herself slowly as a child seeking to comfort itself would. Derek's heart went out to her. He wished he could kiss her and make it all better but recalling her reaction in the bathroom he eased down beside her instead.

Taking the direct approach, he tackled the issue on both their minds.

"The timing for this is not the most opportune, is it?"

The rocking motion of Marissa's body stopped. She did not look at him but he could feel her listening. He continued.

"I want children, and if I had my way, the more the better, but yeah, I'd agree that the timing of this one is a bit early even for me. I also know the plans you had for your career, Rissa, but can we trust God to help us deal with this? Right now it's hard to see His reasons but He knew we'd be facing this moment and I'm sure the power is already available to get us through."

Was it his imagination or did he sense a slight yielding in her stance? Derek couldn't tell for sure. He prayed for more words to do for her what his arms ached to do—hold her tight.

"But think of this, sweetheart. This baby, our baby, was conceived in an environment of love. It couldn't have a better start! And its mother is the joy of my heart. I couldn't imagine life without her."

No, it wasn't his imagination. Marissa shifted position, and was now just slightly leaning toward him. Derek resisted the urge to put his hand over hers.

"Did I ever tell you," he continued, "that on our wedding day, when I saw you walking down the aisle, I asked God to enable me to be the kind of husband who would seek the best for you and not crush your spirit?"

Marissa looked at him then. "What?" she whispered.

"I asked God to help me be the kind of husband who'd seek only the best for you and never, ever crush your spirit."

Salty tracks of tears ran down Marissa's honey-brown face. Her thick lashes were clumped into spikes. Derek thought how they framed her eyes made them look like stars.

He held her gaze. "I love you, Marissa. I love you for who you are and for the joy you bring to my heart, and I hate to see you hurting like this. I know that even though I didn't mean for it to happen, I'm partly responsible for causing you pain. But you know what? I still feel honored—even though you're devastated."

Her face crumpled at that, and she shook her head. He knew what she was thinking and was quick to explain. "I feel honored and blessed to be the father of your child because it's another precious part of you I get to share. And I pray again, just like I did on our wedding day, that God will enable me to be the father I need to be, but to also help you to become the woman God created you to be."

He sighed. "That's all I want to say. I'm going to bed, but if you need to talk just wake me if I've fallen asleep." He gently rubbed her back as he spoke then stood up and slowly walked away.

Marissa watched him go. She could have used a hug, but she needed space more. He'd given her the better gift. No, she'd had no idea that he'd prayed for God to enable him. That touched her.

Maybe this travesty or seeming travesty would one day be a blessing when seen through the perspective of hindsight. But surely, God did not really expect her to just accept this.

Chapter 27

Donald zipped up the small suitcase and checked his pockets for wallet and keys. He wished he could forgo attendance at this conference but he had a presentation to do and plans had been made long before everything else in his life came to a grinding halt.

As far as matters between him and Lisa were concerned nothing had changed even though he could feel a gradual softening of his own heart. Not yet ready to face his wife and talk about the last too many months, he attempted to reconcile with God. But his will balked at yielding to the Spirit. He should be more forgiving. He knew that. He also should be more tolerant, but like the fight the apostle Paul spoke about, the things he wanted to do, he could not, and the very things he wished not to do, those he did. And still continued to do.

He'd hoped that by the time he left for this convention he and Lisa would have at least reopened the conversational door to their marriage. None of that could happen right now, however. Lisa had already left for work. His one attempt a few days ago, a weak one at best, had been met with cold indifference. With only minutes before the airport limousine arrived he had no time to begin the long overdue reparation that required all the time in the world. He'd call her from the hotel, he decided. Maybe with distance between them they could talk more freely.

The ringing of the doorbell put an end to his deliberations. He picked up his bags, looked around the room that had cocooned his agony for months, and prayed that by the time he returned three days hence, his sojourn there would be nearing its end.

• • • • •

Lisa wandered idly through the mall, no real destination in mind. With Donald gone to his convention, there was no need to be home. For once, her work had not been able to hold her attention and restlessness had driven her out. The idea of shopping propelled her to drive the short distance from work to the mall. But even here her mind could not focus on anything in particular to buy.

As she passed the ice cream shop, on impulse she turned back. She'd treat herself to a black cherry ice cream cone.

Completing her purchase, she sat on a bench to enjoy her treat and to watch the people wandering the mall. A young mother gripping several bags walked by, accompanied by two toddlers. She looked harried. The older of the two children held a much maligned rag doll in one hand and a sticky treat in the other while the younger sister ran screaming behind the mother, arms outstretched, begging to be carried.

A teenage couple seemingly glued to each other almost collided with the running child. The spiky haired teen male, sporting a fascinating network of tattoos along one arm and jewelry wedged in painful-looking places gently guided the child in the direction of her mother. Lisa watched in amazement as the mother, not turning around, yelled back to the child to pay attention to where she was going and kept walking. Probably heading home to hide her purchases before hubby gets home, Lisa speculated.

"Hi, Lisa."

Lisa swung her gaze to the left and rose to greet her young friend. "Marissa! What a lovely surprise! How are you?"

Marissa lowered herself on the bench with a sigh. "I'm postponing going home."

"And why is that?" asked Lisa sitting down again.

Marissa gave a shrug. "I just needed some think time. What better place to do that than in a busy mall?"

"I hear you," replied Lisa. "So how is married life with my favorite adopted nephew? I don't know if I had a chance to tell you before, but your wedding ceremony was one of the most beautiful I've attended."

"Thanks," replied Marissa without much enthusiasm. "Derek is fine. Me, I'm not so sure about."

"You're not ill, are you," asked Lisa anxiously. "After Grace, I don't think I can deal with another . . ."

"No." Marissa was quick to assure. "I'm fine. At least physically. It's more my mental health that's in jeopardy."

"Are you and Derek having problems?"

"I wouldn't say we are. But I suppose in a way, we're having problems. At least I'm having problems."

"You don't love him anymore?" Lisa sounded shocked. "Tell me it's not that. Plus I wouldn't believe it anyway. You two are too much in love. You've always been good friends as well as lovers."

"I'm going to have a baby."

Lisa gasped with excitement. "That's excellent news! When?" Seeing the lack of mirrored joy on Marissa's face, Lisa pulled back her excitement. "It's not excellent news?" she asked slowly.

Marissa shook her head. "It's the last thing in the world I want right now. For Pete's sake, Lisa, I've been married for only six months. I'm just getting my head wrapped around what being married is all about—and now I'm going to have a baby! I'm not even sure I want kids."

"I see," replied Lisa.

"I had all these plans, Lisa. I wanted to spend at least three years working for the government and developing my experience so that I could start my own consulting company. I have this great idea for a small business that would not only provide me a good income but help people too. It's the perfect idea. I talked to God about my plans. I thought I had His blessing but this pregnancy has messed up everything!"

"And your walk through the mall is to help you sort out what to do?"

Marissa nodded.

"So have you come to any conclusions?"

Tears sprang into Marissa's eyes. "Have you ever looked into your heart and realized that the person you thought you were is an illusion created by your mind and that the real you is nowhere as nice or decent as you want to believe? That's what I've concluded on my trip through the mall. Tonight I contemplated a way out of my situation. I allowed the idea to take root and grow tentacles. I know the option I'm considering is wrong but in my mind it would solve everything and I don't want to hear what God or anyone else has to say on the matter."

"'Direct my footsteps according to your word,'" Lisa quoted (Ps. 119:133), looking at Marissa. "Do you believe that God knows everything about you?"

"Well, yes."

"This morning when you said your prayers, what did you pray for?"

"I didn't really feel like praying. I think I mumbled something but can't remember what."

"Maybe God looks out for us even when we don't ask Him to. I believe that He directs our steps to situations or people who might be able to help us. I don't think He forces us to do anything but that He allows us to find our way to advice or counsel or even insights that would help us. Then we have to choose what to do with what He's presented to us."

Marissa looked confused. Her mouth opened, then shut. "I suppose," she said at last.

Lisa came to the point. "I feel certain that God directed or ordered your steps to this mall today, Marissa. He ordered mine too. This abortion you're considering . . . it is aborting that you're considering, right?"

Marissa nodded, eyes downcast.

"I think you should trust God to see you through the pregnancy as opposed to taking this alternate step."

Marissa's back went up. "Why? You just don't understand! Neither Derek nor I are ready for a child right now. And it's not even a person yet. Just a few tiny cells. We can have more children later when we're ready for them."

Lisa smiled inwardly at the naivety of the young. Her inward smile vanished however when she recalled her own teenage arguments on this very issue. And look at her life now.

"I would have loved to have children. Donald and I got pregnant two times and I miscarried both. The second pregnancy miscarried at five months. It's an awful thing to birth a child you know is already dead. When they placed our dead baby in my arms—the one I insisted on holding—like Job's wife I came this close to cursing God. At the graveside service that just Donald and I attended, the minister talked about Jesus being the resurrection and the life. But all I could feel was a seething anger at the injustice of a God who had the power to give life yet chose to deny me the life of my child."

"So you think I should just get over myself and deal with this?"

Lisa put her arm around Marissa's shoulders and gave her a gentle squeeze. "I can't tell you what to do. I can only advise. You know what is right and what God expects of you. You do. I just wish I had your 'accident' to deal with. Even though it would resurrect old hurts and pain, it would provide me with another reason to hope for the family I never got. If I was in your shoes, an abortion wouldn't be the option I'd be hugging to my heart right now. Funny isn't it? Sometimes the very thing that's a problem for one person is a gift for another."

Lisa could not continue the conversation. Her whole being screamed to tell Marissa all the very real and personal reasons for not doing what she was contemplating. That it would cause her to suffer beyond belief and may not even get her the very things she hoped to gain by her action. The guilt she'd carried so long, and that she thought she had finally vanquished, now awakened and thoughts whipped against the doors of her heart, wreaking havoc with her peace.

Tell her your story. Tell her your sorry tale. That you're a Christian who is also a baby terminator and that she too can become just like you!

Before the urge to blurt out her pathetic life story took hold, Lisa jumped to her feet and consulted her watch. Marissa stood too, offering profuse thanks to Lisa for listening. She begged her to keep the discussion confidential and Lisa, willing to promise anything to expedite her exit, readily consented. Feeling the threat of tears, Lisa donned her shades, gave Marissa a quick hug, and made herself perform her perfected slow walk-away—with the mad rush firmly confined within the borders of her mind.

She had not gone far before she felt the first run of tears. At that she picked up her pace, careening past shoppers. Her car. She must get to her car. Suddenly she spied an exit. Making a beeline for it, she crashed head first into the glass door. Her sun shades went flying.

Stars of all description danced in front of her eyes as she grabbed her head, completely disoriented. From a distance she heard a voice asking her something that she had the power to respond to, but couldn't because of the pain. The voice spoke again.

"Are you OK, ma'am?"

Unable to respond, Lisa felt a touch on her arm then hands leading her somewhere. Gentle pressure was applied to her shoulder and she knew she was being encouraged to sit. A ringing sound tolled in her ears and she lifted her hand to feel a fast-growing lump on the right side of her forehead.

"Maybe we should call 911," a male someone said to someone else.

"Let's give her another minute. I think she's just winded," a female voice responded.

A light pressure on her hand told her the conversation was directed to her now. "Hello there. Nod if you can hear me."

This voice was male and it had a slight lisp, like when a piece of hard candy got stuck on the tongue. Lisa tried to nod, but it hurt too badly. She managed only a slight motion of her head.

"Good. I think you're going to be OK, but you took quite a wallop. We'll sit with you till you feel better, 'kay?" the male voice continued.

The female voice added, "I picked up your sunglasses but they're all twisted. The right lens is gone. Sorry 'bout that."

Lisa carefully opened her eyes and once the blurriness cleared, found two pairs of concerned eyes staring back at her from heavily made-up faces. Memory returned. These were the teens she'd observed earlier. Her lids fluttered closed again.

"Mrs. Westwood! Lisa, what's the matter?" A new voice.

Oh! This can't be!

"You know her?" It was the female teen asking.

"Yes, I do," Joshua replied.

"That's great! She banged her head pretty hard on that door a few minutes ago. She's a bit disoriented but I think she's coming around. If you can take care of her we'll leave. We have to catch a bus at 7:00," the male voice said.

"Yes, I'll take over from here," said Joshua briskly. "Thank you very much. Can I give you something for your kindness?"

The teenaged male waved Joshua's offer away good naturedly. "No problem. We're just glad we could help. Take care of her, please. She seemed very upset before she crashed into the door." They waved goodbye and walked off but within seconds the guy was back.

"Sir, you're not a serial rapist or someone who's going to take advantage of her, are you?" he asked, adding as an afterthought, "not that you'd actually *tell* me if you were."

"Good thinking, young man. You can't be too careful these days. I promise you that I am completely legit. Here," he said reaching into his pocket. "Here's my business card. Feel free to call me if you want to check up on her or check me out."

The teen looked at the card and mulled the information over in his mind. "You're a lawyer."

Joshua nodded. "I owe you one. If you ever find yourself in the need of legal services, give me a call. If I can't help you, I'll see to it that you get the best referral I can find. How's that?"

"That's good. I'm Gabe Mitchell, and I'll hold you to that." Gabe put out his hand and Joshua shook it firmly. And in the shaking of hands something passed between them that reassured Gabe that this one could be trusted. Shoving the card in his pocket he ran to rejoin his friend who was waiting restlessly for him.

"Lisa?" Joshua called softly to his surprise charge.

Lisa sighed. "I'm here."

"It's Joshua. Joshua Hendricks."

"I know," a small voice replied.

"Can I call your husband for you? I don't think you're in any shape to drive. You're growing one mean looking goose egg on your forehead." Joshua gently touched the area.

Lisa winced and pulled her head back.

"That sore, eh? Give me your husband's cell number."

Lisa shook her head slowly. "He's not home. Away at a conference."

"Then tell me where you live. I'll drive you home. We'll worry about your car later."

Lisa's sudden shake of her head sent bolts of pain across her face, eliciting a moan.

"Come, Lisa. This is not a discussion. I'm taking you home. Now please save us both a lot of trouble by giving me your address. That's all I need. I have a GPS in my car which will do the rest."

Lisa whispered her street address and then strong capable hands were under her armpits, assisting her to stand.

"Just stand for a little. Tell me if you feel the least bit dizzy."

Lisa's legs shook slightly but held her up. She took a step forward, then another. She was not one hundred percent but she could, with assistance, walk out of the mall. Without warning, hot tears again began to make their way down her cheeks. Joshua saw them and said nothing. He just continued his support of her to his car which, thankfully, was parked closer than where she'd left hers. Within a few feet he paused and got his remote out to unlock the doors.

Lisa's legs were starting to feel like jelly.

Please, God, her mind begged.

But if asked, Lisa would have been hard pressed to say exactly what she was begging for. Her head ached something fierce. Her mind felt hot with confused imaginings and Joshua's presence was a mixed comfort. Her head wanted to lay itself against his capable looking chest while the rest of her body poised for flight.

Please, God, her mind prayed again. *Too much today. Don't let me rest my head against this man who is not my husband.*

Joshua opened the car door and guided Lisa into the still warm comfort of the leather seat, making sure that her swollen head did not brush against anything to hurt it even more. He even closed the door without a thud. Lisa closed her eyes and counted off breaths until she heard the driver's side of the car open and felt him lowering his frame behind the steering wheel. Then startled eyes snapped open as she felt his hand reaching across her lap.

Kindness smiled back on her. "I'd hate to have to explain to your husband that I drove you home injured without making sure you had your seatbelt on." His breath was close enough for Lisa to feel its air brushing against her cheek. She panicked.

"I can do that," she cried grabbing for the seatbelt. But the sharp movement sent ribbons of pain bouncing across her face and she clutched her head.

Patiently Joshua replied, "Lisa, like it or not, I'm going to have to help you on with your seatbelt. OK? I'm not trying to take advantage of you. You're hurt. Now please relax and no more sharp turns. Let's just get you home and then we can put some ice on that swelling. I'm not liking the look of it."

Like the proverbial lamb to the slaughter, Lisa allowed herself to be strapped in the seatbelt and driven home. She allowed Joshua to open the door to her house and guide her inside. She allowed herself to be relieved of her coat, seated on her living room sofa, pillows fluffed to support her back. Then her shoes were gently removed, and she was guided to lie down against the pillows, feet elevated on several more brought in from other chairs. Her entire body gave thanks for making it prone while her head continued to throb painfully.

In no time at all Joshua was back with a package of frozen peas. He'd found a kitchen towel to wrap it in and laid it ever so gently against her throbbing head.

"How do you feel?" he asked. "Are you nauseated?"

"No. Not nauseated. Just hurting."

"Look at me. Can you see me? Are you seeing double?"

"Of course not!" Lisa retorted.

"We've got to be sure you don't have signs of a concussion," Joshua explained. "But now we wait. I want you to try to rest. When you feel like it—and I'm hoping you'll have a short nap—I'll ask you a few more questions to make sure you're OK."

Lisa sighed and closed her eyes.

Joshua pulled up a chair close by her head and sat down. Despite her desire to remain alert, Lisa slept. When she awoke her head felt heaps better and Joshua was still seated inches away, keeping his vigil. He gave her a tired smile when she looked in his direction, straightened in his chair and leaned toward her.

"Welcome back," he greeted her. "More questions. Are you ready?"

Lisa nodded.

"Your name?" he asked.

"Lisa Jones Westwood," she replied dutifully.

"And where are you?"

"I'm at my home." She gave the address.

"What's your occupation?"

"I'm a lawyer."

"How old are you?"

"That's none of your business!"

"Any nausea?"

"No."

"Can you still see clearly?"

"Yes."

"Feeling better?"

"Much. Thank you.

"Permission to leave my post ma'am?"

"Permission granted. What time is it?" Lisa asked.

"11:47 p.m."

"Joshua!" Lisa cried rising. "Why did you let me sleep this long? You must be exhausted! Did you even have supper?"

"I tried but there's nothing in your fridge."

"Liar. There's always food in my fridge."

"Well there's nothing ready to eat. I had some juice."

"Let me make you something. An omelette with some toast. That won't take too long."

"Lisa, don't worry about me. I can grab something on the way home. You need your rest. Even though the swelling has reduced somewhat you still need to take things easy."

"I'll take things easy tomorrow. I'll work from home. It's Thursday and things won't be too hectic. Now tell me if you like lots of stuff on your omelette or just plain with a bit of cheese."

"I can't talk you out of this, can I?"

Lisa shook her head.

"And it would make you feel like you've done something for me in return for bringing you home?"

"You're a smart man, Mr. Hendricks. Now, give me exactly seven minutes then join me in the kitchen for your late night repast."

"I'll join you now. I like to know what's going into my food."

"Suit yourself."

Lisa, glad to have something to do and yes, glad to repay him in part for taking care of her, strode off with purpose toward the kitchen with Joshua on her heels. However, she'd have preferred him to stay in the living room until she finished. She could have used the time to get her defenses in shape.

In exactly seven minutes, a succulent looking omelette, four slices of 12-grain toast and three thick tomato slices along with a pot of tea sat in front of Joshua. His stomach rumbled.

"Dig in," Lisa encouraged.

"Tell me you're not going to stand there and watch me eat." Joshua eyed her warily. "Did you have dinner at the mall?"

"I had an ice cream cone. It was good too!"

Joshua slipped off the stool by the breakfast nook where he'd been seated and searched her cupboards. Locating the plates, he removed one and loaded it with two slices of his toast, one slice of tomato and a third of the omelette."

"Sit and eat. Doctor's orders."

"But—"

"Eat, Lisa. You need the energy and I'd like some company while I eat. Now sit. Please." He removed another mug from the nearby mug hook. "There."

Lisa, losing the will to argue, joined him. Her stomach, glad for the food, discouraged conversation and in no time her plate along with Joshua's was clean.

"You make a mean omelette, Mrs. Westwood."

Lisa inclined her head in thanks. "Why do you call me that sometimes?" she asked.

"Call you what?"

"Mrs. Westwood."

Joshua thought about it. "Maybe it's my way of reminding myself that you're a married woman and I can have no claims on you. It helps me to keep my distance both mentally and physically."

"I see." Lisa replied, sorry she'd asked.

"'I see?' That's all you have to say?"

"What else is there to say?"

"Have you never wondered why is it that life seems to be throwing us at each other?" Joshua asked her. "Our first meeting—that wasn't supposed to be your case. Then at the Christmas banquet. Your husband had just left to go home and there I was. And this evening—you could have knocked me over when I entered the mall and saw you sitting there accompanied by those interesting looking young people. And here we are, Lisa. Here we are. Every time we meet I have to talk myself into walking away from the temptation you present."

Lisa looked aghast. "Temptation? I don't set out to tempt you?"

"There's the rub. You don't set out to tempt me, Mrs. Westwood, but you do. I dream of you still. I've tried, Lisa, but I just can't seem to shake you. Tonight I'm here in your house. Your husband is away. I want to kiss you. That's just the beginning. And even though you might not want to admit this even to yourself, I think you want to kiss me too. I'm right, aren't— "

"*Stop.* Stop, stop, stop!"

Lisa swung off the stool, briskly clearing the counter of the plates, mugs, and utensils. She turned on the tap, applied dishwashing liquid to the sponge, scrubbing vigorously at the plates as if trying to rid them of their design as well as the food soil. Back turned, she did not hear Joshua come up behind her. Then he was turning her around to face him. She allowed herself to be turned, hands gripped tightly by her side, one dripping suds onto the floor from the clenched sponge.

Joshua was speaking again, the sincerity in his voice forcing Lisa to drop her eyes and head lest he see what she did not dare show him.

Please, God!

"If there is a heaven, Mrs. Westwood, I'm going to make sure I get there. I want to ask God why He brought you into my life. Why He's made me so drawn to you when I shouldn't even be here. And my biggest question to Him will be why He made you want me too. That's the hardest part to deal with. The knowledge that this desire is mutual."

Lisa dug her toes into the floor mat, her shaking head denying everything. No. No. She felt nothing for this man. Nothing at all.

"Shaking your head changes nothing, Lisa. You see, I know. I know. I've seen it in your eyes before you think to hide it. Desire."

Head still negating his words, Lisa's ever ready tears came again. This time with no shades to hide them they spilled over their lids down her face, dripping off her cheekbones. Rigid, head felled to her chest she stood rooted to the floor, dripping hands mimicking the drips from her face.

Joshua groaned and pulled her into his arms. Only then did her body lose some of its rigidity.

Bent head resting against his solid chest Lisa wept for the past that could no longer be. She wept for her losses—Luke, her first love; her babies, and her dying marriage. She wept tears of defeat tinged with defiance at her longing for this fabulous man who was not her husband, and for being such a pathetic witness for her faith.

Flee!

Run!

Just step away!

But Lisa could not move.

It was Joshua who finally, gently released her and stepped back. Then tilting her face upwards he consoled her.

"There. Don't cry anymore, love."

With the pad of his thumb and a gentleness that took her breath away he wiped her still flowing tears in the same way Derek had done for Marissa at their wedding. His fingers against her cheek shook. Lisa's eyes sought and found his, then slammed shut at what she saw there.

Please, God, lead me not into temptation. Deliver me from the evil within me, please, God, please, God, please-God-please-God, don't let me do this-thing-I-want-to-do, please-oh God, please! God. Help!

"*I can do everything through him who gives me strength*" (Phil. 4:13).

The text popped into Lisa's head with force. Where had she heard it recently? Lisa thought about her Bible study buddies. Yes. Yes. One of the women had read it out loud.

Please, God. Make me do the right thing for once in my life. Make me do what You want me to do despite my aching desire to do otherwise. Please, God. I need deliverance right now, Jesus. Please don't turn Your back on me. Send an angel, send strength. Please, Father in heaven.

Then choose to step away. Choose the right.

That must be Marissa's voice of the Spirit again.

Lord! Is it all up to me? thought Lisa. *I'm being tested! But I need help. I can't do it by myself!*

With bated breath the universe watched the war waging in the mind of one Lisa Jones Westwood. One step away stood Joshua. All she had to do was reach for him. She knew he, too, was barely holding himself in check.

The voice of the Spirit continued.

I cannot make you do the right, Lisa. You must choose. By a simple act of your will, weak as it might be, give Me permission to help you.

Joshua waited.

God waited.

The angels folded their wings and waited.

The powers of darkness hushed.

Please, God, Lisa's heart cried.

She drew in a ragged breath and held it.

Dear God.

Lisa shut her eyes so tight her face hurt.

Then she took one step backwards. That's all she could manage.

But it was enough.

Joshua closed his eyes and sighed so hard it dropped his shoulders a few centimetres. Then his eyes were on hers again but this time ignoring the elephant in the room, he forced a lightness he did not feel into his tone.

"Lisa, I'm not doing either one of us any favors by being here so I'll go. Take care of that head of yours. Take care of yourself, Mrs. Westwood. And plan to be in heaven so together we can ask God about this. Deal?"

He extended his hand.

Dropping the sponge, Lisa took the proffered hand and shook it. And even then desire crackled between them as palm touched palm.

Both pulled back. Shocked.

Lisa rubbed her palm against her side to rid it of the sensation. Joshua tucked his in his pocket.

Please, God, Lisa prayed again.

The phone rang. She ran to answer it.

Joshua collected his coat and keys and let himself out of the house.

Chapter 28

Marissa allowed her mind to travel through the consequences of having an abortion. She'd been to the clinic earlier. Armed with pamphlets, she remained on the mall bench long after Lisa left, giving full consideration to this thing which could be the solution to her problems.

Could she live with herself if she did this? Marissa searched her heart.

She thought about the time in college when she shared a kitchen with another woman. She'd been so tired of her macaroni and cheese dinners supplemented by the occasional can of tuna fish. That was all she could afford. Then one day she'd discovered a nice roast in the refrigerator. She'd begun to salivate. Oh, to have a small slice of that meat. She hadn't had meat in months. Couldn't afford it plus she'd been trying to eliminate red meat on her road to vegetarianism. The roast belonged to Sara, her flatmate, not known for sharing anything at all.

The thought had entered her mind to just carve a tiny piece of the meat. Nothing noticeable. When she put the small morsel in her mouth however, her body begged for more. Three more slices were carved and consumed until sated and guilty, she'd returned the container to the fridge, trying to position it just the same as before.

Later that evening as she studied in her room, she'd heard Sara come home. Her heart hammered with guilt. She timed Sara's change of clothes and counted the steps it took to get to the kitchen. She strained to hear the opening of the refrigerator door and then hid her face in distress as Sara's cursing and slamming of pots and doors indicated that all had been discovered.

For a week Sara had not spoken to her. Then she'd moved away soon afterward. Marissa often thought of Sara and wondered how she could repay her for the four slices of meat.

Guilt. She still felt it. Raw and real, making her cringe with shame every time the memory surfaced. Then she recalled how as a child she'd begged her dad one spring to let her plant some of the peas he was sowing in their garden. He'd given her a few which she'd hidden under the soil just like he told her to. Daddy had said it would take awhile, maybe even 10 days, for the plants to grow. Everyday after school, she'd go to the backyard hoping to see those pea plants. Daddy would remind her to be patient and wait.

But one day, she just couldn't wait any more. She wanted to see; just had to check—only to unearth the delicate babies, just starting to send out shoots but not yet ready for exposure. Marissa recalled how awful she'd felt exposing those fragile plants to the harshness of the sun they were not yet ready for and how her dad had looked on her with disappointment.

If the stealing of a few slices of beef or the exposure of a few seeds could still affect her so powerfully, reviving such strong feelings of guilt, how would it be if she allowed herself to be relieved of this beginning of a life? Guilt can destroy so many things that are good in a person. Just like those exposed seeds, she had a new life starting in her. The question is: would she allow God to see her through this unplanned pregnancy and still work in her to do the things He created her to do?

She knew that God could do whatever. She also knew she needed to give Him the permission to do His "whatever" with her.

Trust.

Faith.

Obedience.

Surrendering.

Submission.

Oh, that God would allow her a glimpse into the future just to reassure her that all would be well!

Then where would the faith be?

Marissa turned in surprise. God had not abandoned her.

Sitting there on the mall bench, Marissa began a whispered conversation with her Maker.

"But I don't want this pregnancy God. I didn't mean for it to happen now."

I knew it would happen. Before you were created I knew. I have already made provisions for you. Will you trust Me with not just your present, but your future?

"I want to trust You. But I'm afraid that what You want for me may be different from what I want for myself. I want to control my own destiny and You desire things I have trouble with. Like submission."

I know the plans I have for you, Marissa. Plans to give you hope and a future. There is nothing that I will allow you to go through that I have not already prepared a way for you to deal with it. So will you trust Me, my daughter?

"Even when I can't see where You're taking me?"

Especially when.

"Can't You provide even a little evidence? After all, three times You came through for Gideon. You showed up especially for Thomas so that he could touch and see You. You did that for a lot of people in Bible times."

"Blessed are they who . . ."

Marissa finished the sentence. "'have not seen and yet have believed' (John 20:29). You want me to be one of those. Why me, Lord?"

Because there will come a day when all the evidence in the world will not be enough. I want My children to trust that I love them no matter what. That when, because of life in a sin-cursed earth, they suffer untold anguish, they will trust that I will be true to My promise of coming again and making all things new. That circumstances here are for their character development, fitting them to become permanent citizens of heaven and that some of the tests and trials they endure are meant to demonstrate to the universe that there are those who love Me enough to give their most precious possession to Me.

"Their most precious possession? What's that?"

Their God-given power to choose.

"You want me to choose to surrender to You because I love You more than anything or anyone else?"

Something like that.

"And in return You will grant me all that I ever dream of."

No. I will do for you immeasurably more than you could ever dream of—both here and in the hereafter.

"Attention shoppers. The mall will be closing in 15 minutes."

Marissa gave a start. How long had she been sitting here?

She searched her heart.

"O taste and see that the Lord is good." Marissa recalled Monica describing that text as a carte blanche invitation to experience God to the full. Could she extend her faith on this matter? Lisa had also told her that her steps had been ordered here tonight. Had God really created this occasion of meeting Lisa so that they could talk? Lisa who had such a perfect life, the one Marissa most wished to emulate—a professional woman happily married and free of children or problems to encumber her. So what if she missed not having children? She could travel at will and spend time on developing herself. Everything this child's arrival threatened in Marissa's life.

Lisa has her life to live and you have yours. Her path cannot be yours.

Marissa took a deep breath.

Trust.

Faith.

Obedience.

Surrender.

Submission.

She considered the requirements of her discipleship, not sure if she even had them in the right order or that it mattered. Could she do it?

Then she thought of the gains:

Love

Joy

Peace

Hope

Gentleness

Goodness

Purpose

Contentment

Eternity

Pressed down, flowing over.

She placed her right hand over her tummy. Inside her, away from what the natural eyes could see, cells were forming even now. Multiplying at a rapid pace. Within her womb a chain reaction had been set in motion, incorporating genetic information from both her and Derek in a way that only God knew the outcome, creating a being that would also one day come to this place of choosing. Her will, or God's.

She, Marissa Clarke, had been granted the opportunity to help shape this being and what she'd become. She could trust God in this, couldn't she?

She would.

Despite the screaming of her will, she would choose this day to continue what she'd started—a walk of surrender. The act of procreation was an invitation from God. Pro-creation. For creation.

She looked at the pamphlets in her hand, stood up, and chucked them in the litter bin close to where she'd sat.

Pro choice. *For choice*. That's what it boiled down to.

She would choose.

Pro life.

For life.

Having decided, Marissa walked purposefully toward the exit. At the door, her foot crunched against an object. It was the lens of someone's sunglasses.

• • • • •

When she walked through the door of her home, Derek hung up the phone, relief washing over his face. "I tried to call your cell but kept getting your voice mail. You OK?"

Marissa nodded.

He helped her off with her coat and led her to the kitchen. He picked up a ladle and dipped it into a pot of soup that simmered on the stove. Three ladles and a bowl was filled. He placed the bowl and a spoon in front of her and sat in the chair opposite. He'd been frightened when she hadn't come home and couldn't be reached on her cell phone. He didn't know what to think. Was she hurt? Had she left him? He'd spent the time between the pacing and the waiting, pondering Thomas' charge. A standing-in-the-gap kind of priest in his home? How was that even possible? But he had remembered to pray. Opening his heart to God, he'd poured out everything to Him—his will, anxiety, and uncertainty about his capability to be that kind of priest. He had so much growing to do!

When Marissa picked up the spoon, Derek watched her with an almost scientific scrutiny. She grew uncomfortable. "Why are you staring at me like that?"

Chin resting in his palm with index finger gently tapping his cheek, Derek started to speak. "I've been doing a lot of thinking and praying since I found out that you, I mean, that we're, going to have a baby and . . . well . . . I have a few things to confess."

Marissa sat back, spoon in hand, prepared for anything.

Derek's hand dropped away from his face. "You were right," he told her. "I expected you to be just like my mom. I didn't even think about it. It's just what I thought."

Marissa let out a long breath. "Well, yeah."

"But that's not fair to you." He shook his head. "God made my mom who she is, but I love you for who you are. Of course, I love the way I was brought up—Mom at home seeing to us kids while dad did the earning. And yeah, I wanted us to be the same way, without even consulting you and asking what your plans were. Worse yet, I didn't consult God. You know, I was in jeopardy of breaking my marriage vows—"

"Your *wedding vows*?" she interrupted.

"Yeah. At our wedding, Rissa, I promised to love you and to seek what's best for you. But I wasn't doing that, and I'm sorry for failing you."

Marissa placed her spoon in the bowl and focused on her husband. She could hardly believe it. God was already providing evidence that she could trust Him. Derek, who'd have loved to keep her a stay-at-home mom—

even though he'd never before come right out and said it—was admitting it now.

Marissa always knew she'd married a special man. Even though, at times, he tended a bit toward arrogance, he had a kind and generous heart. This humility however was new, and when he took her hand in his and asked to pray with and for her and their future, Marissa could only marvel again at God's leading. This man loved her enough to seek God's guidance in the plans for her life even if God's plans differed from his. She would always remember that prayer. Maybe not all the details, but the most personal, important bits.

"Heavenly High Priest, I, Derek, and my wife Marissa approach Your throne with both boldness and awe. Boldness because You encourage it and awe because I know that I am not worthy. We are not worthy to be in the presence of a Holy God but You've made this approach possible through Your redemption plan.

"God, you know this woman," he said, giving her hand a squeeze. "You created her for a special purpose that is only hers to do. You knew we would one day meet, fall in love, and join our lives together. You know how we can help each other and even how we can injure each other. Let the hurts we do against each other be few and the help we provide each other be abundant. You know that Marissa is pregnant, Lord. You also know that I'm extremely happy about this but happy for the wrong reason. I wanted her to be home to meet my needs—not necessarily to do Your will. Forgive me. This child that we have been blessed with has come earlier than we planned. You knew that would happen as well. Support us, Lord, through this adjustment period. Support Marissa, Lord. You know the plans she has for her life.

"Hard as it is, enable us to yield to Your leading in this matter. We submit all our wants to Your perfect will and choose this day to follow the path You've prepared for us, not doing anything to 'assist' You in making what we want happen.

"High priest, Jesus Christ, please show me how to love Marissa the way I need to love her. Help me to model myself only after Your example. Help me to present myself daily to You as a living sacrifice so that the incense emanating from my life may be acceptable in Your sight. Show me how to be the man You created me with the potential to become."

He paused, and what he said next affected Marissa more than anything before.

"I don't know what else to ask for, Jesus. I don't know how to pray for what I really need. My heart is open and You can read it. Work with me, please. There's so much I have to learn, but here I am. Lead me."

And gripping her hand he kept his head bowed and waited. She knew God was speaking to him. He listened. Nodded at times and waited some more.

Never before had Marissa understood the meaning of the song, "Heaven came down and glory filled my soul." But now she did. The glory of the Lord surrounded them right there in their too-small kitchen.

Finally Derek rose from the table and drew her to him. He encircled her in an embrace that went beyond the physical and warmed her right down to her toes. *This must be a piece of agape*, she thought. She hugged him back with a fierce intensity, wanting to hold on to this moment forever.

Interlude

Journal entry #7

Josiah, my dear one:

I've been postponing this moment because saying goodbye to you means so many things. On one hand it means I'm moving on and putting the past behind me. That's good. I need to do that. On the other hand, however, it feels like I'm terminating you again. I know you are real only in my imagination and might even have been a girl, but for these many years, you've always been here waiting for me to talk to within these pages. I loathe letting you go. To me, you are the son I look forward to visiting from time to time. Thanks for the unconditional love you've given me and your willingness to listen to my confessions.

What will I do without you? What am I saying? God will see me through just as He's done these many years. It's been a wonderful journey with Him. Laura-Ann, she writes to me still, talks about the letting go as a way of making peace with the past. I look now with confidence to the future.

All this time I never mentioned that you have a sister, did I? You do. A beautiful person through and through. When I first held her in my arms, I could not stop crying. I was filled with joy and unspeakable pain. I'd been given another chance to have a baby. Your dad and I poured all our love on her. We hoped that she'd be one of many, not to replace you, but to provide tangible examples that God does not hold our past against us. Alas, she ended up being the only one my womb would bring to term.

Lisa. That's what we called her. Your sister's name is Lisa, son. Lisa and Josiah. Josiah and Lisa. Except she doesn't know about you. Not even a whisper.

Some people say that an only child tends to be spoiled and selfish. Lisa is none of those things. She's solid, dependable, and as a teen growing up she had none of the moodiness we'd been prepared for. She loved the Lord, and gave us numerous opportunities to be proud and honored to be her parents. At almost 18, she was the envy of many. A lot of our friends wished they had a child like our Lisa.

The summer she turned 18, our very dear daughter told us over breakfast one morning that she was pregnant. Our daughter! Pregnant! Your dad almost had a heart attack. I still remember how he exploded out of the chair, sending it flying, as he stalked from the room. I still remember Lisa bent over double, sobbing her heart out, apologizing over and over again. "I'm sorry, Mom. I'm so sorry. It was just the one time!"

What could I do, Josiah? I held her. And rocked her. And crooned something I hope was reassuring. But my mind had flown away, following the footsteps of your father up the stairs. As soon as I could, I left your sister and hurried after him.

Please, God, I prayed, let him be OK.

And he was. I found him gazing out the window of our bedroom, his back to me. Your dad had such broad shoulders. He must have sensed my entry because he began to speak to the window at a vista I could not see. What he said set my feet running into his arms to give and receive comfort.

"'Visiting the iniquities of the fathers upon the children . . .'"(Ex. 20:5, KJV). That's what your dad kept repeating, Josiah. He considered this bad dream our just desserts for our own teenage pregnancy.

Retribution.

What he did not know was how prophetic his words would become. We agreed to rally around our child and support her even though your dad wanted to kill the baby's father. Luke. That was his name. But Luke came to us and volunteered to do the "right" thing. He impressed us despite ourselves. So when two weeks later Lisa broke the news to us that she'd aborted the child, it was a blow of defeat before the fight had even started. Your dad had no words this time. But his whole manner communicated the litany that kept ringing in my heart every time I looked at my child: "visiting the iniquities of the mothers upon the daughters to the third and fourth generation of them that hate me."

God was punishing us. He demanded retribution.

Lisa lost that nice young man, Luke, as a result of her decision. She's married now to another sweetheart of a man. His name is Donald. He loves her dearly. But between you and me, I don't think she loves him the way she loved that boy Luke.

My daughter is hurting real bad, Josiah. Not because her husband or life is unkind to her. Her hurting is one I fully understand. She's dying from guilt and self-hate. When you hate yourself you somehow feel as if you are not deserving of any happiness or joy and set about to sabotage all that's good in your life. Fortunately for me, your dad and I decided about you together and still kept together afterwards. But the guilt is always lurking in unexpected places: the kitchen cupboard, the shower stall, the car trunk, and right behind your prayers.

You see, I don't think our Lisa has ever forgiven herself for what she did. I think that she, too, is living all the things I've been writing about in this journal. I must tell her my story and leave her a legacy of peace. I must not rest until my child also, just like I had to do, lets go of the past and all the self-blame and presents it to God as a sacrifice. That kind of guilt will eat away at your sanity. Josiah, I know of which I speak.

"I will lift up my eyes to the hills—where does my help come from? My help comes from the Lord, the Maker of heaven and earth"(Ps. 121:1). This has become one of my favorite psalms. When I look at me and what I've done, I'm mired in guilt, but when I lift my eyes from myself to which is above me, I see all that God has done and wants me to do. My help to endure comes from looking up.

Son, I hope Lisa and I will have an opportunity soon to speak. It never seems the right time to tell her about you—not because I'm ashamed of you but because it's hard for me to admit to my daughter that I, too, have feet of clay.

Lately however I've become convinced that she needs to hear my story of deliverance. God is good. While we sometimes have to deal with the consequences of our unrighteous acts, God looks at our sordid past and covers it with His unblemished life. With one powerful application of His special cleansing blood He deep cleans every stain, no matter how embedded they seem. He's done that for me.

"So wash me thou without within
Or purge with fire if that must be
No matter how if only sin
Die out in me" (SDA Church Hymnal [1941], # 634).

That's the simple truth. We must desire to be clean. Once we desire it and ask God for it, He covers us with a pure white robe and from there on does not hold our past against us. You know, Josiah, it's rather like refusing to give up an adulterous affair even though it's hurting all the good things we want to keep in our lives. In the same way, I clung unto my guilt. God had forgiven me, but I hugged the guilt close, refusing to be separated from it. Not worthy. That was my sin. I am not worthy. What God had done for me was good, but subconsciously I felt that I must never be too happy again because of the weaknesses of my flesh. So I threw God's forgiveness right back at Him, choosing instead to wallow in my misery.

No more! I am a forgiven child of the King of the universe. He loves me and in His eyes I am clean and blemish free because I have surrendered all my dirt to Him.

Goodbye, my dear son. I heard someone say that when Christ returns again He will resurrect those babies who died in infancy and return them to the arms of their mothers. I don't know what God does with the early cells of infants who never got to form faces or bodies. I'd like to think that when He makes all things new I'll get another chance to mother you in heaven and pour out on you all the love that I missed sharing with you here. Wishful thinking, you say? It might be, but I put nothing beyond the power of God. So until then, I will keep on keeping on with joy in my heart.

Sincerely yours,
Mary Jones (your mother)

PS: I will ask God to direct me to the best way to share my story with Lisa. No more running ahead of His will.

Chapter 29

Lisa watched her front door close behind Joshua then collapsed on the floor, the phone in her hand. Her heart beat so hard against her chest wall she could hear it as well as feel it.

Thank You, God. Thank You.

A tinny sound reached her. Recalling the phone still in her hand, Lisa quickly brought it to her ear and heard Catherine's frantic voice.

"Lisa, are you OK? I tell you nothing like this has ever happened to me before. Not so strong. I was in the middle of a deep sleep when it's as if someone shook me awake. 'Call Lisa!' I seemed to hear. There was such urgency in the message that I had to act on it." She stopped to gulp a breath then finished all in a rush. "Tell this old woman you're OK and all this was a figment of an overactive imagination."

Lisa closed her eyes in a prayer of thanksgiving. "'My God sent his angel, and he shut the mouths of the lions. They have not hurt me'" (Dan. 6:22). Then she returned the phone to her ear. "No Catherine. You're not an old woman with an overactive imagination. Your phone call was heaven sent. I needed to be rescued and God chose you to be His angel of mercy tonight."

"Are you going to be all right?"

Dear God, thought Lisa as her tears started up again, but she brushed them aside. "Yes. I think so. But could you pray with me, Catherine? I could use your prayers right now."

"Anything in particular you want me to pray for?"

"Could you thank God for deliverance from temptation and for open hearts like yours that allow the Holy Spirit to work through them to help souls in need of rescue?"

Catherine's prayer drove home to Lisa all the good reasons for Christian support groups. These women not only challenged you and laughed with you, but they were there to surround and prop you up when your own legs had turned to jelly. As Catherine prayed, Lisa felt new strength returning to her limbs and warmth that had been long missing coming back into her heart.

Following Catherine's prayer, Lisa, still bruised in both mind and body, dragged herself upstairs to wash off the day's grit. She felt spent. It seemed an effort to even step into the shower. As the warm sprayed over her body, into her mind came Joshua's face. She flinched. *Why do I want him so much* she wondered. *Is it because my marriage is breaking up?*

"No," she whispered aloud. "It's not." She'd been attracted to him from the first day they met. And even now, with God rescuing her and Joshua out of her house, temptation still beckoned. Then it hit Lisa how much farther she had to go. One prayer for deliverance did not remove the temptation forever. Again and again she would have to choose to step away, gaining strength from each victory but never, ever temptation free.

And she also remembered that temptation is not sin. The sin was in the yielding. She knew she'd yielded though. In the corridors of her mind where fantasies take shape and thoughts provide fodder, she'd allowed images of Joshua to occupy mental real estate that belonged to the man she'd promised before God and witnesses to remain true to. Dear, dull, and now distant, Donald.

How would she bring her mind back from the precipice of forbidden desire? She'd only peeked over it, but it was enough. She wondered if she could do it, or if she'd forever be haunted by two men who briefly touched her life, igniting more passion than her husband ever did. It seemed an overwhelming task—disciplining her mind to prevent her thoughts from even going there.

I can do all things through Christ who gives me strength (Phil. 4:13).

There it was again. The voice. Lisa paused, towel wrapped around her body.

Christ! How could she have forgotten Him? Even more than yielding her mind to forbidden thoughts, she had failed to represent God to Joshua. Suddenly she thought of Joseph. In running away from temptation he had been more concerned that he not sin against God than about what would happen to him if he rejected Potiphar's wife. And the three Hebrew boys had told King Nebuchadnezzar that they'd rather die in the raging fire than disobey God.

Lisa pulled the towel tighter and sat on the edge of the bathtub. She examined her mind and her motives. Mentally she ticked off her wrongs.

In not trusting God to show her how to talk to Donald about her past, she'd sinned.

Guilty.

Allowing thoughts of Joshua to fill her mind had been a sin. Guilty.

Concentrating on the bad in her marriage as opposed to the good. Guilty.

Dwelling on the failures in her past. She stopped at that one. Had that been a sin or just a consequence of her action she must learn to live with? Lisa was not sure, but everywhere her mind traveled, she saw guilt and sin in her life.

That must be what the Apostle Paul meant when he said, "What a wretched man I am! Who will rescue me from this body of death?" (Rom. 7:24).

The weight of her fallen-ness bore down.

Guilty.

Condemned.

Sentenced.

Lisa did not fight the sentence. She submitted to it. She deserved it. She might as well be dead.

No tears greeted this pronouncement. Lisa had gone beyond tears. Nothing about her remained good. All of her, soiled, stained, dirty.

Guilty!

The guilt pressed down, a solid weight, making her breath shallow and squeezing every bit of hope from her heart. Yes. She was a failure and might as well be dead.

She dropped to the floor, head resting against the tub.

"Take me out, God," she prayed. "I've failed You in every way. I've misrepresented You, disobeyed You, ignored You, and sinned against You. You don't need me around as another bad witness for You. I'm sorry I did not live up to Your creative plan for my life and I can see that I'm way past the place where Your redemption can reach me. And even if I wasn't, I'm not deserving of Your mercy. Just take me out and end this."

Lisa hung her head and waited for the guillotine of justice to mete out its punishment. She prayed that it be quick.

"Where sin increased, grace increased all the more" (Rom. 5:20).

Lisa did not move. She remained where she was. Condemned.

Where sin increases, grace increased even more, Lisa. Grace that is greater than all of your sins. Choose grace, My child. Don't worry about your guilt. All's been forgiven. Erased. Flung to the bottom of the sea. Remembered no more. Here, take it.

Lisa raised her condemned head an inch. Could it be true? Her heart pounded at the thought of a clean slate. She reached out her hands toward this incredible offering and saw them trembling. Just like Joshua's.

Her hand fell back. Empty. There she was again. Thinking about Joshua.

O dear God, just let me die.

No Lisa. Think. Think of My words. You learned them as a child, and even thought of them in your sporadic episodes with Me in years since. They're hidden in your heart.

Lisa's tired mind rebelled at the exertion. So much easier to just give over to her self-condemnation. But she tried. One for the road.

She concentrated, slowing her breathing to calm herself.

And one came.

A promise. A very good promise.

"Now unto him who is able to keep you from falling and present you faultless before the presence of his glory with exceeding joy" (Jude 24, KJV).

Could it be that she could be kept from falling? But how? By Him! Still how? And God would present her before His presence without fault? And with exceeding joy?

Lisa's hand reached out again. This time without reservation. Greedy for grace, she grabbed hold of the hem of the garment of Him who dispenses this unmerited favor to hungry souls.

She would be made whole.

And there on the bathroom floor Lisa's tired body and mind finally gave out. She slept.

· · · · ·

Donald hoped the sound of the door opening did not waken Lisa. She was such a light sleeper. Dog tired and bone weary, he'd managed to lug his body from the limo toward his front door. It was 6:30 a.m., almost morning. Slipping off his shoes, he padded softly up the stairs. Perhaps a shower would revive him, then he'd be ready to bare his soul to the woman he loved.

He'd given his presentation last afternoon. But afterward he found that his heart was not in the typical conference networking events. He couldn't make himself do it. As soon as protocol allowed, he'd escaped to his eighteenth floor room to pray and to call his wife. He'd prayed, but he couldn't think of how to pick up the phone and begin the reparation his marriage needed.

He rehearsed opening lines: "Hi, Lisa. How's my favorite girl?"

No. Not good.

"Hi, sweetheart. I miss you."

Yes he missed her, but no. That just wouldn't cut it. She'd think him drunk, as withdrawn as he'd been for the past few months.

"Lisa, I love you and I forgive you" or "Lisa, can we talk?" or "Lisa, I'm sorry for being such a —"

He wished she was there with him so he could talk to her about what was on his heart. Then it hit him. He didn't have to stay at the conference. He could go home. He'd finished his work here, and his heart wasn't into it anyway.

Quickly packing his bags, Donald called the front desk to have a cab waiting for him. At the airport café, he'd ordered some tea and sipped at it slowly, praying that his request to be accommodated as a stand-by would be granted soon.

It had.

And now, thank God, he was home. Donald stowed his suitcase in the room that he hoped would soon return to its guest-room status and headed for the bathroom. He closed the door then turned on the lights. His heart stopped.

Lying on the floor, her body twisted in an uncomfortable position, lay his wife, wrapped in a towel and out cold. Spit dried up in his mouth.

"Lisa!" he whispered, kneeling beside her.

No response.

He shook her. She moaned and moved. That's when he saw a large dark lump on her forehead. She was hurt! Could he risk moving her?

He called to her again. "Lisa, honey, it's Donald. Did you fall in the bathroom and hit your head?"

"No," she answered, eyes still closed and voice weak. "At the mall. Better now."

He put his arms under her, and as gently as if lifting a baby, Donald picked her up and carried her to their bed, laying her down with care.

She opened her eyes and looked at him. Then she started to cry.

"I'm so sorry. For everything."

Donald knelt on the floor beside the bed. "Just tell me that you're OK. I found you on the bathroom floor."

Lisa's weepy voice answered. "I'm OK. Just a very long day and night."

"Are you sure?"

His concern touched her. She really did not deserve this good man. "I'll be fine, Donald."

"Lisa, I came home early so we can talk. There's so much I want to

197

tell you but first—"

The phone's loud ring stopped his voice. It was 6:42 a.m. Who could be calling at this hour? Taking Lisa's hand in one of his, he lifted the receiver with the other. A moment later he dropped her hand and clutched the phone with both of his.

It was Thursday, February 21, and Mary Jones was dead. Lisa's mother, her mama, was gone.

Chapter 30

Lisa stood alone at the graveside, a yellow rose in her hand. Single flowers as well as fancy arrangements covered the mound of earth. The late February cold bit her face, but her coat and gloves kept her warm. She'd asked for this time alone to say goodbye to the woman who meant the world to her and now tears of grief and pain and loss rolled down her cheeks. It seemed she'd been crying for weeks. Long before the early morning phone call, she'd been crying. Then she'd cried all the more for her mama who had died alone without her there by her side.

Yesterday when she'd opened the door of her mother's apartment and seen a tired looking Grace next to Monica, Marissa, Catherine, and Yolanda she'd burst into tears. She was touched beyond belief that these women, who were fast becoming like sisters to her, would come all this way to support and prop her up. She'd gotten a lovely card, sent by Sophie through Janine. Flowers had come from Joshua, again through Janine, each conveying beautiful thoughts or prayers of comfort. More tears had come with those as well.

Lisa took a deep breath, knowing before she uttered them that her words could never convey all that filled her heart.

"Goodbye, Mama." She gulped.

Goodbye had such a final sound. She dabbed at her runny nose with a tissue and tipped her head back, willing her tears not to fall.

"I wish we'd had more time, you know . . . but . . . but I'm glad we had the chance to visit in December. You helped me a lot." Unconsciously, she reached toward the mounded dirt. "Last Thursday I took a hit on my head and it woke me up, Mama. It really, seriously did. So I've given all the stuff I've been carrying around to God and accepted His grace. I hope that one day my faith will be as strong as yours and Daddy's. Maybe it will."

Her voice broke and the tears came again. Crossing her arms around her chest she bent forward and wondered if one could die of grief.

"Listen, I'm going to miss you more than words can say. I can't tell you how bereft I feel to have no mother or father—not even a brother or sister. But God knew how I'd feel, Mama, and He sent me sisters of spirit to be with me. I'm going to try real hard to choose Jesus every day of my life to help me handle the situations life throws at me. My prayer is that we'll be reunited when He comes again—you, Daddy, and me. And when 'this corruptible puts on the incorruptible,' I'll just lay my head against yours and you can see for yourself all the love I hold for you in my heart."

Wind whipped her hair and stung her face. Swallowing against the tears, Lisa pressed the wilting rose petals to release what little was there of its out-of-season perfume. The scent reminded her of her mother. Then she placed the single rose atop the mound, turned, and walked away.

Donald must have stayed out in the cold waiting for her, for he met her halfway. Tucking her arm into his, he walked her to the waiting car.

Back at the funeral home she hosted a reception for friends who had come, discovering how much her mother's kindness had touched the lives of others. Tomorrow, being Monday, Donald and her friends, would return home. He had offered to stay with her, but he'd been away from work for four days and his workload had piled up. Lisa urged him to go, reassuring him that she'd be fine and back home on Tuesday.

Before he left, however, Donald pulled her aside, held her hands, and prayed for her. Then he hugged her. "I know we have to finish that talk," he told her. "We have lots to discuss, but since I have to go and you need to stay, I want to remind you how much I love you. I'm sorry for not acting lovely these past few months, but I do love you, Lisa. I do."

He kissed her then with a passion she'd never seen in him. And then he was gone.

Lisa fingered her tingling lips in wonder.

By Tuesday morning the apartment had been sorted and arrangements made for the Community Services people from the church to pick up the stuff Lisa would not be keeping. Most of the family heirlooms had been passed on to her when her mother moved to the seniors' residence, so now all she took were a few framed photos and her mother's papers which she'd sort through later. She also had a bulky envelope with her name written boldly across the middle. Probably estate stuff. Lisa left that to look through on the train ride back to Windsor.

The nurse who had called to tell them the news of her mother's passing dropped by just as Lisa was about to close the door. Lisa felt cheered by her smile of greeting. She'd had too much time alone.

"How are you holding up?" she asked after introducing herself.

"I don't know *how*, but I am holding up," Lisa replied. "It must be God."

"You think so?"

"I know it's not me. So it must be Him."

"Your mother talked about God a lot. Especially close to the end. I don't understand it. She didn't seem to be afraid of dying. She knew her health was fragile and yet, she looked . . . at peace. That's a good way to go out. Peaceful. I wish I knew what gave her that."

"It's not a 'what,' Megan. It's 'Who.' The Bible talks about Christians, true believers, as possessing a peace that defies understanding. Only God can do that. Death for the Christian is not an end. It's just a respite." Lisa shook her head. "I wish I could have been with her at the end though. Why didn't she call me?"

"I asked her to, but she said she didn't want to add to your troubles. She said you had enough on your plate and that you and she had a long visit back in December. But she'd written you a letter. Did you see it? She had me put it in a large brown envelope with some other stuff and told me to make sure you got it. I forgot all about it till now."

Lisa pulled the bulky envelope from the side of her bag. "This?"

Megan looked relieved. "That's it. To think that I forgot after she made me promise to remember."

"That's OK," Lisa said. "It's been a stressful time for all of us. I miss her so much."

"Me too," said Megan getting teary. "She was my favorite patient. Even though I was the one looking after *her,* she constantly gave me more than I gave her. I especially appreciated her words of encouragement."

Seeing Lisa's glance at her watch, Megan stopped. "Look at me rambling when you have to go."

"I wish I could stay longer and chat but I have to get a train, and with today's uncertain weather, I should get a move on. But Megan, thank you for everything you did for my mom. I really truly appreciate it. I'll pray for you as often as I think of you. God be with you."

"You believe? Like your mom?" asked Megan.

"Yes I do. But even though I've been a believer all my life, I'm just starting to understand what being a Christian is about. If you want to talk with me about it—" Lisa reached in her purse and pulled out a business card—"call me. I mean it. Call me anytime. My cell and work numbers are on the card." She gave Megan a quick hug and received an equally tight hug from the older woman. "Promise me you'll call?"

Megan hesitated then nodded with a smile that held great longing. "I might just take you up on that."

"See that you do." Lisa gave her a quick kiss on the cheek and dashed off, smiling at the shocked look on the nurse's face.

Once she had settled comfortably in her window seat Lisa let her mind roam over the past couple of days. She was glad there were few people in the train car with her, A few more tears escaped but not the torrential downpour she'd expected. Mama was gone. It hardly seemed possible. A week ago . . . she was still here. But no more.

Then Lisa remembered the envelope and stood up, balancing against the rocking motion of the train, to retrieve it from her bag. Tearing open the flap, she pulled out a book.

"I wonder what this is," she mumbled under her breath.

Putting aside the envelope, she opened the book only to discover that it wasn't a typical book. It was a sort of hardcover journal.

The first entry caught her eye. "My dear son . . ."

Puzzled Lisa read on and soon got caught up in this amazing story about a young woman who'd had an abortion.

This is my story, Lisa thought. Did her mother want her to share her story with others and had started this journal on her behalf? A journal like the one she herself had made three entries in and could not bring herself to continue?

Lisa read on, consumed by this saga that so mirrored her life it was uncanny. "God, did you do this?" she asked, but received no reply.

When she got to the part where the mother described seeing the face of her son in the visage of every young man, Lisa had to tear her eyes away from the mesmerizing words.

Staring out the window she concentrated on the snow and the drifts and the whiteness of the scenery. Soon spring would come and cows would be in the meadows. There'd be green grass and leafy trees. She tried to recall if she'd ever seen a river at that location, but could not. The lightly falling snow, so silent and peaceful, relaxed her. When she felt calm enough she returned to the story, trepidation tippy-toeing close by.

What if this woman . . . would she feel as soiled as me?

The miles flew by unnoticed. When Lisa got to Journal entry #5, guilt and self-condemnation screamed from the pages. Both states described her to a T! To think that her mother had known her that well to be able to identify all the things they'd talked about together and some things they never did! Every word she read, every feeling described, they told her very own story.

God must have spoken to her, Lisa thought. *God read her mind and heart and heaven-breathed my feelings into my mother's brain so I could be left this legacy of therapy.*

For that's what it felt like. Despite the ache in her heart and the burning of her throat, Lisa for the first time in years felt *recognized*. Others looked at her but her mom *recognized* her in these pages; authenticated her. When could she have written all this? Lisa searched back through the entries up to that point for a date, but found none. No identifiers either at the end of the entries.

Then she read something that stopped her cold. *If I have to live with the memories, I want release from the guilt. How do I pray for self-forgiveness? God does not seem to answer this prayer of mine. This woman in the book talks about how sometimes we tenaciously hang on to things that aren't good for us because we don't think ourselves deserving of God's grace. Could it be possible that I don't want forgiveness? It's possible, but why would I do that? Could it be that I've come to enjoy being a martyr to my own self-condemnation and by doing so I have limited what God wants to do with and through me?*

Lisa gasped. "Is that what I'm doing, God? So many times in the past You've extended Your grace to me and I've rejected it. I've always considered myself undeserving. Forgive me, please. I'm sorry it had to take a bump on my head to get me to see straight, but I'm glad for the collision."

Eagerly she turned to Journal entry #6. All of this was building to some kind of climax. She could feel it. Could it be that here in these pages she would find a way out and learn through her mother's words to her how to walk with God guilt free?

The entry began, *I wrote to the author that I like so well, and she called me today.*

When she read the next sentence, Lisa's brain screeched to a halt. Like the teller of the story, her hands began to shake as logic kicked in and the facts sorted themselves.

Impossible!

With beads of moisture forming on her upper lip Lisa tried to absorb what could not be.

"This is preposterous! There is no way my mother . . . My mother had an—" She couldn't even let her mind say the word.

This is *her* story?"

Sweet Jesus!

Frantically Lisa flipped the pages forward. A small slip of paper floated to the floor but Lisa ignored it. Probably a page marker. There must be something here. Didn't Megan say that Mama insisted she, Lisa, get this book? There must be a message of explanation because there was no way she could believe that her mother . . .

Here it is.

The last entry.

My dearest Lisa, it began.

"That's me. I'm Lisa. Mom's just telling my story and this will clear up everything. Foolish of me to get worked up over nothing."

She read on.

I don't know where you are or what you're doing as you read this journal I've left you, but I've talked to God and Laura-Ann about it. If you've gotten through the previous pages you should have figured out by now that this is my story.

Jesus, help me! Lisa's heart cried.

When you came to visit in December and I saw how you were suffering I wanted so much to tell you the whole thing. But the timing was not right and you had more important things to deal with.

No way!

I knew of which you spoke, my daughter, when you talked about how soiled you feel. For years, even after you were born, I, too, felt like that. Mine was more a feeling of uncleanness. No matter how many time I mentally justified my decision—and even years later when I recognized why the teen girl I was then made the decision she made—still I could not erase the sense of uncleanness. But God heard my cry and rescued me. He will hear your cry too, my child.

There is no need for me to go into the whole sorry tale about how your father and I got into our particular predicament. You can read it in the pages you hold in your hand. I can only tell you that I was terrified.

When I told your dad, then a young man of 20 with no prospects to speak of, I was frightened by the wild look that came into his eyes. He looked ready to take flight, and I thought he didn't want me anymore. Shamelessly I begged him not to leave me, for how could I face this thing alone?

David had an older friend whom he unburdened to. This friend had been in a similar situation and, well . . . wasn't anymore. He and the girl had it taken care of. We would need money. One hundred dollars in cash. It might as well have been a million. We didn't have it. But this friend lent David the money and so that night, he came to see me.

After my parents had gone to bed I went out to meet him. We walked back and forth in the park going over arguments this way and that way, taking no joy from the stars in the sky or from the holding of each other's hands. We finally agreed that seeing that doctor to have the abortion was the only way out.

But the decision terrified me. Back then, there were no such things as legal abortions. Canada criminalized abortions in the nineteenth century, and back then one could be given life imprisonment for it. I knew none of this then, however. I've since done much research on the topic. Did you know it's estimated that between 4,000 to 6,000 women died in Canada alone because of bungled or illegal abortions? I could have been one of those!

I had so many questions and fears. What if the doctor messed up my insides? What if I bled to death? And, of course, would it hurt?

It hurt like crazy. But I survived. We survived. David stayed with me as far as they would let him and in a bizarre kind of way this nasty business brought us closer together. From then on in our relationship we concentrated on just being friends. I was too shaken up to even feel sexual urges. I think David felt the same way, too, because with the exception of an occasional kiss, until the day we were married we never allowed ourselves to get carried away. We spent time getting to know each other and planning for our future, hoping that our past was indeed left behind.

When David turned 24 and I, 23, we got married in a church with the blessings of our family and community raining down on us.

I wore white.

Honey, decisions against one's conscience have a way of leaving a nasty after-taste. When I became pregnant with you I breathed a sigh of relief, thanking God that my insides had not been irreparably damaged. Your dad smiled that year more than all the years since the day we'd had the abortion. Every time he looked at me, waddling around the house like a fat duck, he'd just smile at me and tell me how beautiful I looked. Yes, God had forgiven us and did not hold our past failures against us.

As I've indicated in the pages of this journal, no other child came to us. When I miscarried for the third time, I accepted the fact that you would be our only blessing and believed the denial of my wish to mother more children was God's way of punishing us for our lack of faith. Stoically we took what was coming to us.

We understood the need for penance. Through you we had been granted a gift of mercy. We dared not beg for more lest God think we were not sufficiently grateful. We took our medicine with thankful hearts.

I remember taking you to the park one day and there you found a little boy who so wanted to play with you. His mother and I got to talking as mothers tend to do when their children play together. She asked me if you were my first. I told her yes.

But that was a lie.

I left the park that day with the first clear picture of the shadow that'd been dogging my dreams over the years. It was a picture of a stain that could not be removed from an otherwise white diaper. That night I could not sleep and started to write in this book. Thank heavens these episodes into guilt were few and far between, but whenever they hit, sleep deserted me. I would leave the side of your father and empty my thoughts in these pages. Then I'd be good again for a season.

Your dad never brought up the subject of the abortion. Somehow we had decided, without discussion, to stay away from it. Yet sometimes I'd find him staring into space, a haunted look in his eyes. I would call him back and he'd come willingly, shaking off whatever it was. There's no doubt in my mind that he too was visited by guilt.

I've done a lot of reading up on abortion; its history and some of the women's stories. I know there are good arguments for why a woman should be the one to decide what to do with her own body. There is a part of me that agrees wholeheartedly with many of the reasoned arguments of the pro-choice advocates, and would go as far as to say that in circumstances like incest or rape I can fully understand why a woman might choose to have those pregnancies terminated.

I know I've railed in these pages against those who would rather a woman be saddled with an unwanted child whom she cannot love or provide for, instead of doing the merciful thing and terminating the pregnancy. But my heart refuses to agree with my mind.

For me, one who has also chosen to call myself Christian, I've discovered that the pendulum of my mental debate on this subject consistently lists to the side of "this is wrong." Some would argue that it is my so-called Christian brainwashing and socialization that causes me to experience guilt. In fact, I've read survey results that show that most women who have abortions bear no significant long-term feelings of remorse such as I've felt, and that those who do usually come from the kind of religious background I have, or are somewhat psychologically vulnerable.

It is saying something that still, after all this time, I do not know with any kind of absolute certainty that, given the same circumstances, I'd choose differently, even if the risks now were the same as then—which if I'm to believe the experts, they're not. Equally telling is the fact that I know I would still feel guilty then as now. I guess I'm one of the exceptions, fated to live within the shadows of grey uncertainty—forgiven, weak, conflicted, and almost persuaded.

But where the pendulum tilts, there I sit. In the heart of me I feel that having the abortion was wrong. And maybe it's all religious programming or it could be guilt of flesh-weakness for not saying no to premarital sex in the first place. But my decision still feels wrong to my heart. Despite the source of it, guilt is what I feel. Naked, reason-defying guilt.

You see, whether the guilt is short-lived or lingering, my belief is that whether she's pro-choice, or not, no woman relishes being in the position of having to terminate a pregnancy except maybe for those reasons I cited above. But they do it, or think they have to do it, or are told they must do it—and so live (some to suffer) with the consequences of their decision.

I've come up with a couple ways of looking at this issue. It could be, as some of the readings I've done seem to suggest, that women who feel the kind of guilt that I do (and I suspect you feel as well, dear), are guilt-ridden personality types in desperate need of therapy to correct faulty religious programming. What do you think?

My other thought, which is the one I tend to lean toward, is that this feeling of wrongness or guilt, or discomfort is God-planted. That because we do not have the power to create life—only to participate in the nurturing of it—we must never take it for granted, even the beginning part of it where no reason or mental functioning yet resides.

Whether or not these ways of looking at things have any basis in truth, I am eternally grateful that God loves me despite my frailties.

So you see, when you told your dad you were pregnant, it brought the whole thing back. Suddenly our past was now. *But heaven help us! We would provide you the support we never would have received from our parents. You, my daughter, would never have to live your life feeling unclean like I did. But you did the one thing we did not expect. On your own, you, too, had an abortion. I knew then the path your future would take and felt afraid. For you.*

Lisa, mothering you has been one of the greatest blessings of my life. You are my constant joy and delight, and thoughts of you make my heart praise God every day. But I suspect that you are carrying a baggage of guilt and self-condemnation just like your mother did for years. My guess is that you believe your miscarriages to be punishments from God.

Not so.

Yes, I know that sin has consequences which must be dealt with but God does not hold our past against us and use it to flail us every time we reach for glimpsed joy. You have asked for His forgiveness. I know you have. Now claim it. Not because you deserve it, but because God loves you.

Say it with me, sweetheart.

"God loves me."

Say it again.

"God loves me."

Every time you begin to feel undeserving of His goodness, run to your closet, your car, or even to your bathroom mirror and look yourself in the eye. Tell yourself that God loves you. Keep saying it aloud until the guilt leaves.

Let it go, my child. Let go of the pain. You've been pardoned. Bought with a price. Glorify God in your body and spirit—which are God's.

Grasp grace and start living a forgiven life.

That's why you have this journal in your hand. It is my story of deliverance. I love you with all of my heart. You know that. But however much I love you, God loves you more.

I look forward to seeing you soon. But peradventure we do not get another opportunity to meet again, plan to meet me and Daddy in the earth made new.

Remember,

God loves you!

You are forgiven!

> *Forgiven too,*
> *Mary Jones, your mother*

Overwhelmed Lisa closed the book. Too much information. Startling, inspiring even, but way too much. She stretched out her legs and heard a rustling of paper. Right. Something had fallen out of the journal. She picked it up, saw that it had her name on it, and tucked it unread within the closed pages.

She wanted no more disclosures today. Maybe tomorrow.

Chapter 31

Thomas Charles lay on his back on the bed, mind flitting from one topic to another. Beside him Catherine stirred.

"You're awake," she said.

"How can you tell that? Your back's to me!"

"I can feel your mind warming up, driving all the sleep out of the room."

Thomas chuckled. "Leave it to you to say something like that."

"Is everything all right?" Catherine asked.

"I don't know. I was trying to be still so I could learn something."

"I'll shut up then."

Thomas reached across the bed and patted her on the hip. "I could do with your perspective if you don't mind talking so early in the morning."

Catherine gingerly turned on to her other side, facing Thomas. "OK. I'm listening."

"What do you make of all this? First you start meeting with the women and that seems to be going OK, but so much has happened. Grace is terminally ill and it seems Lisa and Donald are having problems, but you're taking it all in stride. What's the matter with the Westwoods anyway?"

"I have no idea. Lisa's never volunteered and I haven't pried."

"Me neither." Thomas gave voice to the worry on his mind. "Catherine, have we bitten off more than we can chew? When I met with the men a week ago, I presented them with an idea for ministry and asked them to call and let me know what they'd decided. So far no one has called back?"

Catherine shifted position to ease the cramp making its way up her leg. Her arthritic joints protested. "I suspect men process things a bit differently than women. We tend to consult each other more to help us make our decisions. Men turn inside and try to work it out themselves. You've only had one meeting. Give them a chance. Plus Lisa just lost her mom so obviously she and Donald have other things on their minds."

"But none of them have called. Not Derek, Bill, or Simon," Thomas fretted.

"Everyone's busy," Catherine reminded him. "People intend to call, but they don't. Just pray. That's what we do. We pray and wait. Let's examine our hearts and make sure that we're not about our agenda in this mission. We must allow ourselves to be God's instruments."

Shrugging away his worry, Thomas agreed. "OK, sounds reasonable to me. What's for breakfast?"

Catherine mumbled under her breath but loud enough for Thomas to hear. "Your head on a platter over which I'll say grace!"

At his total look of innocence she chided him. "Is that all you think about? Food? You must have the largest tapeworm of anyone who ever hosted that parasite. Look at you, all lanky, bony and knobbly-kneed!"

Thomas turned on his side and faced her. "And still loving you with every beat of my lanky heart!"

"As if a heart can be lanky!" complained Catherine, nestling.

"It follows that a lanky man should have a lanky heart. Now don't distract me, woman. I was in the process of declaring my love for you. What! Your old heart can't bear up under a little good old-fashioned romance?"

"Thomas Edward Charles!" exclaimed Catherine, trying to move away.

Thomas moved closer, his tone communicating pure mischief. He wagged his eyebrows. "Yes, my love."

"Oh, you!"

He pulled back a little to better see her. "What's that staining your cheeks, Catherine dearest? Is that a blush? I can still make you blush?" In one fluid motion Thomas was standing on the bed, jumping and jigging, and singing—rattling all of Catherine's arthritic bones. "The dude's still got it. Yeah, yeah, yeah."

Dodging the dancing feet Catherine escaped from the bed and bolted for the door, cheeks still blushingly warm. But her husband would not be thwarted. With the friskiness of a cat he leapt in front of her, wincing as his knees rebelled against the sudden landing, and pulled her into his arms. Winded from his exertions, he worked to regulate his breathing then slowly sideways walked them back to the edge of the bed where he sat them down.

"Just give me a few seconds to catch my breath," he wheezed.

Concerned, Catherine made to rise. "I'll get you some water," but he held her fast.

"I'm not dying, love. Not today. But yes, I'm not as young as my mind tells me I am."

He hitched up one leg onto the bed and faced his wife. "As I lay in bed this morning more than the men were in my thoughts. I thought of you, too. I thanked God for giving you to me. We have been through so much tragedy, Catherine. Our little girls would now be grown women, possibly with families of their own. And while I watched and prayed and hurt when the loss of their lives bent you almost double, I am still amazed at how you fought your way back to God and to me. Losing our children devastated me more that I could have imagined. The worst part was that I'm a doctor and still I could do nothing to bring them back. But when I thought I'd lost you, too, Catherine, I could not bear it. Thank you for fighting back. In saving yourself, you saved me too.

"Oh, Thomas!"

"I mean it, love. You're my greatest earthly hero, Catherine Charles. Some time ago I heard a pastor say that marriage is a ministry and that it's our responsibility to pray and love and support our partners into the kingdom. You've done that for me. From day one, you did not compromise your principles to accommodate me even though I knew you cared for me. Thank you for everything, but most of all for introducing me to God and showing me what true discipleship is all about. I bless you, my sweetheart, and pray that God continues to use you to bring others closer to Him just like He's used you for me."

Then Thomas tenderly kissed his wife of 43 years.

Catherine's heart soared to heaven in gratitude. "Thomas, I love you so much. Thank you for the words even though I don't see it the way you do. I especially appreciate your blessing. You loved me and prayed for me even when I was mired in that deep depression. You say I saved you? No. It was you who anchored my world. I leaned against your love when I thought myself undeserving of God's. You modeled Him to me. Many times I felt you were the only good thing between me and giving up."

Thomas swallowed. "So here we are in our dotage at the cusp of another adventure in ministry and already I'm quaking like a babe in Christ at the first little hitch."

"That's when we need to focus on God and not on the problems. The joy of the Lord is our strength."

Thomas grinned. "I hear a praise and thanksgiving session coming on!"

Catherine's eyes crinkled in merriment. "You got that right." She launched into that traditional chorus about seeing what the Lord has done for us and what a mighty God He is. When she got to the part about the walls tumbling down, Thomas joined in and together they blended quaky bass and reedy contralto in an anthem of praise that made the angels smile.

· · · · ·

Donald had expected Lisa to be quiet when she arrived home from Toronto, but not this quiet. At the train station she hugged him with what felt like a bit of urgency but he must have imagined it because for the rest of the evening and over the next few days she seemed removed. He said nothing about it for he wanted to give her time to grieve.

Mary Jones had been a wonderful mother and mother-in-law. Donald had loved her almost as much as Lisa did, and it was a hard loss for them both. He'd hoped that the grief would provide a mutual place for them to reach out and comfort each other and so begin their own healing, but that wasn't happening. Perhaps she seemed a little softer, he pondered, but no less remote. He knew better than to rush her even though he urgently wanted to make up for the damage and lost time.

Earlier today he'd called her to see if she wanted to go out for dinner. She'd agreed, but when he got to the office she was still with a client. Janine told him to wait in her office.

He found a lovely floral arrangement on her credenza and without thinking looked to see which of their friends had sent her flowers. He knew it must be a condolence at the passing of her mom. The card on the arrangement read, "My thoughts are with you during this difficult time. Love, Joshua."

Joshua? His brow knitted. He didn't recall a Joshua. Maybe it was one of her clients.

Donald sat at her desk, careful not to disturb any of her paperwork. A photograph of the two of them taken on one of their trips to Europe sat off to the left side of the desk. He picked it up. They looked so carefree and happy. That trip had taken place back in 2005. Ah!

His wife was a beautiful woman who knew what to wear to accentuate her personality. Spontaneous and fun-loving, she held nothing back in her total enjoyment of life. He loved that about her and had told her so many times over. He'd always been proud to walk down the street with her on his arm, and considered himself a lucky man. Sometimes he wondered what she'd seen in him to agree to marry him.

Yet all this while, he remembered with pain, beneath the banter and joy she had carried a secret. And when she could carry it no more and had dropped it in his lap, he'd fled. Yes, he'd been shocked. Of course he was. He'd never imagined her to be that kind of woman. In his mind she occupied a position of . . . specialness. His ideal woman.

That terrible day, however, she had blasted to bits the pedestal on which he'd placed her. It was almost as if she'd dared him: You think you love me. Can you love this about me? But the blast had not only revealed her to be human and weak, it had drilled holes into his own self-image revealing more character flaws than he ever wanted to see.

Donald set the photograph back in its place. No sooner had he done so, than Lisa breezed into the room.

"Sorry to keep you waiting. I got held up."

There were tired lines around her eyes. Were they always there or did they just recently appear?

"Relax," he assured her. "It's OK. The extra time allowed me to wind down from my day. Come. I've made a reservation at one of your favorite restaurants. I even requested a private room and table in the back so we can have a peaceful meal together."

She smiled at him. "That's nice. I could surely do with some quiet." Lisa turned to get her coat and saw the flowers. "These are nice. I love the bright colors. Did you bring them to cheer me up?"

"Unfortunately not. Dining out was my cheer gift."

Lisa slipped the card from its plastic pole and opened the flap of the envelope. Donald watched as her brows furrowed and cleared. A sigh escaped.

"A client?" he asked.

"Not really. He's a lawyer a client of mine had to deal with."

"You must have made an impression for him to send you flowers." Donald hoped the tightness around his heart did not come through in his voice.

"I guess," Lisa replied absent-mindedly as she put on her coat.

Donald could not stand this but he made himself remain calm. "What's his name?"

Lisa paused in buttoning up the coat and looked at him. "His name is Joshua Hendricks, Donald."

"Should I be worried, Lisa? About this man?"

Lisa dropped her eyes. What had her nonverbal body language communicated to Donald? She thought about her answer. Should her husband be worried about Joshua Hendricks? She remembered the last time they'd seen each other and the tense atmosphere in her kitchen until she'd taken that one step back from—what?

How much of this did her husband need to know anyway? She'd

pulled back with the help of God. Can a Christian lie to be kind and be justified doing it? Would not telling her husband everything further shatter his faith in her? But having lived with secrets her whole married life and finding out that her own mother had secrets of her own, could she hold on to another secret and not just crack into pieces?

Lisa looked up at her husband. Love gave him a vulnerable look. She must not under any circumstances presume on that love—such a sacred trust—to give another your heart. She had to protect it. "No, Donald. You need not worry about this man," she said softly. "I'll tell you all about it after dinner. And some other things I've recently discovered as well. Then assuming you're willing, we'll work on building up walls of protection around our marriage."

Wow! That was . . . different, Donald thought in surprise. He wanted to know so much more. Instead he declared, "I love you, you know."

Lisa stepped over to him and rising on tiptoe, lightly kissed him. "I know."

• • • • •

Donald pushed back from the table and looked at his wife. The meal had been delicious. And now the server had placed a warm white teapot between he and Lisa, and two china cups. At Donald's motion that he'd pour it himself, the man had quietly slipped away.

Now is the time, Donald thought as he poured hot tea into Lisa's cup. He wished they were outside somewhere, a beautiful open space in nature, perhaps a sunken garden or a pine forest. He lifted the miniature pitcher. Lisa nodded, so he added cream to her tea. She liked hot tea the English way while he preferred lemon in his.

It's time! his mind repeated. How much easier it would be to speak of trivial things, but he would not postpone it a moment longer. God help him. He wanted his marriage back on secure ground.

"I want to talk, Lisa, but I also want to listen. I know it's a rough time for you with Mom gone now so tell me if you need more time. I can make myself wait."

Lisa lifted the cup to her lips and took a sip. "I'm fine, Donald. I can talk now if you want. At any rate, I think we're long overdue."

"I'm sorry I left you," he started. "I didn't mean to but it's just that . . ."

". . . it was such a shock?" asked Lisa, anticipating his words.

Donald nodded.

"I'm sorry, too," said Lisa. "It was an awful way to tell you." She closed her eyes for a moment. "You know, I really didn't plan on telling you that night. I don't know that I planned on telling you at all, but during that period I thought I was losing my mind. Everything was too much. And too dull. And too same-old. But it was me and my stuff, Donald. You're a sweet and wonderful husband but—"

"I'm as dull as dishwater."

Lisa started. "I didn't say that. I never told you that!"

"But I am, Lisa. I know what I am. I'm a nice solid guy married to a beautiful butterfly who has to fly, who needs to fly, and yet I've never even tried to fly with you."

"Donald . . ."

"Let me speak, Lisa. I've got to get this out before I lose my nerve. For years I've been content to set your bath, make our meals, travel with you, and basically take care of you every way I thought I should. But none of it required me to live outside my comfort zone. You love dancing and spontaneity and romance and I'm dull, stolid Donald." He noisily sucked in air. "We're never going to have children and even though that broke me up, it didn't drive me to talk to you about how I felt. I just became even more predictably dull. I felt like the life had gone out of me except, well, I didn't know it."

"Oh, Donald," Lisa cried, tears stinging her eyes. "I'm sorry. I—"

He leaned forward. "No, no. It's not your fault. This is about me. But when you dropped that bombshell, telling me you'd had an abortion, it's like a huge hand punched me in the gut. Anger, pain, and frustration I never knew I had came crashing down. I came close to hating you. Not only for what you told me, but because what knowing it made me to see of myself."

Now the tears streamed down her cheeks. "I'm sorry, Donald. I don't know what to say except . . . I'm sorry."

He grasped her hand and lifted it to his lips. "I'm not telling you this to make you feel bad, Lisa. I'm telling you because I need to let you know what's going on in my mind and how God can use the devastations in our lives to reveal our weaknesses to us. Better yet, I've learned that when we bring those frailties to Him, He'll rescue us. God rescued me, Lisa. I blamed you for what was my failing. Yes, I suppose you could've chosen a better time to land that announcement on me, but I'm the one who failed you. After the initial shock, I justified my isolation by blaming you. I stayed away because I wanted you punished.

"What's ironic is that in shutting you out, I shut God out too. For how could I talk with God and have Him talk back to me when I had such venom in me toward you? So I didn't talk to Him either."

"You haven't turned your back on God, have you?" Lisa asked quietly.

"No, not anymore. Thank heavens for His patience." He laughed. "He and I had it out, and as usual I came out the loser yet the winner."

Lisa forced herself to look in her husband's eyes. "Do you want me to tell you about it? Why I did it?"

"Sure. But not tonight. The details can wait for another day. What can't wait is my profuse apology for failing you as a representative for God. I should have been kinder and more forgiving. I should have been more like Jesus." He paused, tears in his eyes. "I beg your forgiveness from the bottom of my heart."

Lisa had to stop this.

"Donald! I'm the one who should be begging your forgiveness. I should have told you about that stuff from years ago long before I did. I was just so afraid that if you knew you wouldn't still want me."

Donald let go of her hand and stirred the cold tea in his cup. Finally he said, "And by my behavior over the past few months, I fulfilled every fear you had."

"But it wasn't just you who duked it out with God," Lisa insisted. "I did too. Last week when you found me on the bathroom floor I had finally submitted all my feelings of guilt and unworthiness to Him. And He promised to keep me from falling and to present me faultless before . . . "

He joined her in saying the last words: ". . . the presence of the Father with exceeding joy."

"I love you, Donald."

Donald closed his eyes and whispered, "Thank You, Father!"

"What?"

Eyes now full on her face he said, "I missed hearing those words. It's been months since you told me you love me. I thought you'd stopped. Not that I would blame you. I've not been a very loving spouse lately, but thank you for still caring."

"I do love you, Donald," Lisa assured him. "Despite everything, I never really stopped."

Donald felt light, almost floating but not quite. A questioning look passed over his face, and he asked, "Do you mind telling me who Joseph is?"

"Joseph?" asked Lisa, confused.

"Yeah. The fancy bouquet guy."

The confusion vanished from her face. "Oh. You mean Joshua."

"This man means something to you?"

The voices filling her mind provided advice of all sorts.

Don't tell him how close you came to kissing that guy.

You still ache for him. I know you do.

Come clean. Tell him everything.

Lie Lisa. No husband can take all this stuff. Lie to preserve your marriage!

Her neck lay on that guillotine again. Would her disclosure cause the blade to drop? She didn't know. The one thing she did know was that she must speak the truth. Slowly Lisa began to address the man who held the blade.

"I think that it must be when we're at our most vulnerable the devil brings the temptation that will take us past the point of grace," she began. "I was feeling so sick with guilt over what I did so many years ago. You had stopped talking to me, and this man was there. He liked me. He was fun. Being around him made me feel good."

Donald's face registered his sorrow at abandoning her.

"No, Donald!" Lisa reached across the table for her husband's hand. "It wasn't your fault. It was just . . . I don't know. Joshua was the enticing, forbidden fruit in the garden. Three times, without planning, I ended up in his company. First was when I agreed to represent that young woman, Sophie, I told you about. Then that night at the Christmas banquet, just as you left, I bumped into him and he sat with me through dinner. And the day I hit my head in the mall, he was there again."

The question Donald so wanted to ask stuck in his throat. Eve had yielded to temptation. She had eaten the forbidden fruit. If his wife told him she'd given in to this man would he be able to survive it or even forgive her? Could he stand in the gap as did Aaron of old, or as Jesus did now? He felt his nostrils siphoning shallow breaths of air and commanded his chest to expand to let in more.

God, please help me represent You to my wife. Please . . .

Lisa saw her husband's face empty of expression.

Give me the right words, Father. Show me how to be truthful without being hurtful. Please, God. Help me again.

Despite the urge, she allowed no image of Joshua to fill her mind. She must step away this time and every time he came into her thoughts. She must make Joshua Hendricks history.

She covered Donald's hands with both of hers. "I'll be truthful with you," she said. A shudder passed through his body and she gripped his hands tighter. "I was tempted. Very tempted. But God saved me and I'm here. Still yours."

She raised one hand to wipe her eyes. "I know that a person shouldn't let their feelings dictate their action. You stay the course of right because that's what your commitment means. So if my love for you cannot survive a bit of temptation and still stay true to my commitment to you, then my wedding promises meant nothing. And back then as now . . ." she looked up with a smile, "I promise you, Donald Westwood, to love you in sickness and in health, through good times and bad, when it's easy and even when it's difficult. However, there's one promise I didn't make on our wedding day that I will make now.

"I promise to be a minister of God to you in our marriage," she told him. "I will love you and support you. I will challenge you and help you in your walk with God so that together we can make it to the kingdom."

Dear God, thought Donald. *Look at what You've done with our mess!*

Throat working against the movement of his heart, he gripped his wife's hands tighter. What could he say? Nothing came, but he gripped her hands as if he'd never let go. How he loved this woman! And she, having had her pick, still chose him.

He had no doubt this Joshua had charm and charisma. Those were the types that were always drawn to his wife. None however had come close to turning her head until the one time in his life when he'd turned away from her.

"I'd like to meet this Joshua."

Shock made Lisa sputter. "M-m-m-meet him? Why?"

"First, I want to shake his hand. Then I'm going to punch him in the face."

"What!"

Dead serious Donald stared back at her. When he spoke, his words were softly emphatic. "I'm a man, Lisa. One who loves you with all my heart. You're my woman. My wife. If somehow I've given you the impression that I'm a pushover, permit me to disabuse you of that notion. When it comes to your love, I want no contenders except God for your affection. Do you hear me?"

"Donald, what's come over you?"

"Do you hear me, Lisa?" His gaze on her was steady.

"Yes, Donald."

Carefully measuring his words, he continued. "Tomorrow when you get to work, get rid of those flowers. I'll see to it that your office as well as our home is supplied with flowers every day of the year, if you like. I've missed you more than words can say, and tonight when we go home I'm going to dance with you. And then I'm going to show you like I've never shown you before how much I love and adore you. And when I'm done, Mrs. Westwood, you will wonder for the rest of your life—just like you asked a minute ago—what's come over dear, dull Donald. Do I make myself clear, love?"

Lisa nodded. For what could she say? This man she thought she knew so well . . . she didn't. Did she?

Donald released her hand, rose from his chair, and walked to her side. He held out his right hand to her. Lisa took it. Looking deeply into her eyes he pulled her up and against him and the kiss he planted on her lips caused the incoming server to quickly turn tail and head back to the kitchen.

"Something to tide you over till we get home," he whispered in her ear.

Lisa's knees buckled. But Donald propped her up. Then he emptied his wallet of the cash, leaving a substantial tip on the table. *A little extra for the server*, he thought as he and Lisa left the room.

That night marked the start of Lisa's wonderment.

Chapter 32

February finally ended, and by the middle of March the women had found time to meet again. They all looked forward to the meeting, for each one had much to report. Each took the spot she now claimed as her own, and Catherine invited them to bow their heads for prayer.

When they opened their eyes Catherine stood up, the better to see each of them. "In order for this meeting not to deviate into talk of expensive blueberries," she began, "I made an agenda. First, we never fully answered Marissa's question about why God would bless her with competencies that have nothing to do with parenting and expect her to just stay at home. We need to tackle that. Second—" Catherine's gaze stopped at one woman. "Lisa," she asked in a musical tone, "are you listening to me?"

All eyes turned to Lisa. She was staring into space, a dreamy expression on her face.

"Seems somebody's savoring a secret candy," Yolanda commented. "Look at her!"

Grace laughed. "I want some of what she's got."

"Me too!" agreed Monica.

"L-i-s-aaaa. Oh, Lisa," Marissa sing-songed. "Come baaaack."

"It's a shameful thing when a person cannot even have a moment to let her mind drift." Lisa glared at them.

"You looked like you'd died and gone to heaven," said Marissa. "Anything you want to share with the rest of us?"

Lisa smiled and stretched like a contented cat. "Nope. Nothing at all."

"Oh, wow!" said Monica.

Catherine refused to comment but her heart gladdened to see Lisa looking so happy after all the tears. *Thank You, God.*

Lisa spoke up. "About that agenda of yours, Catherine, add me to it. I have a few things to say today, hopefully without crying."

"OK. Anyone else?"

"Add me too," said Marissa. "But after Lisa. Oh, and about that unfinished discussion from last meeting," she added. "I'm OK. I asked for and got your opinions." Looking quite like the young woman she was, she tucked her legs under her and smiled. "I think this is something every woman who gets to mother a child has to work through for herself. You know that the thought of having to completely rely on a husband for all my financial needs frightens me. What if I take myself out of the job market and then he ups and leaves me and the kids? Not that *my* sweetie would, of course. Anyway, I decided that if I can find a way to juggle home, family, and career without harming my kids, then that's what I'll do. If not, then I'll cross that bridge with God's help when I get to it. Until then, I'm enjoying my job as well as my husband. Case filed till further notice."

Catherine wrote on the small pad in her hand.

"Excellent."

She sat down, placed the pad in her lap, and clasped her hands on her knees.

"Today, ladies, I want to discuss touch."

"As in one of the five senses—that touch?" asked Monica.

"That very one. I've been thinking a lot about touch and what touch can do. Once a week I go to the nursing home to visit with those a bit older than me. One of the things I've observed over the years is that as we get older, people don't touch us as much. There's a particular resident I visit with who is always crying. I've discovered that when I touch her hand, she calms. Once when she had become inconsolable over whatever was ailing her that day, I cupped her cheek and began to speak softly to her. She turned her face into my palm and rubbed it against my hand, looking for all the world like she'd just been given good medicine.

"So I've come to the conclusion that touch has medicinal powers. We all long for touch. But sometimes our need for touch drives us to seek it in places where it's given with strings attached, or at a cost. God, who created us with the sense of touch, knows its power and how that power can be abused." Subconsciously, she lifted a hand to her face and lay it against her own cheek. "Through the sense of touch we learn so much and can say so much. Remember that people brought their children and their sick to Jesus so He could touch them. The woman with the issue of blood understood the touch of faith. Just check any Bible concordance and you will find many references to touch.

"So here's my idea. Why not start a touch ministry? There are many wounded people on the face of this earth who are desperately in need of touch therapy. All of us here, if we think about it, can recall instances when a touch, the right kind of touch, made all the difference in a load we were carrying—whether it was a hug, the squeeze of a hand, a pat on the shoulder, or the cupping of the face. By wisely using this much abused sense, we can communicate a bit of who God is." She paused, took a deep breath, and let her gaze go around the room.

"Can I say something, Catherine?"

"Sure, Lisa."

"I think it's interesting that you chose to talk about this topic today. It helps me to explain what I want to talk about." She blinked rapidly. "Oh, no; here come the tears!"

"It's OK, Lisa. You communicate best through your tears. Just talk away," encouraged Catherine.

Lisa brushed impatiently at the waterworks. "These last few months have been pretty rough for me. Some stuff that happened a long time ago . . . well . . . it's like . . . it's like it all suddenly erupted in my mind, you know. I felt so unlovely, and couldn't imagine why God would want to forgive me, let alone love me. Then we started these meetings and to tell the truth, it was the last thing I wanted to do—get close to people and to God. I thought no one could love me if they really knew me."

"Oh, Lisa," Grace said, but Lisa went on.

"I have a knack for putting on a happy face. Yet under the mask, I was dying from guilt. Finally one night I blurted out to Donald all the stuff that had been bothering me, and boy, that just about shot a hole in my marriage. Things got pretty rough for me to the point that I almost stopped coming to our group meetings. I just couldn't do the happy face thing anymore.

"The day I got here long after you'd started the meeting, that day in particular had been really rough. And when I came in, I found Grace with bigger problems than mine. Grace, whom I had grown to love, was dying. And when I hugged you, Grace, and cried, it was for you and me both. But something strange happened. In hugging you and sharing your grief, I received comfort for myself.

"Touch did that. Physical and emotional touch. During this time as well, a temptation came at me that looked so enticing. But God delivered me by the skin of my teeth.

"And then my mom died. Oh, man! That broke . . . well, losing a mother is tough, you know . . . but there you were. You all showed up in Toronto to support me. Bless you. Bless you!"

Overcome by tears, Lisa could not speak. Yolanda rose to go to her but Lisa put out a hand to stop her. "I'm OK. Really. All I'm trying to say is that what you've started here, Catherine, what you women bring to this meeting, is more than just your quest to get to know God. You bring something that all of us need. Fellowship.

"In this room, with you dear sisters, I can cry (not that it takes much for me to do that). I can think, question, eat, learn, laugh, sing, pray, and discover God. I read somewhere, maybe something from Mother Teresa, that God has no hands but our hands. All around us are people like me, looking happy and on top of the world but dying inside. We as Christians can offer touch. God's touch. So many want it and don't even know.

"So thanks for touching my life, ladies. And thank you, Catherine, for allowing God to lead you to start this small group. You've rescued me in ways you cannot even imagine. Thank you, Grace, for your faith and you, Marissa, for your strong spirit. Thanks, Monica, for your honesty, and Yolanda, you've been my lifeline for so long. Thank you for being my friend.

"Recently I had a wrestling match with God and surrendered all the stuff to Him. I took hold of grace, guys. My mother left me a testimony journal that God must have inspired her to write for me. And Donald? Well . . . Donald and I are experiencing a new awakening in our marriage. But best of all, I stand clean before God, completely covered with the robe of Christ's righteousness. Saved by grace." Lisa smiled a watery smile. "That's the end of my long speech."

Marissa blew her nose. Catherine dabbed at her eyes. Grace bowed her head and both Monica and Yolanda gathered Lisa to them and hugged her, rocking her back and forth, wanting and sharing touch.

Marissa thought about her announcement. She would wait till next month to tell them about the baby. Lisa's testimony needed no follow up.

• • • • •

When the doorbell rang on the Tuesday afternoon following the women's meeting, Thomas was sitting in his study talking to God about the men. The surprise on his face when he found Donald standing in his doorway was comical to see.

"Don't tell me you left a patient in the chair with his mouth still propped open?" he teased, glad to see this man in particular.

"I know. I'm a sorry excuse for a dentist," Donald deadpanned. "Someone should write to the Association to register a complaint."

"Yeah. But how is that going to help the poor guy stuck in your chair as we speak, getting lockjaw?"

Donald shrugged. "No clue. Can I come in or do you need to call my office first to rescue the bloke?"

Thomas stepped back to let him in. "Come in. I guess I'll just have to trust your good judgment. Taking the afternoon off?"

At Donald's nod, Thomas asked, "You OK?"

A slow smile broke over Donald's face. "You could say that. But I need to talk to you so I decided to drop by since some of us have the luxury of a retirement lifestyle."

"Don't you start with me," replied Thomas. "I put in my time and have earned every single minute of this retirement." He had his friend by the arm now, gently ushering him in as he spoke. "Unlike you pseudo-doctors, calling yourselves dentists, with regular daytime schedules and an answering service telling your patients that if they have an emergency they should go to the closest walk-in clinic, we *real* doctors had to burn the candle on both ends."

Donald rolled his eyes. "Oh, here we go again. Did you know that dentists have the highest stress level and burnout rate of any medical practitioner?"

"Well, yes, but I've never understood that statistic. It's the patients who have sharp whining objects whirring around in their mouths. Every visit draws blood or causes us some kind of pain, and despite our efforts to swallow with our mouth open, we still end up with spit drooling down our chins into our necks. And if that's not sufficient, you guys insist on having conversations with us when we are in no position to answer you—"

Donald opened his mouth to speak but Thomas overrode him.

"—don't say a word," he laughed. "I'm on a roll. And when you guys are finished torturing us and we've rinsed our mouths of chalk, brain matter, sandy stuff, and cotton balls, and we're ready to talk to you, you disappear and have your assistant hurry us out of the office before we can say a word."

"Are you finished?"

Thomas tipped his head to the side in thought. Finally he nodded. "I am. Now can I offer you a drink?"

"No. Go to your study. I'll talk to you there. Where's Catherine? She's the only one in this house who truly appreciates me."

"Nursing home today. You're stuck with just poor old me."

Now they both laughed as they stepped toward the study. It was in this same room that the group of men had met the last time, each seated on one of a hodgepodge of mismatched chairs that nestled in sections of the room, inviting one to sit and read.

Dropping on one of these chairs, Thomas pointed Donald to one nearby. "What's on your mind, my friend?"

Donald thought about the things he'd mentally prepared his mind to discuss. Thanks featured prominently on the list. Thomas had been a means for him to reconcile with his wife. He had no desire to lay bare before this man he so admired the details of what went down between him and Lisa but felt that some kind of explanation was necessary. That and a decision he'd come to.

"I'm going to ask you a personal question," Donald finally said. "Then I have a few things to discuss with you."

Thomas settled back in his chair. Knowing Donald's propensity for accuracy, he would need his wits about him.

"Ask away."

"After you and Catherine had come to terms with the loss of your girls—" Thomas' eyelids closed against a memory but Donald, whose own eyes had turned inward, missed it—"did you ever consider adoption?"

Jumbled thoughts flew around in Thomas' head. The just-getting-through-the-next-hour period. Then the getting-through-a-day or a week. Falling into despair so deep you could not see your way out. Some days you didn't want to come out. Fighting against the feeling that life had no meaning, fighting to hold on to faith, to God and finding Him not there, and when He came to visit, providing no concrete answers to your silent screams of "why." When, indeed, had he come to terms with the loss of their girls?

It might have been the day he found a photograph in the back of his desk drawer, taken on their fifth birthday, and seeing their cheeks puffed out with air, faces aglow as they got ready to blow out their candles. He'd reached out and touched their sweet faces, a bittersweet smile on his face instead of wanting to howl with pain.

Perhaps it was the time when he'd come home from work and found his wife in the girls' bedroom surrounded by baby clothes and frilly dresses she could not bear to part with but wanted to give to someone who needed them for something practical rather than a memorial. That was the day she'd looked up at him from amid the pile and begged him to hold her. The first time she'd allowed him to share grief with her. Together they'd cried for hope lost, but on that day, at last, they began to take delight in the touch of comfort they could provide each other.

"Have I touched a raw nerve, Thomas? If so, then don't bother answering my question."

Thomas dragged his feelings back to the present, running his long, blue-veined fingers through what was left of his totally gray hair.

"Sometimes you just don't see it coming. Someone says something and you're back there, in the memories. But I'll try to see if I can answer your question. I want to," he added. But a full two minutes passed before he spoke.

"By the time we could put one foot in front of the other without stumbling, and finally got to the stage of walking and leaping, it just never came up. Then we went overseas to work. Each day was a lesson in survival. The needs were so great that we had no time to think about us. We were looking after children who desperately needed the medical help we could provide and when we dropped in bed at nights, sleep and the touch of each other's hand became enough. Those years saved us. Why do you ask?"

"Lisa and I can't have children. One of the things that have been at the root of our recent problems is the unwillingness on both our sides, to discuss how this has affected our marriage. I miss not being a father, even though I've never been one. If it seems I'm dancing around what I want to say, let me come to the point now. Your coming to see me at the office and our talk afterward, set me on the path back to reconciliation with my wife. I wanted her to be perfect and discovered she was human. Big surprise! Without consciously meaning to, I blamed her for all the things I was angry about (like not having children), for not being some model of perfection, and worst of all, for showing me up to be less loving and forgiving than I thought myself to be."

He leaned forward, hands open toward his friend. "Thanks to you, greater thanks to God, Lisa and I are going to be OK. These past couple of weeks we've been doing a lot of talking. Working through stuff we should have worked through a long time ago. One of the things we discovered is that even though we cannot have children of our own, there's nothing preventing us from being parents. So we are seriously going to look into adoption. There must be kids available right now who could do with a couple of flawed but good-intentioned parents."

Thomas jumped to his feet and reached for Donald's hand. Pulling him to his feet he simultaneously pumped his hand while back-slapping him with hearty enthusiasm. "That's great news! Excellent news! Way to go! You guys will make excellent parents! And that means Catherine and I get to be the 'grand' ones. Just hurry it up. I'm not getting any younger, y'know."

"One more thing," said Donald, sitting back down. "I thought about what you asked us men to do. You can count me in. If I'm going to be not just a husband but a father, I want to make sure I set a good example. Stand in the gap and all that. Staying committed to your marriage vows can be tough sometimes but a brotherhood of sorts might be a way to help us guys deal with our stuff and learn how to mentor each other and our young men. So yes. Count me in. This is needed."

Thomas looked up to heaven and acknowledged the Great One. Just that very morning Bill and Simon had called with similar sentiments. Derek he'd heard from last week. God who'd begun a good thing would see them through. Using even their tragedies to lead them to this place of ministry.

Chapter 33

Lisa pulled the soccer chair from its bag and positioned it against the tree sheltering Grace's graveside. September already! This Labor Day Monday was a balmy one. While everyone went about their typical end of summer activities, Lisa knew that this spot on this day would afford her some much needed quiet time to catch her breath and reflect.

What a difference a year made. Had someone told her a year ago less two weeks, when she sat in the church watching Marissa and Derek exchanging their wedding vows, that so much in her life would change she'd have laughed in their face.

Yet so much had. So very much.

She'd eventually gotten around to reading the note tucked in her mother's journal. She hung on to it—a memento, part of her mom to be forever treasured. Lowering herself in the chair, she opened the journal and there it was. Lisa read it again. She could just picture her mama, writing her a swan song.

Sweetheart,

My time is almost gone. Megan wants me to call you but I told her No. She's not happy. I can tell by the way she's tightening her lips. This dying passage is not as scary as I thought it would be. I'm ready to go. Forgive me for being selfish but this is how I want it. Megan promised me she'd make sure you got the journal I left you. In it you will find a part of my story you don't know. My prayer is that my testimony will help to expedite your own healing. I love you with all my heart and leave you in the capable hands of my Heavenly Father.

See you in heaven,
Mom

Lisa re-folded the note and tucked it back in the journal. For the past few months she had come back again and again to read this most fascinating of stories, giving her mind time to absorb the now altered perception of her mother. Mostly however she came back for the heady fragrance of recognition and the prescription for guilt—God's love.

Grace had finally succumbed to the cancer, dying in late July. Lisa missed her so much. Her final days had not been pain free. It had gotten so bad she'd begged God for the release of death. By then, all of them wished it for her too, so great was her suffering. But on the last night, in a moment of pure lucidity, Grace, true to her lived life rose above the pain, voice reedy with suffering. There and then she committed herself and her friends again to God asking Him to give them peace. Lisa could not get over it. Grace, whose faith in God remained unshakable even to the end, died moments after uttering what was to be her last amen.

Lisa came often to her graveside. It became a way to touch base with her own mortality. So much loss this year, she reflected! Her mom. Then Grace. So much change!

Her marriage which had been on a fast track collision course toward disaster had taken an incredible turn for the better. Following that restaurant "cheer gift" from Donald back in the spring, they had taken time to talk like never before. But the most breathtaking of all the miracles was the change in Donald. It's like he'd had a personality makeover.

Gone was the predictable guy of old. Not completely, but enough. He dressed differently, walked differently, and loved her differently. Oh, he was still conservative, but he often surprised her with bouts of unpredictable spontaneity. Whatever it was—her mental mind shift or his—it was enough to banish Joshua from her thoughts. Truth was, every day she fell a little bit more in love with her husband. They shared a passion like never before. Her mind just had to let go of wishing for what was not hers to have in the first place.

Not all had been smooth sailing. In addition to the loss of dear Grace, the child she and Donald hoped to adopt had not yet put in an appearance. However Sophie's little one, Laurel, provided much opportunity for practicing parenthood.

At Lisa's invitation, Sophie had joined their Bible study group, their first recruit in the "touch of care" outreach program. To see her thriving so much in God, so hungry to learn more about how to be the mother God needed her to be made the rest of them buck up—especially after losing Grace. And miracle of miracles, Sophie's mom, just last week, had tagged along with her daughter to the meeting. Shyly she'd sat for most of it saying nothing much, but had promised to come again.

Marissa now sported a cute little tummy. Derek and Yolanda were over the moon with joy.

Lisa's thought drifted to the men. Our men, she owned. Just last week they'd taken six young guys from the community on a wilderness trek.

Thomas' idea. Donald had grumbled about it, claiming that a good game of cricket was *the* best way to teach a boy how to be a man. However he'd returned from the trip full of mosquito bites with tail between his legs. They'd gone white water rafting and had had themselves a whale of a time. Nature had proved a more effective and terrifying instructor than a cricket game ever could. Already the young men were pestering them for a repeat adventure.

Lisa opened the journal to remove another letter. This one given to her by Catherine. Word of their "touch of care" ministry had gotten to their church's district Women's Ministry leader. In a letter to Catherine, she'd invited them to submit a contribution for the fall issue of their newsletter. Catherine had informed Lisa that she must write it.

But what could she write about? What could she say that would help other women?

The words of her mother's journal came to her. *But what of the ones like me?*

How do we help those haunted by decisions made a long time ago and to which they are afraid to confess before the people? . . . Is there a support group in the church for well-meaning "baby killers"?

No way could she write about that! No way!

But then again, what if there were women like her in the church who were living with the guilt that had for so long crippled her? The same way her mother's story had helped her and Laura-Ann's story had helped her mother! Could she not reach out to another woman with her own story?

Lisa wrestled with herself. Going public on this would be suicidal. Wouldn't it? Then everyone would know. And they'd judge her.

"God," Lisa prayed by the graveside of her friend, "tell me You don't want me to do this thing. I don't want to do it."

God did not answer. Neither did the grave make utterance.

What to do? What to do?

Opening her bag, she pulled out her own journal, long discarded, and reread her last entry written so many years ago.

I went back the next day and got it done. I skipped church and did what I had to do.

When I told____ what I had done he got very upset. How could I have done this thing without even talking to him? I told him I did it for us, for our future. Men don't understand that sometimes one has to make tough decisions for the greater good.

From the first time I saw him I felt as if I'd been reborn. We were both in our late teens when we met and I can't recall ever being so happy in my entire life as when I was with him. Being with him made me more of me. He was so hand-

some—closely copped hair, lean, bow-legged, and sexy. He loved the Lord just as much as I did. We were . . .

Once the deed was done, _____ never talked about it much after that. And then, well, he . . . I'll come back to that another time. It's too painful even now to write about . . .

Heart accelerating at the memories, a sound escaped from within her—an involuntary reaction when she recalled embarrassing moments. Could she tell it? Her parents knew, yes. But they were dead. And Donald. And Yolanda. And Luke. And Luke's mom. And maybe even Luke's friend of old. Not many!

But to go public?

"God," Lisa cried again. "This is no time to go quiet on me. What do You want me to do? I promised I'd submit to Your leading and *You* promised that You would tell me 'this is the way, walk in it' (Isa. 30:21). So tell me what to do!"

The Spirit's voice which had become her constant companion of late gave her no answers. Nothing firm. Just this question:

Why are you fighting so hard against your heart?

For the very first time Lisa understood her mother's reference to feet of clay. Really understood it. She wanted no one else to know that she, too, had feet of clay and had done this very private of things. Yet, she knew what her heart wanted to do.

Was it necessary however for it to be *her* that told the tale? Could she not assume a pseudonym and be just as effective? And what of Donald? How would he feel to have her openly write about her abortion?

Lisa prayed again. "God, You know I love You. Right now, however, You make me want to scream. You choose the most inappropriate times to keep Your peace. What's that about? Other times I hear from You on everything, even stuff I don't want to hear! Yet now, when I beg You for a clear word, You're mum! Tell me what to do. You know how badly I've messed up in the past from not listening to or ignoring You. Just tell me plainly. 'Yes, Lisa, I want you to write your story' or 'No, Lisa, bad idea!' What's so hard about that?"

A soft late summer breeze cooled Lisa's face. No still small voice whispered to her.

Trust.

Even when you cannot trace.

Trust.

Lisa made her decision. She'd do this much. She'd finish the story she'd started so long ago. Finish her journal. This time, however, she'd write it with a public audience in mind and end it just like her mom did, with a letter. A letter to a sister who might be suffering from guilt. Then she'd bring it back to her friends and seek their counsel. Maybe even there someone might benefit. Then she'd see. Maybe through the wisdom of these sisters in fellowship God would give her a clear answer.

She looked toward the skies. "I'm not happy with You right now, God. But I am going to trust You to work out Your perfect will so that what needs to be done can be done. Just don't leave me, please, or desert me. I couldn't last a day without Your presence."

Bolstered by quiet assurance, Lisa picked up the pen and applied it to paper. She started with the end in mind.

Dear sister,

My name is Lisa and this is my story. I've tried to be as honest as I can in what I've written while protecting the privacy of those involved in my life. This story is not about them but about me and my deliverance. My prayer is that it will help you if you too are weighed down by guilt, either the kind I suffered or another kind.

You've read about the abortion I had several years ago and the praise-stopping, joy-stealing, peace-denying guilt I lived with. But now, thanks to the amazing power of God's love, I'm free.

Maybe you, too, have gone through an abortion and feel guilty? Not every day but sometimes? Maybe the source of your guilt is something else? Whatever your guilt, this message is for you.

"God loves you."

Did you think I'd say something different?

The only thing that could fix the kind of guilt I had was this love.

My sister, you who suffer in silence within the church of God. God loves you!

It might be hard to believe, but it's true. For years I fought against that love, thinking myself unworthy of it. I sat in church and heard grace preached. I walked to the altar to get some, I went to prayer meetings to ask for some, only to come away time after time empty-handed. Why? Did God pull back His hand whenever I reached for grace?

No!

I pulled back. No way could this be for me. I was not worthy. I had, with open eyes and calm defiance, done something that I knew in my heart to be wrong. So how could I now brazenly come to the throne of grace and take this gift. I didn't deserve it!

You will see through the pages of this journal how Jesus rescued me. Now I can say, and relish in the saying, "God loves me."

I've also beaten myself up with remorse more times than I can recall. Don't do that to yourself. If you're doing it, stop. Right now. Trust God when He says He's forgiven you and even if you don't feel forgiven, act as if you do. Your mind will follow your behavior. Just accept it. You'll never feel deserving of it. Just claim it as a gift given from the heart of God to a child He desires to have sweet fellowship with.

Submit to God. Don't argue with me about this. Just submit. You know you've tried to run things on your own for a long time. Are you happy with your efforts? Are you at peace? That's what I mean when I say don't fight me on this. God is the answer and He's the only one who can fix you for good. I am a living testimony.

Next, find a support group within your church or community. Women who have compassionate hearts and are seriously committed to knowing God. Study with them, share food for body and soul. Touch their lives even though you think you have nothing to give. God will use you to add some color to someone else's life and they will add to yours.

This walking daily with God is educational. Problems come, but somehow they're not so overwhelming because I've started to cast my cares on Him. My sisters in Christ are there to provide a perspective whenever I need a point of view. Their friendships and prayers bolster me in my walk. "Let us not give up meeting together as some are in the habit of doing" (Heb. 10:25). The author of this quote knew of which he spoke. Fellowship strengthens. Touch does too.

Touch.

Such a powerful thing! God touched me. It is my hope that these words will convey the hug of understanding I cannot give to you in person. And I dare you to allow God to touch you in all the soiled places of your life. I dare you to reach for forgiveness. Therein and only there lies the antidote for your suffering.

And what will you get?

Wonderful peace. Whether or not you've been gifted with a voice to sing, you'll find a song of deliverance on your lips. And you will sing it. You won't be able to help yourself. Because how can you keep silent when the King of the Universe loves you, pardons you, cleanses you, and bestows on you the kiss of grace?

God loves you, my sister. Believe it and live!

Your sister in Christ,
Lisa

The peace Lisa wrote about settled within her and with it a sense of rightness about her decision. There! She would ponder no longer.

Clicking her pen shut with finality, she rose from her seat. Moving purposefully but without haste, she gathered up her life lessons, folded the chair, and headed for the car and home.

This time she'd have a surprise waiting for Donald. Time for her to take the initiative in providing her version of touch therapy. Oh yes, they'd dance! Her heart fluttered in anticipation.

Who woulda thought!

Let it Go
Introduction to discussion questions.

I strongly believe in the power of discussion to stimulate our minds in ways we could not have done working alone. A number of issues were raised in this book that just beg for a healthy debating session. Indulge yourself. Do it. Tackle the issues head on. Keep an open mind and listen.

One more thing. I'd love to hear from you. When a writer weaves a story together, she is never sure how it will connect with the reader. So please tell me what you think, or what I should have tackled in the story but didn't. You can write to me at rodneybooks@rogers.com.

Now let's get on with the discussion. Here are a few topics to get things started.

Guilt and forgiveness
A number of characters in this book are dealing with guilt. Many find forgiving themselves a difficult thing to do. How can we assist those who cannot seem to forgive themselves?

Donald ends up forgiving Lisa. Is he a wimp or a man of strong character?

What situation or deed would you find it most difficult to forgive?

What does it mean to forgive?

Temptation
When the Christian experiences sexual temptation, what's the most effective way of handling it?

From all we know about him, Joshua Hendricks sounds like a really great guy. A good, decent man, and fun as well. What would you do if faced with the same temptation Lisa faced?

Is it wrong to feel sexual desire for someone who is not your spouse? How would you help someone who was not able to step away from sexual temptation and as a result ended up hurting others? Potentially, how many people can be hurt by such a situation?

When does temptation become sin? In the contemplation, the dalliance, or in the act itself?

Touch and God

The book briefly explores different kinds of touch: the touch evidence that some of us need to verify our belief; the inappropriate kinds of touch some might have been subjected to over the years which cripples their ability to be whole persons; and the touch that can heal/restore. Discuss the various kinds of touch and how a person's touch experience might color his/her ability to exercise faith in people or in God.

Do you think you are a lovable person? Do you personally believe that God loves you? Would you say most Christians really believe that God loves them? If yes, how would that show in our daily lives? If no, why is it hard to believe?

Reading the Bible

Do you believe that Bible study is necessary for your spiritual growth and development? Why, or why not?

Can a person develop a close relationship with God without access to a Bible?

The women in *Let It Go* formed a fellowship group to study the Bible. Their approach was to make the scriptures relevant to their lived circumstances. Would that method work for people you know who struggle with reading the Bible?

What methods have you found successful in helping you enjoy personal Bible study? What would your advice be to someone for whom Bible study is not appealing?

Disclosure

Mary Jones asks in her journal: "Is there a support group in the church for well-meaning 'baby killers?'" Do you think that things like abortion should be disclosed within a church/group *or* should that be a private matter between the person and God?

If a partner is tempted or succumbs to sexual temptation, should she/he confess to the husband or wife? Are there times when nondisclosure is the more prudent option? Is nondisclosure the same as lying?

How can we ensure that when private information is shared with us, we can be trusted to keep it secure?

Lisa blurts out the story about her abortion to her husband. He reacts by withdrawing and for a while privately blames her for possibly denying him the children he wanted. Discuss Lisa's disclosure. What could she have done differently? Do you think Donald's response was reasonable/appropriate?

Marriage and Family

What if you're bored in your marriage and your spouse has no desire or interest in "spicing" things up—what do you do?

Marissa thinks Derek is changing from the man she thought she'd married. Is what she's experiencing just a normal part of marital adjustment or do you think that even when you take time to get to know your partner prior to marriage there will always be surprises?

Thomas Charles presents a challenge to the men to see their marriages as ministries. How can that happen?

Grace laments the fact that God did not grant her two of the things she most wanted—marriage and children. Do you believe that marriage is for everyone? If you answer yes, why do you think so? If your answer is no, indicate why you are of that opinion.

THE HEALING POWER OF FORGIVENESS

MAY SAVE YOUR LIFE!

Dr. Tibbits has done the research and scientifically documented the healing power of forgiveness. READ IT AND LIVE!
— HAROLD G. KOENIG, M.D., ASSOCIATE PROFESSOR OF PSYCHIATRY AND MEDICINE, DUKE UNIVERSITY MEDICAL CENTER, AND AUTHOR OF *THE HEALING POWER OF FAITH*

Forgive to Live

HOW FORGIVENESS CAN SAVE YOUR LIFE

Dr. Dick Tibbits with Steve Halliday

Anger kills . . . every day . . . through a host of ailments such as depression, stress, broken relationships, and heart disease. Dr. Dick Tibbits reveals a solution for this silent killer: forgiveness. He provides a step-by-step plan that will help you forgive in a workable plan that can effectively reduce your anger and improve your health. Hardcover, 978-1-591-45470-0.

Forgive to Live Workbook
978-1-591-45471-7.

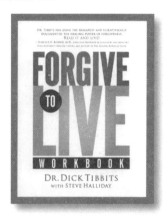

**Forgive to Live
God's Way Workbook**
978-0-9820409-4-2.

Forgive to Live Devotional
Hardcover, 978-0-97190-748-

BOOKS TO ENRICH YOUR RELATIONSHIP WITH JESUS

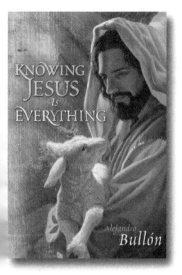

Knowing Jesus Is Everything

The Christian life is too difficult—if you don't know Jesus personally. No matter what you do (or don't do), you don't stand a chance without Him. Alejandro Bullón offers guidance for pursuing a genuine friendship with Jesus. 978-0-8280-2381-8

Savior

You've read the greatest story ever told—but never quite like this. Written in modern language without the disjointed interruption of chapter or verse, Jack Blanco merges the four Gospel accounts into one fresh, unified narrative. This is the timeless, captivating story of Jesus, our Savior. 978-0-8127-0469-3

Revelation's Great Love Story

Larry Lichtenwalter explores the final book of the Bible and unveils a side of Revelation that is seldom portrayed: Christ's passionate love for humanity. Open your eyes to the extraordinary love of our Savior for His rebellious, undeserving children—and the incredible reasons we can love Him in return. 978-0-8127-0460-0

3 Ways to Shop
- Visit your local Adventist Book Center®
- Call 1-800-765-6955
- Order online at www.AdventistBookCenter.com

Ordinary women—
extraordinary stories

Trudy Morgan-Cole draws back the dusty curtains of time and takes an intimate look into the souls of women in the Bible—women whom the world has never forgotten but never really knew. What made them so unique . . . so special? They were like you. Paperback.

3 WAYS TO SHOP